JC

MANLY WADE WELLM[...] [...] west Africa (now Angola), where his fat [...] as a medical officer. His family moved to the United States when he was a small boy, and he attended school in Washington, D.C. and prep school in Salt Lake City before eventually attending Fairmount College in Kansas, where he earned a B.A. in English.

His first published story, "When the Lion Roared" (*Thrilling Tales*, May 1927), was based on stories told to him in Africa in his childhood; it would be followed by dozens more stories in early- and mid-century pulp magazines, including *Weird Tales*, *Wonder Stories*, and *Astounding Stories*. His many creations include Judge Keith Hilary Pursuivant, a World War I hero and retired judge who is an expert on the occult; John Thunstone, a Manhattan playboy and dilettante who fights supernatural perils with potent charms and a silver sword-cane; and perhaps his most beloved character, John the Balladeer (or "Silver John"), a folk song-strumming wanderer of the Appalachian hills who debuted in 1951 and would feature in numerous short stories, five novels, and a film adaptation.

Wellman's considerable output also includes science fiction novels, stories for young readers, and works of history and nonfiction. His many honors include an Edgar Award for best story in 1956, a World Fantasy Award for his collection *Worse Things Waiting*, and another World Fantasy Award for Life Achievement in 1980. He died in 1986.

MANLY WADE WELLMAN

JOHN THE BALLADEER

Edited with an introduction by
KARL EDWARD WAGNER

Foreword by DAVID DRAKE

VALANCOURT BOOKS

John the Balladeer by Manly Wade Wellman
Originally published by Baen Books in 1988
First Valancourt Books edition 2023

Published by Valancourt Books, Richmond, Virginia
http://www.valancourtbooks.com

Valancourt Books and the Valancourt Books logo are registered trademarks of Valancourt Books, LLC

ISBN 978-1-960241-03-0 (trade paperback)
ISBN 978-1-960241-02-3 (trade hardcover)
Also available as an electronic book.

Cover by Ilan Sheady / Uncle Frank Productions
Set in Dante MT

CONTENTS

FOREWORD

Manly in the Mountains

Music brought Manly to the North Carolina mountains. Folk music—the old songs, real songs—had been an interest of Manly's since the 1920s when he tramped the Ozarks with Vance Randolph, the famed folklorist. He was drawn by the folk festival that he found when he moved with his family to Chapel Hill in 1951; became a friend of the organizer, Asheville native Bascom Lamar Lunsford; and traveled with Lunsford to meet "the best banjo player in the country."

That was Obray Ramsey of Madison County, high in the Smokies where they divide North Carolina from Tennessee. It was the start of a life-long friendship, and the genesis as well of this book: the tales of John the Balladeer, hiking the hills of North Carolina with his silver-strung guitar.

Manly and his wife Frances visited the mountains regularly, staying in the Ramseys' house when they were alone and in a tourist cabin farther down on the French Broad River if they had their son or another friend with them. By the early '60s they had a little cabin of their own, next to the Ramseys and built in fits and starts over the years by them and their friends.

It wasn't fancy, but it was a place to sleep and eat; and a place to have friends in to pick and sing and pass around a bottle of liquor, tax-paid or otherwise. That was where they were when my wife and I visited the mountains with them and with Karl Wagner in the Fall of 1971.

The Ramseys' house is close by the road, Highway 25-70, which parallels the course of the French Broad River snaking through hard rock. The mountains lowered down behind the house, and the river dropped away sharply on the other side of the road.

One statistic will suffice to indicate the ruggedness of the terrain. There were seven attorneys in practice in Madison County when 25-70 was the direct route from Asheville to Knoxville. Shortly after Interstate 40 was completed, cutting off the business that had resulted from auto accidents on 25-70, six of the lawyers left.

The seventh was the District Attorney.

Manly's cabin was a little farther back from the road and a little higher up the mountain he called Yandro. The water system was elegant in its simplicity, a pipe that trailed miles from a high, clear spring to a faucet mounted four feet up above a floor drain in the cabin. There was a pressure-relief vent and settling pond partway down the mountainside. The vent could become blocked with debris, especially if the water hadn't been run for a time. The way you learned that it was plugged was—

"Let me fix you a drink, Dutch," Manly said to Karl as we settled into the cabin. He poured bourbon into a plastic cup, held it under the spigot, and just started to open the tap.

The water, with over a thousand feet of head, blew the cup out of his hand to shatter on the drain beneath.

Nobody said anything for a moment.

We stumbled up the mountainside in the dark—there was a moon, but the pines and the valley's steep walls blocked most of its light as they did the sun in daytime. Manly went partway, but when Obray guided Karl and me off the road-cut, he decided he'd wait. Wisely: he was 68 even then, though that was hard to remember when you saw him.

He had fresh drinks waiting for those as used it when we got back—and fresh laughter as he always did, this time because Karl had slipped off the catwalk into one of Obray's trout ponds as we neared the cabin.

Manly was in his element that evening, watching the incredible fingerings of Obray and a neighbor while lamplight gleamed from the gilded metalwork of the banjo and guitar; pouring drinks; singing "Will the Circle be Unbroken" and "Birmingham Jail" and "Vandy, Vandy." . . .

Which brings up a last point about Manly and the mountains. I said he called the mountain Yandro, but I don't know you'd find that name on a map. Manly blended past reality with new creations in his life as well as his writing. Many of the songs he sang and quoted in this volume are very old; he once claimed to have written "Vandy, Vandy" himself.

And that may be part of the magic of these stories. They were written by a man who knew and loved the folkways he described so well that he became a part of them, weaving in his own strands and keeping the fabric alive instead of leaving it to be displayed behind the sterile glass of a museum.

May you read them with a delight as great as that of the man who wrote them.

DAVE DRAKE
Chapel Hill, N.C.

INTRODUCTION
Just Call Me John

There are moments in literature—very rare and very marvelous—when a writer creates a unique character. One such moment occurred in 1951 when Manly Wade Wellman began to write stories about John the Balladeer.

He had no last name, no other name: he was known only as John. Some reviewers suggested that Wellman intended John to be a Christ figure. Manly firmly denied this, but he often hinted that there might exist some mystic link to John the Baptist (*cf.* Mark 1. 2-3).

We never knew a lot about John's past. He was born in Moore County, North Carolina, and Manly said he sort of pictured John as a young Johnny Cash. He also told us that John was a veteran of the Korean War, and that he could hold up his end of things in a barroom brawl. John had a profound knowledge of Southern folklore and folksongs—as did Manly. John had a guitar strung with silver strings, a considerable knowledge of the occult, and his native wit. He needed all three as he wandered along the haunted ridges and valleys of the Southern Appalachians—sometimes encountering supernatural evil, sometimes seeking it out.

John first appeared in the December 1951 issue of *The Magazine of Fantasy and Science Fiction,* but Wellman had given us foreshadowings. He sometimes liked to claim that two stories from *Weird Tales,* "Sin's Doorway" (January 1946) and "Frogfather" (November 1946), were stories about John before he got his silver-strung guitar, but usually he grouped them instead with his other regional fantasies. Not coincidentally, following his move from New Jersey to Moore County, North Carolina after the War, Wellman began to make use of Southern legends and locales in his stories. When he moved to Chapel Hill in 1951, his subsequent acquaintance with folk musicians of the Carolina mountains combined with Manly's lifelong interest in folklore to generate the stories of John. The transition can be seen in Wellman's abandonment of his then-popular series character, John Thunstone, an urbane occult detective who worked the New York night-club set. Thunstone's final appearance in *Weird Tales* ("The Last Grave of Lill Warran" in the May 1951 issue) finds him in hiking gear and stomping through the Sand Hills in search of a backwoods vampire. Seven months later John the Balladeer made his first appearance in "O Ugly Bird!". The difference was the mountains—and the music.

There hadn't been anything like the John stories at that time, and there hasn't been since. No one but Manly Wade Wellman could have written these stories. Here his vivid imagination merged with authentic Southern folklore and a heartfelt love of the South and its people. Just as J.R.R. Tolkien brilliantly created a modern British myth cycle, so did Manly Wade Wellman give to us an imaginary world of purely American fact, fantasy, and song.

Between 1951 and 1962 Wellman wrote eleven stories about John, in addition to a grouping of seven short vignettes. These were collected in the 1963 Arkham House volume, *Who Fears the Devil?*. The original magazine versions were somewhat revised (Manly grumbled that this was done to give the collection some semblance of a novel), and four new vignettes were added. When I first met Manly in the summer of 1963, he gave me the grim news that he was all through writing about John. Fortunately, this wasn't to be true. Manly loved his character too much.

John would next appear on film, with folksinger Hedges Capers miscast as John. The film was partially shot in Madison County, North Carolina (the general setting for the John stories) in October 1971. Despite a surprisingly good supporting cast and the incorporation of two of the best stories ("O Ugly Bird!" and "The Desrick on Yandro"), the film was an embarrassment— largely due to its shoestring budget and stultifying script. It was released in 1972 as *Who Fears the Devil?* and flopped at the box office. It was then re-edited and re-released the following year as *The Legend of Hillbilly John*, with equal success. Sometimes it turns up on videocassette.

But it would take more than a bad film to finish off John. Renewed interest in his earlier fantasy work coupled with summer trips to his cabin in Madison County soon had Wellman writing about the mountains again. John returned—this time in a series of novels.

In 1979 Doubleday published *The Old Gods Waken,* the first of five John novels. This was followed by *After Dark* (1980), *The Lost and the Lurking* (1981), *The Hanging Stones* (1982), and *The Voice of the Mountain* (1984). A sixth John novel, *The Valley So Low,* was planned but never started due to Wellman's final illness; instead it was published by Doubleday in 1987 as a collection of Wellman's recent mountain stories.

But there was more to be heard from John. Wellman always maintained that he preferred to write about John in short-story form rather than in novel length. And to prove he could still do both, Manly wrote six new John stories in between work on his novels. Shortly after completing his final novel for Doubleday (*Cahena,* 1986), Manly wrote a new John story, "Where Did She Wander?". This was to be his final story. A few days after completing it, Wellman suffered a crippling fall, shattering his shoulder and elbow. Despite the weakness and pain, he managed to revise and polish the final draft of "Where Did She Wander?".

Five years before Manly would have been back at his desk before the plaster cast hardened, but at age 82 complication followed complication. Death came on April 5, 1986, a few weeks short of his 83rd birthday.

John will live on, as long as there are readers who love good stories—and good storytelling.

John the Balladeer is the complete collection of all of the short stories of John. All of the stories in this book are Manly Wade Wellman's original versions, reprinted from their initial magazine or anthology appearances. To approximate as closely as possible the order in which they were written, I have arranged these stories according to date of original publication. I regret a certain awkwardness in the clustering of the vignettes between two stories which are directly connected (albeit having been written twenty-one years apart). Think of this as an interlude, perhaps, between the old and the new.

While the John stories can be read in any order one wishes, I chose this method of presentation deliberately. John is one of the most significant characters in all of fantasy literature. For thirty-five years John lived in the marvelous imagination of Manly Wade Wellman, one of fantasy's foremost authors. As such it is desirable to provide a definitive, orderly text so that we may consider the growth and development of both character and creator over those three-and-one-half decades.

On the other hand, if you're simply looking for a good read, you're holding one of the best. Dip into it anywhere. These stories are chilling and enchanting, magical and down-to-earth, full of wonder and humanity. They are fun. They are like nothing else you've ever read before.

Savor this book. Treasure it to reread in years to come.

I wish you the joy and wonder I have found here.

KARL EDWARD WAGNER
Chapel Hill, N.C.

JOHN THE BALLADEER

O UGLY BIRD!

I swear I'm licked before I start, trying to tell you all what Mr. Onselm looked like. Words give out—for instance, you're frozen to death for fit words to tell the favor of the girl you love. And Mr. Onselm and I pure poison hated each other. That's how love and hate are alike.

He was what country folks call a low man, more than calling him short or small; a low man is low otherwise than by inches. Mr. Onselm's shoulders didn't wide out as far as his big ears, and they sank and sagged. His thin legs bowed in at the knee and out at the shank, like two sickles point to point. On his carrot-thin neck, his head looked like a swollen pale gourd. Thin moss-gray hair. Loose mouth, a bit open to show long, even teeth. Not much chin. The right eye squinted, mean and dark, while the hike of his brow twitched the left one wide. His good clothes fitted his mean body like they were cut to it. Those good clothes were almost as much out of match to the rest of him as his long, soft, pink hands, the hands of a man who never had to work a tap.

You see what I mean, I can't say how he looked, only he was hateful.

I first met him when I came down from the high mountain's comb, along an animal trail—maybe a deer made it. Through the trees I saw, here and there in the valley below, patch-places and cabins and yards. I hoped I'd get fed at one of them, for I'd run clear out of eating some spell back. I had no money. Only my hickory shirt and blue duckin pants and torn old army shoes, and my guitar on its sling cord. But I knew the mountain folks. If they've got ary thing to eat, a decent spoken stranger can get the half part of it. Towns aren't always the same way.

Downslope I picked, favoring the guitar in case I slipped and fell, and in an hour made it to the first patch. Early fall was browning the corn out of the green. The cabin was two-room, dog-trotted open in the middle. Beyond was a shed and a pigpen. In the yard the man of the house talked to who I found out later was Mr. Onselm.

"No meat at all?" said Mr. Onselm. His voice was the last you'd expect him to have, full of broad low music, like an organ in a town church. I decided against asking him to sing when I glimpsed him closer, sickle-legged and gourd-headed and pale and puny in his fine-fitting clothes. For he looked mad and dangerous; and the man of the place, though he was a big, strong old gentleman with a square jaw, looked afraid.

"I been short this year, Mr. Onselm," he said, begging like. "The last bit of meat I fished out of the brine on Tuesday. And I don't want to have to kill the pig till December."

Mr. Onselm tramped over to the pen. The pig was a friendly one, it reared its front feet against the boards and grunted up to him. Mr. Onselm spit into the pen. "All right," he said, "but I want some meal."

He sickle-legged back to the cabin. A brown barrel stood in the dog trot. Mr. Onselm lifted the cover and pinched some meal between his pink fingertips. "Get me a sack," he told the man.

The man went indoors and brought out the sack. Mr. Onselm held it open while the man scooped out meal enough to fill it. Then Mr. Onselm held it tight shut while the man lashed the neck with twine. Finally Mr. Onselm looked up and saw me standing there.

"Who are you?" he asked, sort of crooning.

"My name's John," I said.

"John what?" Then, without waiting for my answer, "Where did you steal that guitar?"

"It was given to me," I replied. "I strung it with silver wires myself."

"Silver," he said, and opened his squint eye by a trifle.

With my left hand I clamped a chord. With my right thumb I picked a whisper from the silver strings. I began to make a song:

> Mister Onselm,
> They do what you tell 'em—

"That will do," said Mr. Onselm, not so musically, and I

stopped playing. He relaxed. "They do what I tell 'em," he said, half to himself. "Not bad."

We studied each other a few ticks of time. Then he turned and tramped out of the yard in among the trees. When he was out of sight the man of the place asked, right friendly, what he could do for me.

"I'm just walking through," I said. I didn't want to ask right off for some dinner.

"I heard you name yourself John," he said. "So happens my name's John too, John Bristow."

"Nice place you've got," I said, looking around. "Cropper or tenant?"

"I own the house and the land," he told me, and I was surprised; for Mr. Onselm had treated him the way a mean boss treats a cropper.

"Then that Mr. Onselm was just a visitor," I said.

"Visitor?" Mr. Bristow snorted. "He visits everybody here around. Lets them know what he wants, and they pass it to him. Thought you knew him, you sang about him so ready."

"Shucks, I made that up." I touched the silver strings again. "I sing a many a new song that comes to me."

"I love the old songs better," he said, and smiled, so I sang one:

> *I had been in Georgia*
> *Not a many more weeks than three,*
> *When I fell in love with a pretty fair girl,*
> *And she fell in love with me.*
>
> *Her lips were red as red could be,*
> *Her eyes were brown as brown,*
> *Her hair was like the thundercloud*
> *Before the rain comes down.*

You should have seen Mr. Bristow's face shine. He said: "By God, you sure enough can sing it and play it."

"Do my possible best," I said. "But Mr. Onselm don't like it." I thought a moment, then asked: "What way can he get everything he wants in this valley?"

"Shoo, can't tell you way. Just done it for years, he has."

"Anybody refuse him?"

"Once Old Jim Desbro refused him a chicken. Mr. Onselm pointed his finger at Old Jim's mules, they was plowing. Them mules couldn't move ary foot, not till Mr. Onselm had the chicken. Another time, Miss Tilly Parmer hid a cake when she seen him come. He pointed a finger and dumbed her. She never spoke one mumbling word from that day to when she died. Could hear and understand, but when she tried to talk she could just wheeze."

"He's a hoodoo man," I said, "which means the law can't do anything."

"Not even if the law worried about anything this far from the county seat." He looked at the meal back against the cabin. "About time for the Ugly Bird to fetch Mr. Onselm's meal."

"What's the Ugly Bird?" I asked, but he didn't have to answer.

It must have hung over us, high and quiet, and now it dropped into the yard like a fish hawk into a pond.

First out I saw it was dark, heavy-winged, bigger than a buzzard. Then I saw the shiny gray-black of the body, like wet slate, and how it seemed to have feathers only on its wide wings. Then I made out the thin snaky neck, the bulgy head and long stork beak, the eyes set in front of its head—man-fashion in front, not to each side.

The feet that taloned onto the sack showed pink and smooth with five graspy toes. The wings snapped like a tablecloth in a wind, and it churned away over the trees with the meal sack.

"That's the Ugly Bird," said Mr. Bristow. I barely heard him. "Mr. Onselm has companioned with it ever since I recollect."

"I never saw such a bird," I said. "Must be a scarce one. You know what struck me while I watched it?"

"I do know, John. Its feet look like Mr. Onselm's hands."

"Might it be," I asked, "that a hoodoo man like Mr. Onselm knows what way to shape himself into a bird?"

He shook his head. "It's known that when he's at one place, the Ugly Bird's been sighted at another." He tried to change the subject. "Silver strings on your guitar—never heard of any but steel strings."

"In the olden days," I told him, "silver was used a many times for strings. It gives a more singy sound."

In my mind I had it the subject wouldn't be changed. I tried a chord on my guitar, and began to sing:

> You all have heard of the Ugly Bird
> So curious and so queer,
> That flies its flight by day and night
> And fills folks' hearts with fear.
>
> I never come here to hide from fear,
> And I give you my promised word
> That I soon expect to twist the neck
> Of the God damn Ugly Bird.

When I finished, Mr. Bristow felt in his pocket.

"I was going to bid you eat with me," he said, "but—here, maybe you better buy something."

He gave me a quarter and a dime. I about gave them back, but I thanked him and walked away down the same trail Mr. Onselm had gone. Mr. Bristow watched me go, looking shrunk up. My song had scared him, so I kept singing it.

> O Ugly Bird! O Ugly Bird!
> You snoop and sneak and thieve!
> This place can't be for you and me,
> And one of us got to leave.

Singing, I tried to remember all I'd heard or read or guessed that might help toward my Ugly Bird study.

Didn't witch people have partner animals? I'd read and heard tell about the animals called familiars—mostly cats or black dogs or the like, but sometimes birds.

That might be the secret, or a right much of it, for the Ugly Bird wasn't Mr. Onselm's other self. Mr. Bristow had said the two of them were seen different places at one time. Mr. Onselm didn't turn into the Ugly Bird then. They were just close partners. Brothers. With the Ugly Bird's feet like Mr. Onselm's hands.

I awared of something in the sky, the big black V of a flying creature. It quartered over me, half as high as the highest woolly scrap of cloud. Once or twice it seemed like it would stoop for me, like a hawk for a rabbit, but it didn't. Looking up and letting my feet find the trail, I rounded a bunch of bushes and there, on a rotten log in a clearing, sat Mr. Onselm.

His gourd-head sank on his thin neck. His elbows set on his knees, and the soft, pink, long hands hid his face, as if he was miserable. His look made me feel disgusted. I came toward him.

"You don't feel so brash, do you?" I asked.

"Go away," he sort of gulped, soft and sick.

"Why?" I wanted to know. "I like it here." Sitting on the log, I pulled my guitar across me. "I feel like singing, Mr. Onselm."

> His father got hung for horse stealing,
> His mother got burned for a witch,
> And his only friend is the Ugly Bird,
> The dirty son of—

Something hit me like a shooting star from overhead.

It hit my back and shoulder, and knocked me floundering forward on one hand and one knee. It was only the mercy of God I didn't fall on my guitar and smash it. I crawled forward a few scrambles and made to get up, shaky and dizzy.

The Ugly Bird had flown down and dropped the sack of meal on me. Now it skimmed across the clearing, at the height of the low branches, its eyes glinting at me, and its mouth came open a little. I saw teeth, sharp and mean, like a garpike's teeth. It swooped for me, and the wind of its wings was colder than a winter storm.

Without stopping to think, I flung up my both hands to box it off from me, and it gave back, flew backward like the biggest, devilishest hummingbird ever seen in a nightmare. I was too dizzy and scared to wonder why it gave back; I had barely the wit to be thankful.

"Get out of here," moaned Mr. Onselm, who hadn't stirred.

I shame to say that I got. I kept my hands up and backed across the clearing and into the trail beyond. Then I half realized where my luck had been. My hands had lifted the guitar toward the Ugly Bird, and somehow it hadn't liked the guitar.

Just once I looked back. The Ugly Bird was perching on the log and it sort of nuzzled up to Mr. Onselm, most horrible. They were sure enough close together. I stumbled off away.

I found a stream, with stones to make steps across. I turned and walked down to where it made a wide pool. There I knelt and washed my face—it looked pallid in the water image—and sat with my back to a tree and hugged my guitar and rested. I shook all over. I must have felt as bad for a while as Mr. Onselm looked like he felt, sitting on the log waiting for his Ugly Bird and—what else?

Had he been hungry? Sick? Or just evil? I couldn't say which.

After a while I walked back to the trail and along it again, till I came to what must have been the only store thereabouts.

It faced one way on a rough road that could carry wagon and car traffic, and the trail joined on and reached the door. The building wasn't big but it was good, made of sawed planks well painted. It rested on big rocks instead of posts, and had a roofed open front like a porch, with a bench where people could sit.

Opening the door, I went in. You'll find a many such stores in back country places through the land. Counters. Shelves of cans and packages. Smoked meat hung one corner, a glass-front icebox for fresh meat another. One point, sign says U.S. POST OFFICE, with half a dozen pigeonholes for letters and a couple of cigar boxes for stamps and money-order blanks. The proprietor wasn't in. Only a girl, scared and shaking, and Mr. Onselm, there ahead of me, telling her what he wanted.

He wanted her.

"I don't care if Sam Heaver did leave you in charge here," he said with the music in his voice. "He won't stop my taking you with me."

Then he swung around and fixed his squint eye and wide-open eye on me, like two mismated gun muzzles. "You again," he said.

He looked hale and hearty. I strayed my hands over the guitar strings, and he twisted up his face as if it colicked him.

"Winnie," he said to the girl, "wait on him and get him out of here."

Her eyes were round in her scared face. I never saw as sweet a face as hers, or as scared. Her hair was dark and thick. It was like the thundercloud before the rain comes down. It made her paleness look paler. She was small, and she cowered for fear of Mr. Onselm.

"Yes, sir?" she said to me.

"Box of crackers," I decided, pointing to a near shelf. "And a can of those sardine fish."

She put them on the counter. I dug out the quarter Mr. Bristow had given me, and slapped it down on the counter top between the girl and Mr. Onselm.

"Get away!" he squeaked, shrill and mean as a bat. He had jumped back, almost halfway across the floor. And for once both of his eyes were big.

"What's the matter?" I asked him, purely wondering. "This is a good silver quarter." And I picked it up and held it out for him to take and study.

But he ran out of the store like a rabbit. A rabbit with the dogs after it.

The girl he'd called Winnie just leaned against the wall as if she was tired. I asked: "Why did he light out like that?"

She took the quarter. "It doesn't scare me much," she said, and rung it up on the old cash register. "All that scares me is—Mr. Onselm."

I picked up the crackers and sardines. "He's courting you?"

She shuddered, though it was warm. "I'd sooner be in a hole with a snake than be courted by Mr. Onselm."

"Why not just tell him to leave you be?"

"He'd not listen. He always does what pleases him. Nobody dares stop him."

"I know, I heard about the mules he stopped and the poor lady he dumbed." I returned to the other subject. "Why did he squinch away from money? I'd reckon he loved money."

She shook her head. The thundercloud hair stirred. "He never needs any. Takes what he wants without paying."

"Including you?"

"Not including me yet. But he'll do that later."

I laid down my dime I had left. "Let's have a coke drink, you and me."

She rang up the dime too. There was a sort of dry chuckle at the door, like a stone rattling down the well. I looked quick, and saw two long, dark wings flop away from the door. The Ugly Bird had spied.

But the girl Winnie smiled over her coke drink. I asked permission to open my fish and crackers on the bench outside. She nodded yes. Out there, I worried open the can with my pocket knife and had my meal. When I finished I put the trash in a garbage barrel and tuned my guitar. Winnie came out and harked while I sang about the girl whose hair was like the thundercloud before the rain comes down, and she blushed till she was pale no more.

Then we talked about Mr. Onselm and the Ugly Bird, and how they had been seen in two different places at once—

"But," said Winnie, "who's seen them together?"

"Shoo, I have," I told her. "Not long ago." And I told how Mr. Onselm sat, all sick and miserable, and the conjer bird crowded up against him.

She heard all that, with eyes staring off, as if looking for something far away. Finally she said, "John, you say it crowded up to him."

"It did that thing, as if it studied to get right inside him."

"Inside him!"

"That's right."

"Makes me think of something I heard somebody say about hoodoo folks," she said. "How the hoodoo folks sometimes put a stuff out, mostly in dark rooms. And it's part of them, but it takes the shape and mind of another person—once in a while, the shape and mind of an animal."

"Shoo," I said again, "now you mention it, I've heard the same thing. It might explain those Louisiana stories about werewolves."

"Shape and mind of an animal," she repeated herself. "Maybe the shape and mind of a bird. And they call it echo—no, ecto— ecto—"

"Ectoplasm," I remembered. "That's right. I've even seen pictures they say were taken of such stuff. It seems to live—it'll yell, if you grab it or hit it or stab it."

"Could maybe—" she began, but a musical voice interrupted.

"He's been around here long enough," said Mr. Onselm.

He was back. With him were three men. Mr. Bristow, and a tall, gawky man with splay shoulders and a black-stubbled chin, and a soft, smooth-grizzled man with an old fancy vest over his white shirt.

Mr. Onselm acted like the leader of a posse. "Sam Heaver," he crooned at the soft, grizzled one, "can tramps loaf at your store?"

The soft old storekeeper looked dead and gloomy at me. "Better get going, son," he said, as if he'd memorized it.

I laid my guitar on the bench. "You men ail my stomach," I said, looking at them. "You let this half-born, half-bred hoodoo man sic you on me like hound dogs when I'm hurting nobody and nothing."

"Better go," he said again.

I faced Mr. Onselm, and he laughed like a sweetly played horn. "You," he said, "without a dime in your pocket! You can't do anything to anybody."

Without a dime . . . the Ugly Bird had seen me spend my silver money, the silver money that ailed Mr. Onselm. . . .

"Take his guitar, Hobe," said Mr. Onselm, and the gawky man, clumsy but quick, grabbed the guitar from the bench and backed away to the door.

"That takes care of him," Mr. Onselm sort of purred, and he fairly jumped and grabbed Winnie by the wrist. He pulled her along toward the trail, and I heard her whimper.

"Stop him!" I bawled, but they stood and looked, scared and dumb. Mr. Onselm, still holding Winnie, faced me. He lifted his free hand, with the pink forefinger sticking out like the barrel of a pistol.

Just the look he gave me made me weary and dizzy. He was going to hoodoo me, like he'd done the mules, like he'd done the woman who tried to hide her cake from him. I turned from him, sick and afraid, and I heard him giggle, thinking he'd won already. In the doorway stood the gawky man called Hobe, with the guitar.

I made a long jump at him and started to wrestle it away from him.

"Hang onto it, Hobe," I heard Mr. Onselm sort of choke out, and, from Mr. Bristow:

"There's the Ugly Bird!"

Its wings flapped like a storm in the air behind me. But I'd torn my guitar from Hobe's hands and turned on my heel.

A little way off, Mr. Onselm stood stiff and straight as a stone figure in front of a courthouse. He still held Winnie's wrist. Between them the Ugly Bird came swooping at me, its beak pointing for me like a stabbing bayonet.

I dug in my toes and smashed the guitar at it. Full-slam I struck its bulgy head above the beak and across the eyes, and I heard the polished wood of my music-maker crash to splinters.

And down went the Ugly Bird!

Down it went.

Quiet it lay.

Its great big wings stretched out on either side, without a flutter. Its beak was driven into the ground like a nail. It didn't kick or flop or stir once.

But Mr. Onselm, standing where he stood holding Winnie, screamed out the way you might scream if something had clawed out all your insides with a single tearing grab.

He didn't move, I don't even know if his mouth came open. Winnie gave a pull with all her strength and tottered back, clear of him. And as if only his hold on her had kept him standing, Mr. Onselm slapped over and down on his face, his arms flung out like the Ugly Bird's wings, his face in the dirt like the Ugly Bird's face.

Still holding my broken guitar by the neck like a club, I ran to him and stooped. "Get up," I said, and took hold of what hair he had and lifted his face up.

One look was enough. From the war, I know a dead man when I see one. I let go his hair, and his face went back into the dirt as if it belonged there.

The others moved at last, tottering a few steps closer. And they didn't act like enemies now, for Mr. Onselm who had made them act so was down and dead.

Then Hobe gave a scared shout, and we looked that way.

The Ugly Bird all of a sudden looked rotten mushy, and was

soaking into the ground. To me, anyhow, it looked shadowy and misty, and I could see through it. I wanted to move close, then I didn't want to. It was melting away like snow on top of a stove; only no wetness left behind.

It was gone, while we watched and wondered and felt bad all over.

Mr. Bristow knelt and turned Mr. Onselm over. On the dead face ran sick lines across, thin and purple, as though he'd been struck down by a blow of a toaster or a gridiron.

"The guitar strings," said Mr. Bristow. "The silver guitar strings. It finished him, like any hoodoo man."

That was it. Won't a silver bullet kill a witch, or a silver knife a witch's cat? And a silver key locks out ghosts, doesn't it?

"What was the word you said?" whispered Winnie to me.

"Ectoplasm," I told her. "Like his soul coming out—and getting struck dead outside his body."

More important was talk about what to do now. The men decided. They allowed to report to the county seat that Mr. Onselm's heart had stopped on him, which it had. They went over the tale three or four times to make sure they'd all tell it the same. They cheered up as they talked. You never saw gladder people to get rid of a neighbor.

"And, John," said Mr. Bristow, "we'd sure enough be proud if you stayed here. You took this curse off us."

Hobe wanted me to come live on his farm and help him work it on shares. Sam Heaver offered me all the money out of his old cash register. I thanked him and said no, sir, to Hobe I said thank you kindly, I'd better not. If they wanted their story to stick with the sheriff, they'd better forget that I'd been around when Mr. Onselm's heart stopped. All I was sorry for was my broken guitar.

But while we'd talked, Mr. Bristow was gone. He came back, with a guitar from his place, and he acted honored if I'd take it in place of mine. So I tightened my silver strings on it and tried a chord or two.

Winnie swore she'd pray for me by name each night of her life, and I told her that would sure see me safe from any assaults of the devil.

"Assaults of the devil, John!" she said, almost shrill in the voice, she was so earnest. "It's you who drove the devil from this valley."

The others all said they agreed on that.

"It was foretold about you in the Bible," said Winnie, her voice soft again. "'There was a man sent from God, whose name was John.'"

But that was far too much for her to say, and I was that abashed, I said goodbye all around in a hurry. I strummed my new guitar as I walked away, until I got an old song back in my mind. I've heard tell that the song's written in an old-time book called *Percy's Frolics,* or *Relics,* or something:

> *Lady, I never loved witchcraft,*
> *Never dealt in privy wile,*
> *But evermore held the high way*
> *Of love and honor, free from guile. . . .*

And though I couldn't bring myself to look back to the place I was leaving forever, I knew that Winnie watched me, and that she listened, listened, till she had to strain her ears to catch the last, faintest end of my song.

THE DESRICK ON YANDRO

The folks at the party clapped me such an encore, I sang that song.

The lady had stopped her car at the roadside when she saw my thumb out and my silver-strung guitar under my arm. Asked me my name, I told her John. Asked where I was headed, I told her nowhere special. Asked could I play that guitar, I played it as we rolled along. Then she invited me most kindly to her country house, to sing to her friends, and they'd be obliged, she said. And I went.

The people there were fired up with what they'd drunk, lots of ladies and men in costly clothes, and I had my bothers not getting drunk, too. But, shoo, they liked what I played and sang. Staying off wornout songs, I smote out what they'd never heard before—*Witch in the Wilderness* and *Rebel Soldier* and *Vandy, Vandy, I've Come to Court You*. When they clapped and hollered for more, I sang the Yandro song, like this:

> *I'll build me a desrick on Yandro's high hill,*
> *Where the wild beasts can't reach me or hear my sad cry,*
> *For he's gone, he's gone away, to stay a little while,*
> *But he'll come back if he comes ten thousand miles.*

Then they strung around and made me more welcome than any stranger could call for, and the hostess lady said I must stay to supper, and sleep there that night. But at that second, everybody sort of pulled away, and one man came up and sat down by me.

I'd been aware that, when first he came in, things stilled down, like with little boys when a big bully shows himself. He was built short and broad, his clothes were sporty, cut handsome and costly. His buckskin hair was combed across his head to baffle

folks he wasn't getting bald. His round, pink face wasn't soft, and
his big, smiling teeth reminded you there was a bony skull under
that meat. His pale eyes, like two gravel bits, prodded me and
made me remember I needed a haircut and a shine.

"You said Yandro, young man," said this fellow. He said it
almost like a charge in court, with me the prisoner.

"Yes, sir. The song's mountainy, not too far from the Smokies.
I heard it in a valley, and the highest peak over that valley's called
Yandro. Now," I said, "I've had scholar-men argue me it really
means yonder—yonder high hill. But the peak's called Yandro.
Not a usual name."

"No, John." He smiled toothy and fierce. "Not a usual name.
I'm like the peak. I'm called Yandro, too."

"How you, Mr. Yandro?" I said.

"I never heard of that peak or valley, nor, I imagine did my
father before me. But my grandfather—Joris Yandro—came
from the Southern mountains. He was young, with small education, but lots of energy and ambition." Mr. Yandro swelled up
inside his fancy clothes. "He went to New York, then Chicago.
His fortunes prospered. His son—my father—and then I, we con-
trived to make them prosper still more."

"You're to be honored," I said, my politest; but I judged, with
no reason to be sure, that he might not be too honorable about
how he made his money, or used it. The way the others drew
from him made me reckon he scared them, and that kind of folks
scares worst where their money pocket's located.

"I've done all right," he said, not caring who heard the brag. "I
don't think anybody for a hundred miles around here can turn a
deal or make a promise without clearing it with me. John, I own
this part of the world."

Again he showed his teeth. "You're the first one ever to tell me
about where my grandfather might have come from. Yandro's
high hill, eh? How do we get there, John?"

I tried to think of the way from highway to side way, side way
to trail, and so in and around and over. "I fear," I said, "I could
show you better than I could tell you."

"All right, you'll show me," he said, with no notion I might
want something different. "I can afford to make up my mind on a

moment's notice like that. I'll call the airport and charter a plane. We leave now."

"I asked John to stay tonight," said my hostess lady.

"We leave now," said Mr. Yandro, and she shut right up, and I saw how it was. Everybody was scared of him. Maybe they'd be pleasured if I took him out of there for a while.

"Get your plane," I said. "We leave now."

He meant that thing. Not many hours had died before the hired plane set us down at the airport between Asheville and Hendersonville. A taxi rode us into Hendersonville. Mr. Yandro woke up a used car man and bought a fair car from him. Then, on my guiding, Mr. Yandro took out in the dark for that part of the mountains I pointed out to him.

The sky stretched over us with no moon at all, only a many stars, like little stitches of blazing thread in a black quilt. For real light, only our headlamps—first on a paved road twining around one slope and over another and behind a third, then a gravel road and pretty good, then a dirt road and pretty bad.

"What a stinking country!" said Mr. Yandro as we chugged along a ridge as lean as a butcher knife.

I didn't say how I resented that word about a country that stoops to none for prettiness. "Maybe we ought to have waited till day," I said.

"I never wait," he sniffed. "Where's the town?"

"No town. Just the valley. Three-four hours away. We'll be there by midnight."

"Oh, God. Let's have some of that whiskey I brought." He reached for the glove compartment, but I shoved his hand away.

"Not if you're going to drive these mountain roads, Mr. Yandro."

"Then you drive a while, and I'll take a drink."

"I don't know how to drive a car, Mr. Yandro."

"Oh, God," he said again, and couldn't have scorned me more if I'd said I didn't know how to wash my face. "What is a desrick, exactly?"

"Only old-aged folks use the word any more. It's the kind of cabin they used to make, strong logs and a door you can bar, and loophole windows. So you could stand off Indians, maybe."

"Or the wild beasts can't reach you," he quoted, and snickered. "What wild beasts do they have up here in the Forgotten Latitudes?"

"Can't rightly say. A few bears, a wildcat or two. Used to be wolves, and a bounty for killing them. I'm not sure what else."

True enough, I wasn't sure about the tales I'd heard. Not anyway when Mr. Yandro was ready to sneer at them for foolishment.

Our narrow road climbed a great slant of rock one way, then doubled back to climb opposite, and became a double rut, with an empty, hell-scary drop of thousands of feet beside the car. Finally Mr. Yandro edged us into a sort of nick beside the road and shut off the power. He shook. Fear must have been a new feel in his bones.

"Want some of the whiskey, John?" he asked, and drank.

"Thank you, no. We walk from here, anyway. Beyond's the valley."

He grumped and mad-whispered, but out he got. I took a flashlight and my silver-strung guitar and led out. It was a downways walk, on a narrow trail where even mules would be nervous. And not quiet enough to be easy.

There were mountain night noises, like you never get used to, not even if you're born and raised there, and live and die there. Noises too soft and sneaky to be real murmuring voices. Noises like big flapping wings far off and then near. And, above and below the trail, noises like heavy soft paws keeping pace with you, sometimes two paws, sometimes four, sometimes many. They stay with you, noises like that, all the hours you grope along the night trail, all the way down to the valley so low, till you bless God for the little crumb of light that means a human home, and you ache and pray to get to that home, be it ever so humble, so you'll be safe in the light.

I've wondered since if Mr. Yandro's constant blubber and chatter was a string of curses or a string of prayers.

The light we saw was a pine-knot fire inside a little coop above the stream that giggled in the valley bottom. The door was open, and someone sat on the threshold.

"Is that a desrick?" panted and puffed Mr. Yandro.

"No, it's newer made. There's Miss Tully at the door, sitting up to think."

Miss Tully remembered me and welcomed us. She was eighty or ninety, without a tooth in her mouth to clamp her stone-bowl pipe, but she stood straight as a pine on the split-slab floor, and the firelight showed no gray in her tight-combed black hair. "Rest your hats," said Miss Tully. "So this stranger man's name is Mr. Yandro. Funny, you coming just now. You're looking for the des-rick on Yandro, it's still right where it's been," and she pointed with her pipe stem off into the empty dark across the valley and up.

Inside, she gave us two chairs bottomed with juniper bark and sat on a stool next to the shelf with herbs in pots, and one or two old paper books, *The Long Lost Friend* and *Egyptian Secrets*, and *Big Albert* the one they say can't be thrown away or given away, only got rid of by burying with a funeral prayer, like a human corpse. "Funny," she said again, "you coming along as the seventy-five years are up."

We questioned, and she told us what we'd come to hear. "I was just a little pigtail girl back then," she said, "when Joris Yandro courted Polly Wiltse, the witch girl. Mr. Yandro, you favor your grandsire a right much. He wasn't as stout-built as you, and younger by years, when he left."

Even the second time hearing it, I listened hard. It was like a many such tale at the start. Polly Wiltse was sure enough a witch, not just a study-witch like Miss Tully, and Polly Wiltse's beauty would melt the heart of nature and make a dumb man cry out, "Praise God Who made her!" But none dared court her save only Joris Yandro, who was handsome for a man like she was lovely for a girl. For it was his wish to get her to show him the gold on top of the mountain named for his folks, that only Polly Wiltse and her witching could find.

"Certain sure there's gold in these mountains," I answered Mr. Yandro's interrupting question. "Before ever the California rush started, folks mined and minted gold in these parts, the history-men say."

"Gold," he repeated, both respectful and greedy. "I was right to come."

Miss Tully said that Joris Yandro coaxed Polly Wiltse to bring down gold to him, and he carried it away and never came back. And Polly Wiltse pined and mourned like a sick bird, and on Yandro's top she built her desrick. She sang the song, the one I'd sung, it was part of a long spell and charm. Three quarters of a century would pass, seventy-five years, and her lover would come back.

"But he didn't," said Mr. Yandro. "My grandfather died up north."

"He sent his grandson, who favors him," said Miss Tully. "The song you heard brought you back at the right time." She thumbed tobacco into her pipe. "All the Yandro kin moved away, pure down scared of Polly Wiltse's singing."

"In her desrick, where the wild beasts can't reach her," quoted Mr. Yandro, and chuckled. "John says they have bears and wildcats up here." He expected her to say I was stretching it.

"Oh, there's other creatures, too. Scarce animals, like the Toller."

"The Toller?" he said.

"It's the hugest flying thing there is, I guess," said Miss Tully. "Its voice tolls like a bell, to tell other creatures their feed's near. And there's the Flat. It lies level with the ground, and not much higher. It can wrap you like a blanket." She lighted the pipe. "And the Bammat. Big, the Bammat is."

"The Behemoth, you mean," he suggested.

"No, the Behemoth's in the Bible. The Bammat's something hairy-like, with big ears and a long wiggly nose and twisty white teeth sticking out of its mouth—"

"Oh!" And Mr. Yandro trumpeted his laughter. "You've got some story about the Mammoth. Why, they've been extinct— dead and forgotten—for thousands of years."

"Not for so long, I've heard tell," she said, puffing.

"Anyway," he went on arguing, "the Mammoth—the Bammat, as you call it—is of the elephant family. How would anything like that get up in the mountains?"

"Maybe folks hunted it there," said Miss Tully, "and maybe it stays there so folks will think it's dead and gone a thousand years. And there's the Behinder."

"And what," said Mr. Yandro, "might the Behinder look like?"

"Can't rightly say, Mr. Yandro. For it's always behind the man or woman it wants to grab. And there's the Skim—it kites through the air—and the Culverin, that can shoot pebbles with its mouth."

"And you believe all that?" sneered Mr. Yandro, the way he always sneered at everything, everywhere.

"Why else should I tell it?" she replied. "Well, sir, you're back where your kin used to live, in the valley where they named the mountain for them. I can let you two sleep on my front stoop tonight."

"I came to climb the mountain and see the desrick," said Mr. Yandro with that anxious hurry to him that I kept wondering about.

"You can't climb up there until it's light," she told him, and she made us two quilt pallets on the split-slab stoop.

I was tired and glad to stretch out, but Mr. Yandro grumbled, as if we were wasting time. At sunup next morning, Miss Tully fried us some side meat and slices of hominy grit porridge, and she fixed us a snack to carry, and a gourd to put water in. Mr. Yandro held out a ten dollar bill.

"No, I thank you," said Miss Tully. "I bade you stay, and I won't take money for that."

"Oh, everybody takes money from me," he snickered, and threw it on the door-sill at her feet. "Go on, it's yours."

Quick as a weasel, Miss Tully's hand grabbed a stick of stove wood.

"Lean down and take back that money-bill, Mister," she said.

He did as she told him. With the stick she pointed out across the stream that ran through the thickets below us, and up the height beyond. She acted as if there wasn't any trouble a second before.

"That's the Yandro Mountain," she said. "There, on the highest point, where it looks like the crown of a hat, thick with trees all the way up, stands the desrick built by Polly Wiltse. You look close, with the sun rising, and you can maybe make it out."

I looked hard. There for sure it was, far off and high up, and tiny, but I could see it. It looked a lean sort of a building.

"How about trails going up?" I asked her.

"There's trails up there, John, but nobody walks them."

"Now, now," said Mr. Yandro, "if there's a trail, somebody must walk it."

"May be a lot in what you say, but I know nobody in this valley would set foot to such a trail. Not with what they say's up there."

He laughed at her, as I wouldn't have dared. "You mean the Bammat," he said. "And the Flat, and the Skim, and the Culverin."

"And the Toller," she added for him. "And the Behinder. Only a gone gump would go up there."

We headed away down to the waterside, and crossed on logs laid on top of rocks. On the far side a trail led along, and when the sun was an hour higher we were at the foot of Yandro's high hill, and a trail went up there, too.

We rested. Mr. Yandro needed rest worse than I did. Moving most of the night before, unused to walking and climbing, he had a gaunted look to his heavy face, and his clothes were sweated, and dust dulled out his shoes. But he grinned at me.

"So she's waited seventy-five years," he said, "and so I look like the man she's waiting for. And so there's gold up there. More gold than my grandfather could have carried off."

"You believe what you've been hearing," I said, and it was a mystery.

"John, a wise man knows when to believe the unusual, and how it will profit him. She's up there, waiting, and so is the gold."

"What when you find it?" I asked.

"My grandfather was able to go off and leave her. It sounds like a good example to me." He grinned wider and toothier. "I'll give you part of the gold."

"No thanks, Mr. Yandro."

"You don't want your pay? Why did you come here with me?"

"Just made up my mind on a moment's notice, like you."

He scowled then, but he looked up at the height. "How long will it take to climb, John?"

"Depends on how fast we climb, how well we keep up the pace."

"Then let's go," and he started up the trail.

It wasn't folks' feet had worn that trail. I saw a hoofmark.

"Deer," grunted Mr. Yandro; and I said, "Maybe."

We scrambled up on a rightward slant, then leftward. The trees marched in close around us, with branches above that filtered only soft green light. Something rustled, and we saw a brown, furry shape, big as a big cat, scuttling out of sight.

"Woodchuck," wheezed Mr. Yandro; again I said, "Maybe."

After an hour's working upward we rested, and after two hours more we rested again. Around 11 o'clock we reached an open space where clear light touched the middle, and there we sat on a log and ate the corn bread and smoked meat Miss Tully had fixed. Mr. Yandro mopped his face with a fancy handkerchief, and gobbled food for strength to glitter his eye at me. "What are you glooming about?" he said. "You look as if you'd call me a name if you weren't afraid."

"I've held my tongue," I said, "by way of manners, not fear. I'm just thinking about how and why we came so far and sudden to this place."

"You sang me a song, and I heard, and thought I'd come to where my people originated. Now I have a hunch about profit. That's enough for you."

"It's not just that gold story," I said. "You're more than rich enough."

"I'm going up there," said Mr. Yandro, "because, by God, that old hag down there said everybody's afraid to do it. And you said you'd go with me."

"I'll go right to the top with you," I said.

I forebore to say that something had come close and looked from among the trees behind him. It was big and broad-headed, with elephant ears to right and left, and white tusks like bannisters on a spiral staircase. But it was woolly-shaggy, like a buffalo bull. The Bammat. How could such a thing move so quiet-like?

He drank from his whiskey bottle, and on we climbed. We could hear those noises in the woods and brush, behind rocks and down little gulleys, as if the mountain side thronged with living things as thick as fleas on a possum dog and another sight sneakier. I didn't let on I was nervous.

"Why are you singing under your breath?" he grunted after a while.

"I'm not singing," I said. "I need my breath for climbing."

"I hear you!" he charged me, like a lawyer in court.

We'd stopped dead on the trail, and I heard it, too.

It was soft, almost like some half-remembered song in your mind. It was the Yandro song, all right:

> Look away, look away, look away over Yandro,
> Where them wild things are flyin'
> From bough to bough, and a-mating with their mates,
> So why not me with mine?

"That singing comes from up above us," I told Mr. Yandro.

"Then," he said, "we must be nearly at the top."

As we started climbing again, I could hear the noises to right and left in the woods, and then I realized they'd quieted down when we stopped. They moved when we moved, they waited when we waited. There were lots of them. Soft noises, but lots of them.

Which is why I myself, and probably Mr. Yandro too, didn't pause any more on the way up, even on a rocky stretch where we had to climb on all fours. It may have been an hour after noon when we came to the top.

Right there was a circle-shaped clearing, with the trees thronged around it all the way except an open space toward the slope. Those trees had mist among and between them, quiet and fluffy, like spider webbing. And at the open space, on the lip of the way down, perched the desrick.

Old-aged was what it looked. It stood high and looked the higher, because it was built so narrow of unnotched logs, set four above four, hogpen fashion, as tall as a tall tobacco barn. The spaces between the logs were clinked shut with great masses and wads of clay. The steep-pitched roof was of shingles, cut long and narrow, so that they looked almost like thatch. There was one big door, made of an axe-chopped plank, and the hinges must have been inside, for I could see none. And one window, covered with what must have been rawhide scraped thin, with a glow of soft light coming through.

"That's it," puffed Mr. Yandro. "The desrick."

I looked at him then, and knew what most he wanted on

this earth. He wanted to be boss. Money was just something to greaten him. His idea of greatness was bigness. He wanted to do all the talking, and have everybody else do the listening. He had his eyes hung on that desrick, and he licked his lips, like a cat over a dish of cream.

"Let's go in," he said.

"Not where I'm not invited," I told him, as flatly as anybody could ever tell him. "I said I'd come to the top. This is the top."

"Come with me," he said. "My name's Yandro. This mountain's name is Yandro. I can buy and sell every man, woman and child in this part of the country. If I say it's all right to go into a house, it's all right to go into a house."

He meant that thing. The world and everybody in it was just there to let him walk on. He took a step toward the desrick. Somebody hummed inside, not the words of the song, but the tune. Mr. Yandro snorted at me, to show how small he reckoned me because I held back, and he headed toward the big door.

"If she's there, she'll show me the gold," he said.

But I couldn't have moved from where I stood at the edge of the clearing. I was aware of a sort of closing in all around the edge, among the trees and brushy clumps. Not that the closing in could be seen, but there was a *gong-gong* farther off, the voice of the Toller norating to the other creatures their feed was near. And above the treetops sailed a round, flat thing, like a big plate being pitched high. A Skim. Then another Skim. And the blood inside my body was cold and solid as ice, and my voice turned to a handful of sand in my throat.

I knew, plain as paint, that if I tried to back up, to turn around even, my legs would fail and I'd fall down. With fingers like twigs with sleet stuck to them, I dragged around my guitar, to pluck at the silver strings, because silver is protection against evil.

But I didn't. For out of the bushes near me the Bammat stuck its broad woolly head, and it shook that head at me once, for silence. It looked me between the eyes, steadier than a beast should look at a man, and shook its head. I wasn't to make any noise. And I didn't. When the Bammat saw that I'd be quiet, it paid me no more mind, and I knew I wasn't to be included in what would happen then.

Mr. Yandro was knocking at the axe-chopped door. He waited, and knocked again. I heard him growl, something about how he wasn't used to waiting for people to answer his knock.

Inside, the humming had died out. After a moment, Mr. Yandro moved around to where the window was, and picked at the rawhide.

I could see, but he couldn't, as around from behind the corner of the desrick flowed something. It lay out on the ground like a broad, black, short-furred carpet rug. But it moved, humping and then flattening out, the way a measuring worm moves. It moved pretty fast, right toward Mr. Yandro from behind and to one side. The Toller said *gong-gong-gong,* from closer in.

"Anybody in there?" bawled Mr. Yandro. "Let me in!"

The crawling carpet brushed its edge against his foot. He looked down at it, and his eyes stuck out all of a sudden, like two door knobs. He knew what it was, and named it at the top of his voice.

"The Flat!"

Humping against him, it tried to wrap around his foot and leg. He gasped out something I'd never want written down for my last words, and pulled loose and ran, fast and straight, toward the edge of the clearing.

Gong-gong, said the Toller, and Mr. Yandro tried to slip along next to the trees. But, just ahead of him, the Culverin hoved itself half into sight on its many legs. It pointed its needle-shaped mouth and spit a pebble. I heard the pebble ring on Mr. Yandro's head. He staggered against a tree. And I saw what nobody's ever supposed to see.

The Behinder flung itself on his shoulders. Then I knew why nobody's supposed to see one. I wish I hadn't. To this day I can see it, as plain as a fence at noon, and forever I will be able to see it. But talking about it's another matter. Thank you, I won't try.

Then everything else was out—the Bammat, the Culverin, and all the others. They were hustling him across toward the desrick, and the door moved slowly and quietly open for him to come in.

As for me, I was out of their minds, and I hoped and prayed they wouldn't care if I just went on down the trail as fast as I could set one foot below the other.

Scrambling and scrambling down, without a noise to keep me company, I figured that I'd probably had my unguessed part in the whole thing. Seventy-five years had to pass, and then Mr. Yandro come there to the desrick. And it needed me, or somebody like me, to meet him and sing the song that would put it in his head and heart to come to where his granddaddy had courted Polly Wiltse, just as though it was his own whim.

No. No, of course, he wasn't the man who had made Polly Wiltse love him and then had left her. But he was the man's grandson, of the same blood and the same common, low-down, sorry nature that wanted money and power, and didn't care who he hurt so he could have both. And he looked like Joris Yandro. Polly Wiltse would recognize him.

I haven't studied much about what Polly Wiltse was like, welcoming him into the desrick on Yandro, after waiting inside for three quarters of a century. Anyway, I never heard of him following me down. Maybe he's been missed. But I'll lay you anything you name he's not been mourned.

VANDY, VANDY

That valley hadn't any name. Such outside folks as knew about it just said, "Back in yonder," and folks inside said, "Here." The mail truck dropped a few letters in a hollow tree, next to a ridge where a trail went up and over and down. Three, four times a year, bearded men in homemade clothes and shoes fetched out their makings—clay dishes and pots, mostly, for dealers to sell to tourists. They carried back coffee, salt, gunpowder, a few nails. Things like that.

It was a day's scramble on that ridge trail, I vow, even with my long legs and no load but my silver-strung guitar. No lumberman had ever cut the thick, big old trees. I quenched my thirst at a stream and followed it down. Near sunset, I heard music jangling.

Fire shone out through an open cabin door, to where folks sat on a stoop log and frontyard rocks. One had a guitar, another fiddled, and hands slapped so a boy about ten or twelve could jig. Then they all spied me and fell quiet. They looked, and didn't know me.

"That was pretty, ladies and gentlemen," I said, but nobody remarked.

A long-bearded old man with one suspender and no shoes held the fiddle on his knee. I reckoned he was the grandsire. A younger, shorter-bearded man with the guitar might be his son. There was a dry old mother, there was the son's plump wife, there was a younger yellow-haired girl, and there was that dancing little grandboy.

"What can we do for you, young sir?" asked the old man. Not that he sounded like doing anything—mountain folks say that even to the government man who's come hunting a still on their place.

"Why," I said, "I sort of want a place to sleep."

"Right much land to stretch out on yonder," said the guitar man.

I tried again. "I heard you all playing first part of *Fire in the Mountains.*"

"Is they two parts?" That was the boy, before anyone could silence him.

"Sure enough, son," I said. "Let me show you the second part."

The old man opened his beard, likely to say wait till I was asked, but I strummed my own guitar into second part, best I knew how. Then I played first part through, and, "You sure God can pick that," said the short-bearded one. "Do it again."

I did it again. When I reached second part, the old man sawed fiddle along with me. We went around *Fire in the Mountains* once more, and the ladyfolks clapped hands and the boy jigged. Still nobody smiled, but when we stopped the old man made me a nod. "Sit on that rock," he said. "What might we call you?"

"My name's John," I told him.

"I'm Tewk Millen. Mother, I reckon John's a-tired, coming from outside. He might relish a gourd of cold water."

"We're just before having a bite," the old lady said to me. "Ain't but just smoke meat and beans, but you're welcome."

"I'm sure honored, Mrs. Millen," I said. "But it's a trouble."

"No trouble," said Mr. Tewk Millen. "Let me make you known to my son Heber and his wife Jill, and this here is boy Calder."

"Proud to know you," they all said.

"And my girl Vandy," Mr. Tewk finished.

I looked at her hair like yellow corn silk and her eyes like purple violets. "Vandy?" I said after her father.

Shy, she dimpled at me. "I know it's a scarce name, Mr. John, I never heard it anywhere but among my kinfolks."

"I have," I said, "and it's what brought me here."

Mr. Tewk Millen looked funny above his whiskers. "Thought you said you was a young stranger man."

"I heard the name outside in a song, sir. Somebody allowed the song's known here. I'm a singer. I go far after a good song." I looked around. "Do you all know that Vandy song, folks?"

"Yes, sir," said little Calder, but the others studied a minute. Mr. Tewk rubbed up a leaf of tobacco into his pipe.

"Calder," he said, "go in and fetch me a chunk of fire to light up with. John, you certain you never met my daughter Vandy?"

"Certain sure," I made reply. "Only I can figure how ary young fellow might come a far piece to meet her."

She stared down at her hands where she sat. "We learnt the song from papa," she half-whispered, "and he learnt it from his papa—"

"And my papa learnt it from his," Mr. Tewk finished for her. "It goes a way back, that song, I figure."

"I'd sure enough relish hearing it," I said.

"After you heard it," said Mr. Tewk. "After you learnt it, what would you do?"

"Why," I said, "I reckon I'd go back outside and sing it some."

I could see that's what he wanted to hear.

"Heber," he told his son, "you pick it out and I'll scrape this fiddle, and Calder and Vandy can sing it for John."

They played the tune once without words. The notes were put together strangely, in what schooled folks call minors. But other folks, better schooled yet, say such tunes sound strange and lonesome because in old times folks had another note scale from our do-re-mi-fa today. And little Calder piped up, high and young but strong:

> Vandy, Vandy, I've come to court you,
>   Be you rich or be you poor,
> And if you'll kindly entertain me,
>   I will love you forever more.
>
> Vandy, Vandy, I've gold and silver,
>   Vandy, Vandy, I've a house and land,
> Vandy, Vandy, I've a world of pleasure,
>   I would make you a handsome man.

He got that far, singing for the fellow come courting, and Vandy sang back the reply, sweet as a bird:

> I love a man who's in the army,
>   He's been there for seven long year,
> And if he's there for seven year longer,
>   I won't court no other dear.
>
> What care I for your gold and silver,
>   What care I for—

She stopped, and the guitar and fiddle stopped, and it was like the death of sound. The leaves didn't rustle in the trees, nor the fire didn't stir on the hearth inside. They all looked with their mouths half open, where somebody stood with his hands crossed on the gold knob of a black cane and grinned all on one side of his toothy mouth.

Maybe he came up the down-valley trail, maybe he'd dropped from a tree like a possum. He was built spry and slim, with a long coat buttoned to his pointed chin, and brown pants tucked into elastic-sided boots, like what your grandsire had. His hands on the cane looked slim and strong. His face, bar its crooked smile, might be handsome. His dark brown hair curled like buffalo wool, and his eyes were the shiny pale gray of a new knife. Their gaze crawled all over the Millens and he laughed a slow, soft laugh.

"I thought I'd stop by," he crooned, "if I haven't worn out my welcome."

"Oh, no *sir!*" said Mr. Tewk, standing up on his two bare feet, fiddle in hand. "No sir, Mr. Loden, we're proud to have you, mighty proud," he jabber-squawked, like a rooster caught by the leg. "You sit down, sir, make yourself easy."

Mr. Loden sat down on the seat-rock Mr. Tewk had left, and Mr. Tewk found a place on the stoop log by his wife, nervous as a boy stealing apples.

"Your servant, Mrs. Millen," said Mr. Loden. "Heber, you look well, and your good wife. Calder, I brought you candy."

His slim hand offered a bright striped stick, red and yellow. You'd think a country child would snatch it. But Calder took it slow and scared, as he'd take a poison-snake. You'd think he'd decline if he dared.

"For you, Mr. Tewk," went on Mr. Loden, "I've fetched some of my tobacco. An excellent weed." He handed Mr. Tewk a pouch of soft brown leather. "Empty your pipe. Enjoy it, sir."

"Thank you kindly," said Mr. Tewk, and sighed and began to do what he'd been ordered.

"And Miss Vandy." Mr. Loden's croon petted her name. "I wouldn't venture here without hoping you'd receive a trifle at my hands."

He dangled it from a chain, a gold thing the size of his pink thumbnail. In it shone a white jewel, that grabbed the firelight and twinkled red.

"Do me the honor, Miss Vandy, to let it rest on your heart, that I may envy it."

She took the jewel and sat with it between her soft little hands. Mr. Loden turned his eye-knives on me. "Now," he said, "we come around to the stranger within your gates."

"Yes, we come around to me," I agreed, hugging my guitar on my knee. "My name's John, Mr. Loden."

"Where are you from, John?" It was sudden, almost fierce, like a lawyer in a courtroom.

"From nowhere," I said.

"Meaning, from everywhere," he supplied me. "What do you do?"

"I wander," I said. "I sing songs. I mind my own business and watch my manners."

"*Touché!*" he cried in a foreign tongue, and smiled on that same side of his mouth. "You oblige me to remember how sometimes I err in my speech. My duties and apologies, John. I'm afraid my country ways seem rude at times, to world travellers. No offense."

"None taken," I said, and kept from adding on that real country ways were polite ways.

"Mr. Loden," put in Mr. Tewk again, "I make bold to offer you what poor rations my old woman's made—"

"Sir," Mr. Loden broke him off, "they're good enough for the best man living. I'll help Mrs. Millen prepare them. After you, ma'am."

She walked in, and he followed. What he said there was what happened.

"Miss Vandy," he said next, "you might help us."

She went in, too. Dishes clattered. Through the open door I saw Mr. Loden put a tweak of powder in the skillet on the fire. The menfolks sat outside and said nothing. They might have been nailed down, with stones in their mouths. I studied about what could make a proud, honorable mountain family so scared of a guest and I knew there was only the one thing. And that one thing wouldn't be just a natural thing. It would be a thing beyond nature or the world.

Finally little Calder said, "Maybe we can finish the song after a while," and his voice was a weak young voice now.

"I recollect about another song from here," I said. "About the fair and blooming wife."

Those closed mouths all snapped open, then shut again. Touching the guitar's silver strings, I began:

> There was a fair and blooming wife
>   And of children she had three.
> She sent them away to Northern school
>   To study gramaree.
>
> But the King's men came upon that school,
>   And when sword and rope had done,
> Of the children three she sent away,
>   Returned to her but one. . . .

"Supper's made," said Mrs. Millen from inside.

We all went in to where there was a trestle table and a clean homewoven cloth and clay dishes set out. Mr. Loden, by the pots at the fire, waved for Mrs. Millen and Vandy to dish up the food.

It wasn't smoke meat and beans I saw on my plate. Whatever it was, it wasn't that. Everyone looked at their helps of food, but not even Calder took any till Mr. Loden sat down, half-smiling.

"Why," he said, "one would think you feared poison."

Then Mr. Tewk forked up a big bait and put it into his beard. Calder did likewise, and the others. I took a mouthful and it sure enough tasted good.

"Let me honor your cooking, sir," I told Mr. Loden. "It's like witch magic."

His eyes came on me, as I knew they'd come after that word. He laughed, so short and sharp everybody jumped.

"John, you sang a song from this valley," he said. "About the blooming wife with three children who went north to study gramaree. John, do you know what gramaree means?"

"Grammar," spoke up Calder. "The right way to talk."

"Hush," whispered his father and he hushed.

"I've heard, sir," I replied to Mr. Loden; "gramaree is witch stuff, witch knowledge and magic and power. That Northern school could be only one place."

"What place, John?" he almost sang under his breath.

"A Massachusetts Yankee town called Salem, sir. Around 300 years back—"

"Not by so much," said Mr. Loden. "In 1692, John."

I waited a breath and everybody stared above those steaming plates.

"Sixteen ninety-two," I agreed. "A preacher man named Cotton Mather found them teaching witch stuff to children. I hear tell they killed twenty folks, and mostly the wrong folks, but two, three were sure enough witches."

"George Burroughs," said Mr. Loden, half to himself. "Martha Carrier. And Bridget Bishop. They were real. Others got away safely, and one of the young children of the three. Somebody owed that child the two lost young lives of his brothers, John."

"I call to mind something else I heard," I said. "They scare young folks with the story outside here. The one child lived to be a hundred years old. And his son had a hundred years of life, and his son's son had a hundred years more. Maybe that's why I thought the witch school at Salem was 300 years past."

"Not by so much," he said again. "Even give the child that got away the age of Calder there, it would be only about 270 years."

He was daring any of Mr. Tewk's family to speak up or even breathe heavy, and nobody took the dare.

"From 300, that leaves 30 years," I figured. "A lot can be done in 30 years, Mr. Loden."

"That's the naked truth," he said, his eye-knives on Vandy's young face, and he got up and bowed all around. "I thank you all for your hospitality. I'll come again if I may."

"Yes, sir," said Mr. Tewk in a hurry, but Mr. Loden looked at Vandy, waiting.

"Yes, sir," she told him, as if it would choke her.

He took up his gold-headed cane and gazed at me a hard gaze. Then I did a rude thing, but it was all I could think of.

"I don't feel right, not paying for what you all gave me," I allowed, getting up myself. From my dungaree pocket I took a silver quarter and dropped it on the table, almost in front of Mr. Loden.

"Take it away!" he squeaked, almost like a bat, and out of the house he was gone, bat-swift and bat-sudden.

The others sat and gopped after him. The night was thick outside, like black wool around the cabin. Mr. Tewk cleared his throat.

"John, you're better brought up than that," he said. "We don't take money from nobody we bid to eat with us. Pick it up."

"Yes, sir," I said. "I ask pardon, sir."

Putting away the quarter, I felt a trifle better. I'd done that once before with a silver quarter. I'd scared a man named Onselm almost out of his black art. So Mr. Loden was another witch man, and so he could be scared, too. I reckon I was foolish to think it was as easy as that.

I walked outside, leaving Mrs. Millen and Vandy doing up the dishes. The firelight showed me the stoop log to sit on. I touched my silver guitar strings and began to pick out the *Vandy, Vandy* tune, soft and gentle. After while, Calder came out and sat beside me and sang the words. I liked best the last verse:

> *Wake up, wake up! The dawn is breaking,*
> *Wake up, wake up! It's almost day.*
> *Open up your doors and your divers windows,*
> *See my true love march away. . . .*

Calder finished, and then he said, "Mr. John, I never made out what divers windows is."

"An old time word," I said. "It means different kinds of windows. Another thing proves it's a mighty old song. A man seven years in the army must have gone to the war with the English, the first one. It lasted longer here in the south than other places, from 1775 to 1782." I figured a moment. "How old are you, Calder?"

"Rising onto ten."

"Big for your age. A boy your years in 1692 would be 90 in 1782 if he lived, what time the English war was near done and somebody or other had served seven years in the army."

"In Washington's army," said Calder, to himself. "King Washington."

"King who?" I asked.

"Mr. Loden calls him King Washington. The man that hell-drove the English soldiers and rules in his own name town."

That's what they must think in that valley. I never said that Washington was no king but a president, and that he'd died and gone to rest when his work was done and his country safe. I kept thinking about somebody 90 years old in 1782, courting a girl with her true love seven years marched away in the army.

"Calder," I said, "don't the *Vandy, Vandy* song tell about your own folks?"

He looked into the cabin, where nobody listened, then into the black-wool darkness. I struck a chord on the silver strings. Then he said, "Yes, Mr. John, so I've heard tell."

I hushed the strings with my hand and he talked on.

"I reckon you've heard lots of this, or guessed it. About that witch child that lived to a hundred—he came courting a girl named Vandy, but she was a good girl."

"Bad folks sometimes come to court good ones," I said.

"But she wouldn't have him, not with all his money and land. And when he pressed her, her soldier man came home, with his discharge writing in his hand, and on it King Washington's name, he was free from soldiering. He was Hosea Tewk, my grandsire some few times removed. And my own grandsire's mother was Vandy Tewk, and my sister is Vandy Millen."

"How about the hundred-year witch man?"

Calder looked around again. Then he said, "He had to get somebody else, I reckon, to birth him a son before his hundred years was gone and he died. We think that son married at another hundred years, and his son is Mr. Loden, the grandson of the first witch man."

"I see. Now, your grandsire's mother, Vandy Tewk. How old would she be, Calder?"

"She's dead and gone, but she was born the first year her pa was off fighting the Yankees."

Eighteen sixty-one, then. In 1882, end of the second hundred years, she'd be ripe for the courting. "And she married a Millen," I said.

"Yes, sir. Even when the Mr. Loden that lived then tried to court her. But she married Mr. Washington Millen."

"Washington," I said. "Named after the man who whipped the English."

"He was my great-grandsire and he feared nothing, like King Washington."

I picked a silver string. "No witch man got the first Vandy," I reminded him. "Nor the second Vandy."

"A witch man wants the Vandy that's here now," said Calder. "Mr. John, I'm right sorry you won't steal her away from him."

I got up. "Tell your folks I've gone for a night walk."

"Not to Mr. Loden's." He got up, too. His face was pale beside me. "He won't let you come."

The night was more than black, it was solid. No sound in it and no life. I won't say I couldn't have stepped off into it, but I didn't. I sat down again. Mr. Tewk spoke my name, then Vandy.

We all sat in front of the cabin and spoke about weather and crops. Vandy was at my one side, Calder at the other. We sang—*Dream True,* I recollect, and *Rebel Soldier.* Vandy sang the sweetest I ever heard, but as I played I couldn't but think somebody listened in the blackness. If it was on Yandro Mountain and not in that valley, I'd have figured the Behinder sneaking close, or the Flat under our feet. But Vandy sounded happy, her violet eyes looked at me, her rose lips smiled.

Finally Vandy and Mrs. Millen said good night and went into a back room. Heber and his wife and Calder laddered up into the loft. Mr. Tewk offered me a pallet bed by the fire.

"I want to sleep at the door," I told him.

He looked at me, at the door, and, "Have it your way," he said.

I pulled off my shoes. I said a prayer and stretched out on the quilt he gave me. But when all others slept, I lay and listened.

Hours afterward, the sound came. The fire was just a coal ember, red light was soft in the cabin when I heard the snicker. Mr. Loden stooped over me at the door sill, and couldn't come closer.

"You can't get in," I said to him.

"Oh, you're awake," he said. "The others are asleep. They'll stay so, by my doing. And you won't move, any more than they will."

I couldn't sit up. It was like being dried into clay, like a frog or a lizard that must wait for the rain.

"Bind," he said to someone over me. "Bind, bind. Unless you can count the stars, or the drops in the ocean, be bound."

It was a spell-saying. "From the *Long-Lost Friend?*" I asked.

"Albertus Magnus," he answered, "or the book they say he wrote."

"I've seen the book."

"You'll stay where you lie till sunrise. Then—"

I tried to get up. It was no use.

"See this?" He held it to my face. It was my picture, drawn true to me. He had the drawing gift. "At sunrise I'll strike it with this."

He laid the picture on the ground. Then he brought forward his gold-headed cane. He twisted the handle, and out of the cane's inside came a blade of pale iron, thin and mean as a snake. There was writing on it, but I couldn't read in that poor light.

"I touch my point to your picture," Mr. Loden said, "and you won't bother Vandy or me. I should have done that to Hosea Tewk."

"Hosea Tewk," I said after him, "or Washington Millen."

The tip of his blade wiggled in front of my eyes. "Don't say that name, John."

"Washington Millen," I said it again. "Named after George Washington. Why don't you like George Washington's name? Did you know him?"

He took a long, mean breath, as if cold rain fell on him. "You've guessed what these folks haven't guessed, John."

"I've guessed you're not a witch man's grandson, but a witch woman's son," I said. "You got away from that Salem school in 1692. You've lived near 300 years, and when they're over, you know where you'll go."

His blade hung over my throat, like a wasp over a ripe peach. Then he drew it back. "No," he told himself. "The Millens would know I stabbed you. Let them think you died in your sleep."

"You knew Washington," I said over again. "Maybe—"

"Maybe I offered him help, and he was foolish enough to refuse it. Maybe—"

"Maybe Washington scared you away from him," I broke in the way he had, "and maybe he won his war without witch magic. And maybe that was bad for you, because the one who gave you 300 years expected pay—good folks turned into bad folks. Then you tried to win Vandy for yourself. The first Vandy."

"Maybe a little for myself," he half sang, "but mostly for—"

"Mostly for the one who gave you 300 years," I finished another sentence.

I was tightening and swelling my muscles, trying to pull loose from what held me down. I might as well have tried to wear my way through solid rock.

"Vandy," Mr. Loden's voice touched her name. "The third Vandy, the sweetest and best. She's like a spring day and like a summer night. When I see her with a bucket at the spring or a basket in the garden, my eyes swim, John. It's as if I see a spirit walking past."

"A good spirit. Your time's short. You want to win her from a good way to a bad way."

"Her voice is like a lark's," he crooned, with the blade low in his hand. "It's like wind over a bank of roses and violets. It's like the light of stars turned into music."

"You want to lead her down to hell," I said.

"Maybe we won't go to hell, or heaven either. Maybe we'll live and live. Why don't you say something about that, John?"

"I'm thinking," I made answer.

And I was. I was trying to remember what I had to remember.

It's in the third part of the Albertus Magnus book Mr. Loden mentioned, the third part full of holy names he sure enough wouldn't read. I'd seen it, as I'd told him. If the words would come back—

Something sent part of them. "The cross in my right hand," I said, too soft for him to hear, "that I may travel the open land. . . ."

"Maybe 300 years more," said Mr. Loden, "without anybody like Hosea Tewk, or Washington Millen, or you, John, coming to stop us. Three hundred years with Vandy, and she'll know the things I know, do the things I do."

I'd been able to twist my right forefinger over my middle one, for the cross in my right hand. I said more words as I remembered:

". . . So must I be loosed and blessed, as the cup and the holy bread. . . ."

Now my left hand could creep along my side as far as my belt. But it couldn't lift up just yet, because I didn't know the rest of the charm.

"The night's black before dawn," Mr. Loden was saying. "I'll make my fire. When I've done what I'll do I can step over your dead body, and Vandy's mine."

"Don't you fear Washington?" I asked him, and my left fingertips were in my dungaree pocket.

"Will he come from where he is? He's forgotten me."

"Where he is, he remembers you," I allowed.

He was on his knee. His blade point scratched a circle around him on the ground of the dooryard. The circle held him and the paper with my picture. Then he took a sack from his coat pocket, and poured powder into the scratched circle. He stood up, and golden-brown fire jumped around him.

"Now we begin," he told me.

He sketched in the air with his blade. He put his boottoe on my picture. He looked into the golden-brown fire.

"I made my wish before this," he spaced out the words. "I make it now. There was no day when I did not see my wish fulfilled." His eyes shone, paler than the fire. "No son to follow John. No daughter to mourn him."

My fingers in my pocket touched something round and thin. The quarter he'd been scared by, that Mr. Tewk Millen made me take back.

He spoke names I didn't like to hear. "Haade," he said. "Mikaded. Rakeben. Rika. Tasarith. Modeca."

My hand worried out and in it the quarter.

"Tuth," Mr. Loden said. "Tumch. Here with this image I slay—"

I lifted my hand, my left hand, three inches and flung the quarter. My heart went rotten with sick despair, for it didn't hit him—it fell into the fire—

And then up shot white smoke in one place, like a steam-puff from an engine, and the fire had died around everywhere else. Mr. Loden stopped his spellspeaking and wavered back. I saw the glow of his goggling eyes and of his teeth in his open mouth.

Where the steamy smoke had puffed, it made a shape, taller than a man. Taller than Mr. Loden or me, anyway. Wide shouldered, long legged, with a dark tail coat and high boots and hair tied back of its head. It turned, and I saw the big, big nose to its face—

"King Washington!" screamed Mr. Loden, and tried to stab.

But a long hand like a tongs caught his wrist, and I heard the bones break like sticks, and Mr. Loden whinnied like a horse that's been hurt. That was the grip of the man who'd been America's strongest, who could jump twenty-four feet broad or throw a dollar across the Rappahannock or wrestle down his biggest soldier.

The other hand came across, flat and stiff, to strike. It sounded like a door slamming in a high wind, and Mr. Loden never needed to be hit the second time. His head sagged over sidewise, and when the grip left his broken wrist he fell at the booted feet.

I sat up, and stood up. The big nose turned to me just a second. The head nodded. Friendly. Then it was gone back into steam, into nothing.

I'd been right. Where George Washington had been, he'd remembered Mr. Loden. And the silver quarter, with his picture on it, had struck the fire just when Mr. Loden was conjuring with a picture that he was making real. And there happened what happened.

A pale streak went up the black sky for the first dawn. There was no fire left and no quarter, just a spatter of melted silver. And there was no Mr. Loden, only a mouldy little heap like a rotten stump or a hummock of loam or what might be left of a man that death had caught up with after two hundred years. I picked up his iron blade and broke it on my knee and flung it away into the trees. I picked up the paper with my drawn picture. It wasn't hurt a bit.

I put that picture inside the door on the quilt where I'd lain. Maybe the Millens would keep it to remember me by, after they found I was gone and Mr. Loden didn't come around any more to court Vandy.

I started away, carrying my guitar. I meant to be out of the valley by noontime. As I went, pots started to rattle—somebody was awake in the cabin. And it was hard not to turn back when Vandy sang to herself, not thinking what she sang:

Wake up, wake up! The dawn is breaking,
   Wake up, wake up! It's almost day.
Open up your doors and your divers windows,
   See my true love march away. . . .

ONE OTHER

Up on Hark Mountain I climbed all alone, by a trail like a ladder. Under my old brogans was sometimes mud, sometimes rock, sometimes rolling gravel. I laid hold on laurel and oak scrub and sourwood and dogwood to help me up the steepest places. Sweat soaked the back of my hickory shirt and under the band of my old hat. Even my silver-strung guitar, bouncing behind me, felt weighty as an anvil. Hark Mountain's not the highest in the South, but it's one of the steepest.

I reckoned I was close to the top, for I heard a murmuring voice up there, a young-sounding woman's voice. All at once she like to yelled out a name, and it was my name.

"John!" she said, and murmured again, and then, "John. . . ."

Gentlemen, you can wager I sailed up the last stretch, on hands and knees, to the very top.

On top of Hark Mountain's tipmost top was a pool.

Hush, gentlemen, without a stream or a draw or a branch to feed it, where no pool could by nature be expected, was a clear blue pool, bright but not exactly sweet-looking. That highest point of Hark Mountain wasn't bigger, much, than a well-sized farmyard, and it had room for hardly the pool and its rim of tight rocks. And the trees that grew between those tight rocks at its rim looked leafless and gnarled, but alive. Their branch-twigs crooked like claw nails.

Almost in reach of me, by the pool's edge, burned a fire, and tending it knelt a girl.

She was tall, but not strong-built like a country girl. She was slim-built, like a town girl, and she wore town clothes—a white blouse-shirt, and blue jeans fold-rolled high up on her long legs, and soft slipper-shoes on her feet. Her arms and legs and neck were brown as nutmeat, the way fashiony girls seek to be brown. She put a tweak of stuff in the fire, and I saw her long, sharp, red fingernails. My name rose in her speech as she sang, almost:

"... it is the bones of JOHN that I trouble. I for JOHN burn his laurel."

She put in some laurel leaves. "Even as it crackles and burns, even thus may the flesh of JOHN burn for me."

In went something else. "Even as I melt this wax, with ONE OTHER to aid, so speedily may JOHN for love of me be melted."

From a little clay pot she dripped something. *Drip*, the fire danced. *Drip*, it danced again, jumping up. *Drip*, a third jumpup dance.

"Thrice I pour libation. Thrice, by ONE OTHER, I say the spell. Be it with a friend he tarries, a woman he lingers, may JOHN utterly forget them."

Standing up, she held out something red and wavy that I knew. "This from JOHN I took, and now I cast it into—"

But quietly I was beside her, and snatched the red scarf away.

"I've been wondering where I lost that," I said, and she turned and faced me.

Slightly I knew her from somewhere. She was yellow-haired, blue-eyed, brown-faced. She had a little bitty nose and a red mouth. Her blue eyes widened almost as wide as the blue pool itself, and she smiled, with big, even white teeth.

"John," she sang, halfway, "I was saying it for the third time, and you came to my call." She licked her red lips. "The way Mr. Howsen promised you would."

I didn't let on to know Mr. Howsen. I stuffed the red scarf into the hip pocket of my blue duckins. "Why were you witch-spelling me? What did I ever do to you? I disremember even where I've met you."

"You don't remember me? Remember Enderby Lodge, John."

Of course. A month ago I'd strolled through with my guitar. Old Major Enderby bid me rest my hat awhile. He was having a dance, and to pleasure him I sang for his guests.

"You must have been there," I said. "But what did I do to you?"

Her lips tightened, red and hard and sharp as her nails. "Nothing at all, John. You did nothing, you ignored me. Doesn't it make you furious to be ignored?"

"Ignored? I never notice such a thing."

"I do. I don't often look at a man twice, and usually they look at me at least once. I don't forgive being ignored." Again she licked her mouth, like a cat. "I'd been told a charm can be said three times, beside Bottomless Pool on Hark Mountain, to burn a man's soul with love. And you came when I called. Don't shake your head, John, you're in love with me."

"Sorry. I beg your pardon. I'm not in love with you."

She smiled in pride and scorn, like at a liar. "But you climbed Hark Mountain."

"Reckoned I'd like to see the Bottomless Pool."

"Only people like Mr. Howsen know about the Bottomless Pool. Bottomless pools usually mean the ones near Lake Lure, on Highway 74."

"Those aren't rightly bottomless," I said. "Anyway, I heard about this one, the real one, in a country song."

Slinging my guitar forward, I strummed and sang:

> *Way up on Hark Mountain*
> *I climb all alone,*
> *Where the trail is untravelled,*
> *The top is unknown.*

> *Way up on Hark Mountain*
> *Is the Bottomless Pool.*
> *You look in its waters*
> *And they mirror a fool.*

"You're making that up," she charged me.

"No, it was made up before my daddy's daddy was born. Most country songs have truth in them. The song brought me here, not your witch-spell."

She laughed, short and sharp, almost a yelp. "Call it the long arm of coincidence, John. You're here, anyway. Look in the water and see whether it mirrors a fool."

Plainly she didn't know the next verse, so I sang that

You can boast of your learning
And brag of your sense,
It won't make no difference
A hundred years hence.

Stepping one foot on a poolside rock, I looked in.

It mirrored neither a fool nor a wise man. I could see down forever and ever, and I recollected all I'd ever heard norrated about the Bottomless Pool. How it was blue as the sky, but with a special light of its own; how no water ran into it, excusing some rain, but it stayed full; how you couldn't measure it, you could let down a sinker till the line broke of its own weight.

Though I couldn't spy out the bottom, it wasn't rightly dark down there. Like looking up into blue sky, I looked down into blue water, and in the blue was a many-color shine, like deep lights.

"I didn't need to use the stolen scarf," she said at my elbow. "You're lying about why you came. The spell brought you."

"I'm sorry to say, ma'am," I replied, "I don't even call your name to my mind."

"Do names make a difference if you love me? Call me Annalinda. I'm rich. I've been loved for that alone, and for myself alone."

"I'm plain and poor," I told her. "I was raised hard and put up wet. I don't have more than 60 cents in my old clothes. It wonders me, Miss Annalinda, why you need to bother."

"Because I'm not used to being ignored," she said again.

Down in the Bottomless Pool's blueness wasn't a fish, or a weed of grass. Only that deep-away sparkly flash of lights, changing as you spy changes on a bubble of soap blown by a little child.

Somebody cleared his throat and spoke, "I see the spell I gave you worked, ma'am."

I knew Mr. Howsen as he came up the trail to Hark Mountain's top.

He was purely ugly. I'd been knowing him ten years, and he looked as ugly that minute as the first time I'd seen him, with his mean face and his big hungry nose and the black patch over one eye. When he'd had both his eyes, they were so close together you'd swear he could look through a keyhole with the two of them at once.

"Yes," said Miss Annalinda. "I want to pay you what I owe you."

"No, you pay One Other," said Mr. Howsen, his hands in the pockets of the long black coat he wore summer and winter. "For value received, ma'am. I only passed his word along to you."

He tightened his lips at me, in what wasn't any smile. "John," he said, "you relish journeying. You've relished it since you were just a chap, going what way you felt like. You've seen a right much of this world. But she tolled you to her, and you'll stay with her, and you're obliged to One Other."

"One other what?" I asked him.

Though that was just a defy. Of course, hearing of Hark Mountain and the Bottomless Pool, I'd heard of One Other. That mountain folks say he's got the one arm and the one leg, that he runs on the one leg and grabs with the one arm, and what he grabs goes with him into the Bottomless Pool; that it's One Other's power and knowledge that lets witches do their spells next to Bottomless Pool.

"Be here with the lady when One Other asks payment," he said. "That spell was good a many years before Theocritus written it down in Greek. It'll be good when English is as old as Greek is now. It tolled you here."

For the life of me, I couldn't remember seeing Miss Annalinda at Major Enderby's. "My will brought me, not hers," I said. "I wanted to see the Bottomless Pool. I wonder at the soap bubble color in it."

"Ain't any soap in there, John," said Mr. Howsen. "Soap bubbles don't get so big as to have that much color."

"You're rightly sure how big soap bubbles get, Mr. Howsen? Once I heard a science doctor say this whole life of ours, the heaven and the earth, the sun and moon and stars, hold a shape like a big soap bubble. He said it stretched and spread like a soap bubble, all the suns and stars and worlds getting farther apart as time passed."

"Both of you stay where you are," said Mr. Howsen. "One Other will want to find the both of you here."

"But—" Miss Annalinda made out to begin.

"Both of you stay," Mr. Howsen said again, and with his shoe toe he scuffed a mark across the trail. He hawked, and spit on the mark. "Don't cross that line. It would be worse for you than if fire burned you behind and before, inside and out."

Like a lizard he had bobbed over the edge and down the trail.

"Let's go, too," I said to Miss Annalinda, but she stared at the mark of Mr. Howsen's shoe toe, and the healthy blood had paled out from under the tan on her face.

"Pay him no mind," I said. "Let's start, it's toward evening."

"He said not to cross the mark," she reminded me, scared.

"I don't care a shuck for his saying. Come on, Miss Annalinda," and I took her by the arm.

That quick she was fighting me. Holding her arm was like holding the spoke of a runaway wheel. Her other hand racked hide and blood from my cheek, and she tried to bite. I couldn't hang on without hitting her, so I let her go, and she sat on a rock by the poolside and cried into her hands.

"Then I'll have to go alone," I said, and took a step.

"John!" she called, loud and shaky as a horse's whinny. "If you cross that mark, I'll throw myself into this Bottomless Pool!"

Sometimes you can tell a woman means her words. This was such a time. I walked back, and she looked to where the down-sunk sun made the sky's edge red and fiery. It would be cold and dark when the sun went. With trembling brown hands she rolled the blue jeans down her long legs.

"I'll build up the fire," I said, and tried to break a branch from a claw-looking tree.

But it was tough and had thorny stickers. So I went to the edge of the clearing, away from where Mr. Howsen had drawn his mark on us, and found an armful of dead-fallen wood to freshen the fire she'd made for her witching. It blazed up, the color of the setting sun. High in the sky, that grew pale before it would grow dark, slid a big buzzard. Its wings flopped, slow and heavy, spreading their feathers like long fingers.

"You don't believe all this, John," said Miss Annalinda, in a voice that sounded as if she was just before freezing with cold. "But the spell was true. The rest of it's true, too—about One Other. He must have been here since the beginning of time."

"There's one thing peculiar enough to the truth," I answered her. "Nothing's been norrated about One Other until the last year or so. Nothing about his being here at the Bottomless Pool, or about folks being able to do witch stuff, or how he aids the witches and takes payment for his aid. It's no old country tale, it's right new and recent."

"Payment," she said after me. "What kind of payment?"

I poked the fire. "That depends. Sometimes one thing, sometimes another. You notice Mr. Howsen goes around with only one eye. I've heard it sworn that One Other took an eye from him. Maybe he won't want an eye from you, but he'll want something. Something for nothing."

"What do you mean?" and she frowned her brows.

"You witched me to love you, but you don't love me. It was done for spite, not love."

"Why—why—"

Nothing flurries a woman like being caught in the truth. She laid hold on a poolside rock next to her.

"That will smash my head or either my guitar," I gave her warning. "Smash my head, you're up here alone with a dead corpse. Smash my guitar, I'll go down the trail."

"And I'll jump into the pool."

"All right, jump. I won't stay where people throw rocks at me. Fair warning's as good as a promise."

She let go the rock. She was ready to cry again. My foot at the edge, I looked down in the water.

The sky was getting purely dark, but low and away down was that soap bubble shiny light. I remembered an old tale they say came from the Indians that owned the mountains before white folks came. It was about people living above the sky and thinking their world was the only one, till somebody pulled up a big long root, and through the hole they could see another world below, where people lived. Then Miss Annalinda began to talk.

She was talking for company, and she talked about herself. About her rich father and her rich mother, and her rich aunts and uncles, the money and automobiles and land and horses she owned, the big chance of men who wanted to marry her. One was the son of folks as rich as hers. One was the governor of a state, who'd put his wife away if Miss Annalinda said the word. One was a nobleborn man from a foreign country. "And you'd marry me too, John," she said.

"I'm sorry," I said. "Sorry to death. But I wouldn't."

"You're lying, John."

"I never lie, Miss Annalinda."

"Well, talk to me, anyway. This is no place for silence."

I talked in my turn. How I'd been born next to Drowning Creek and baptized in its waters. How my folks had died in two days of each other, how an old teacher lady taught me to read and write, and I taught myself to play the guitar. How I'd roamed and rambled. How I'd fought in the war, and a thousand fell at my side and ten thousand at my right hand, but it hadn't come nigh me. I left out things like meeting up with the Ugly Bird or visiting the desrick on Yandro. I said that though I'd never had anything and never rightly expected to have anything, I'd always made out for bread to eat and sometimes butter on it.

"How about girls, John?" she asked me. "You must have had regiments of them."

"None to mention," I said, for it wouldn't be proper to name them, or the like of that. "Miss Annalinda, it's full dark."

"And the moon's up," she said.

"No, that's the soap bubble light from down in the pool."

"You make me shiver!" she scolded, and drew up her shoulders. "What do you mean with that stuff about soap bubbles?"

"Only what I told Mr. Howsen. The science man said our whole life, what he called our universe, was swelling and stretching out, so that suns and moons and stars pull farther apart all the time. He said our world and all the other worlds are inside that stretching skin of suds that makes the bubble. We can't study out what's outside the bubble, or either inside, just the suds part. It sounds crazyish, but when he talked it sounded true."

"It's not a new idea, John. James Jeans wrote a book, *The Expanding Universe.* But where does the soap bubble come from?"

"I reckon Whoever made things must have blown it from a bubble pipe too big for us to figure about."

She snickered, so she must be feeling better. "You believe in a God Who blew only one lone soap bubble." Then she didn't snicker. "How long must we wait here?"

"No time. We can go."

"No, we have to stay."

"Then we'll wait till One Other comes. He'll come. Mr. Howsen's a despicable man, but he knows about One Other."

"Oh!" she cried out. "I wish he'd come and get it over with."

And her wish came true.

The firelight had risen high, and as she spoke something hiked up behind the rocks on the pool's edge. It hiked up like a wet black leech, but much bigger by a thousand times. It slid and oozed to the top of a rock and as it waited a second, wet and shiny in the firelight, it looked as if somebody had flung down a wet coat. Then it hunched and swelled, and its edges came apart.

It was a hand, as broad in the back as a shovel, with fingers as long as a hayfork's tines.

"Get up and start down trail," I said to Miss Annalinda, as quiet and calm as I could make out to be. "Don't argue, just start."

"Why?" she snapped, without moving, and by then she saw, too, and any chance for escape was gone.

The hayfork fingers grabbed the rock, and a head and shoulder heaved up where we could see them.

The shoulder was a cypress root humping out of water, and the head was a dark pumpkin, round and smooth and bald, with no face, only two eyes. They were green, not bright green like cat eyes or dog eyes in the night. They were stale rotten green, like something spoiled.

Miss Annalinda's shriek was like a train at a crossing. She jumped up, but she didn't run. Maybe she couldn't. Then a big knee lifted into sight, and all of One Other came out of the water and rose straight up above us.

Miss Annalinda wilted down on her knees, almost in the fire. I dropped the guitar and jumped to pull her clear. She mumbled a holy name—not a prayer or either a curse, just the tag end of a habit most of us almost lose, the reminding of Someone that we're hurting for a little help. I stood, holding her sagging slim body against me, and looked high up at where One Other loomed.

One Other was twice as tall as a tall man, and it was sure enough true that he had only one arm and one leg. The arm would be his left arm, and the leg his left leg. Maybe that's why the mountain folks named him One Other. But his stale green eyes were two, and both of them looked down at us. He made a sure hop toward us on his big single foot, big and flat as a table top, and he put out his hand to touch or to grab.

I dragged Miss Annalinda clear around the fire. I reckon she'd fainted, or near to. Her feet didn't work under her, she only moaned, and she was double heavy, the way a limp weight can be. My strength was under tax to pull her toward where I'd dropped the guitar. I wanted to get my hands on that guitar. It might be a weapon—its music or its silver strings might be a distaste to an unchancey thing like One Other.

But One Other had circled the fire the opposite way, so that we came almost in touch again. He stood on his one big foot, between me and my guitar. It might be ill or well to him, but I couldn't reach it and find out.

Even then, I never thought of running across Mr. Howsen's mark and down the mountain in the night. I stood still, holding Miss Annalinda on her feet that were so limp her shoes were like to drop off, and looked up twice my height into what wasn't a face save for the two green eyes.

"What have you got in mind?" I asked One Other, as if he could understand my talk; and the words, almost in Miss Annalinda's ear, brought back her strength and wits. She stood alone, still shoving herself close against me. She looked up at One Other and said the holy name again.

One Other bent his big lumpy knee, and sank his bladdery dark body down and put out that big splay paw of his. The firelight showed his open palm, slate gray, with things dribbling out in a clinking, jangling little strew at our feet. He straightened up again.

"Oh!" And Miss Annalinda dropped down to grab. "Look—he's giving us—"

Tugging my eyes from One Other's, I looked at what she held out. It shone and lighted up, like a hailstone by lantern light. It was the size of a hen egg, and it had a many little edges and flat faces, all full of fire, pale and blue outside and innerly many-colored like the soap bubble light in the Bottomless Pool. She shoved it into my hand, and it felt sticky and slippery, like soap. I let it fall on the ground again.

"You fool, that's a diamond!" she squeaked at me. "It's bigger than the Orloff! Bigger than the Koh-i-noor!"

She scrabbled with both hands for more of the shiny things, that lighted up with every color you could call for. "Here's an emerald," she yipped, "and here's a ruby! John, he's our friend, he likes us, he's giving us things worth more money than—"

On her knees before One Other, she gathered two fistfuls of those things he'd flung down for her to pick up. But I had my eyes back on him. He looked at me—not at her, he was sure of her. He knew humankind's greed for shiny stones. About me he wasn't sure yet. He studied me as I've seen folks study an animal, to see where to hit with a stick or slice with a skinning knife. The shiny stones didn't fetch me. He'd find something that would.

I know how like a crazy tale to scare young ones this sounds. But there and then, One Other was so plain to see and make out, the way you'd see him if I was to make a clay image of him and stand it up on one leg in your sight, and it grew till it was twice as tall as you, with stale green eyes and one hayfork paw and one tabletop foot. In a moment with no sound, he and I looked at each other. Miss Annalinda, down on the ground between us, gopped and goggled at the stones she gathered in her hands. Then the silence broke. A drip of water fell. Another. *Drip, drip, drip,* like what Miss Annalinda had dripped into the fire—water from the Bottomless Pool, dripping off of One Other's body and head and his one arm and one leg.

Then he turned his eyes and mind back to Miss Annalinda, for long enough to spare me for a jump past him at my guitar.

He turned quick and swung down at me with his paw, but I had it and was running backward. I got the guitar across me, my left hand on the frets, and my right hand clawing the silver strings. They sang out, and One Other teetered on his broad sole, cocked his head to listen.

I started the Last Judgment Song, that in my boyhood old Uncle T. P. Hinnard had said was good against evil things:

> *Three holy kings, four holy saints,*
> *At heaven's high gate that stand,*
> *Speak out and bid all evil wait,*
> *And stir no foot or hand. . . .*

But he came at me. The charm didn't serve against One Other, as I'd been vowed to it'd serve against any evil in the world. One Other wasn't of this world, though just now he was in it. He was from the Bottomless Pool, and from whatever was beyond, below, behind where its bottom should be.

I ran around the fire and around Miss Annalinda still crouched down among those jewels. After me he hopped, like the almightiest big one-legged rabbit in song or story. He had me almost headed off, coming alongside me, and I ran right through the fire that was less fear to face than he was. My shoes spumed its coals as I ran through. On the far side I made myself stop and look back. I still had to face him somehow. I couldn't just run from him and leave Miss Annalinda to pay, all alone for her foolishness.

He'd stopped, too, in his one track. The fire, scattered by my feet, blazed up in scattered chunks, and he was sort of pulling himself together, back away from it. *Drip, drip,* the water fell from him. I felt I couldn't stand that dripping noise, and I sang another verse of the Last Judgment Song:

> *The fire from heaven will fall at last*
> *On wealth and pride and power,*
> *We will not know the minute, and*
> *We will not know the hour. . . .*

One Other hopped a long hop back, away from the fire and from me and from the song.

Something whispered me what I'd needed to know.

From out of the water he'd come. If I didn't want him to get me, to make me sell out at a price I'd never redeem—as jewels beyond all reckoning could buy Miss Annalinda—I'd have to fight him like any water-thing.

Fight fire with water, the wise folks say for a saying. Fire and water are enemies. Fight water with fire.

He circled around again, and I didn't flee this time. I grabbed toward the scattered fire. One Other's flat hand slapped me spinning away, but my own fist had snatched a burning chunk. When I staggered back onto my feet, I still held my guitar in one hand, and the chunk in the other.

I whipped that fire around my head, and it blazed up like pure lightwood. As One Other stooped for me again, I rushed to meet him and shoved the fire at him.

He couldn't face it. He broke back from it. I jumped sidewise, myself, so he was between me and the fire, and sashayed the burning stick at him again. He jumped back. His foot slammed down into the fire.

I hope none of you all ever hear such a sound as he made, with no mouth to make it. Not a yell or a roar or a scream, but Hark Mountain's whole top hummed and danced to it. He flung himself out of the fire again, and I dashed my torch like a spear for where his face should be, and made a direct hit.

I tell you, he couldn't face fire, he couldn't stand it. He spun around and dived into the water from which he'd come, into the Bottomless Pool, with a splash like a wagon falling from a bridge. Running to the rocks, I saw him cleave down below there into the deep clearness like a diving one-legged frog—among the soap bubble colors, getting so small he looked a hand's size, a finger's size, a bean's size. And then light gulped him. Then I stepped back to the scattered fire.

Miss Annalinda still huddled on the ground. I question whether she'd paid any attention to what had gone on. Her hands were full of jewels, shining green, red, blue, white.

I put out my hand and pulled her to her feet. "Give those to me," I said.

Her eyes stabbed at me like fish-gigs. She couldn't believe that I'd said such words. I took her right wrist and pried open her right hand, trying not to hurt her, and got the jewels out of it. Into the Bottomless Pool I plugged them, one by one. They splashed and sank like pebbles.

"Don't!" she screamed, but I took her other hand and pried away the rest of them. *Plop.* I threw one after the first bunch. *Plop.* I threw another. *Plop, plop, plop,* more.

"They were a fortune," she whimpered, clawing at my arm. "The greatest fortune ever dreamed of."

"No, not a fortune," I said. "A misfortune. The greatest misfortune ever dreamed of."

"But—no—"

I threw the rest in. *Plop, plop,* the rest of the jewels. "What would you have given for them?" I asked her.

"Anything—anything—"

"You mean everything. If he paid high for us, he meant to have his worth from us. He needs folks to serve him, more folks than Mr. Howsen." I waved for her to look into the pool. "I hope he stays where things are more comfortable than what I gave him to taste."

She looked down to where the pool should have a bottom. "John, you're right," she said, as if she dreamed. "Those colors do look like soap bubble tints, stretched out, with nothing we can imagine beyond the film of suds. A great big soap bubble, like the one you say the Creator blew."

"Maybe," I said, "there's more than one soap bubble. Maybe there's a right many. Each one a life and universe strange to us."

The pain of that new thought made her silent. I went on.

"Maybe there's two soap bubbles touching. Maybe the spot where they come together is where something can leave one sort of life and come into another."

She sat down. The new thought was weight as well as pain. "Oh," she said.

"Maybe some born venturer would dare try to move into the new bubble," I said, "through whatever maybe matches the Bottomless Pool on the far side, in that other world. Maybe, I say. There's a God's plenty of maybes."

"They aren't maybes," she said all of a sudden. "You saw him. No such creature was ever born in our world. A creature looking like that must be—"

"You still don't understand," and I shook my head. "I don't reckon he looks like that in his own soap bubble. He made himself look like that, to be as much as possible like our kind, here in this world. We can't guess what he looks like naturally."

"I don't want to guess," she said, as if she was about to cry.

"A stranger like that needs friends and helpers in the strange place. Some of the things he knows from his own home are like power here, power we don't understand and think is witch stuff. But he'd pay high for helpers, like Mr. Howsen and like us."

"Will he come back?" she asked.

"Not right away." I picked up my guitar. "Let's head down trail as far as we can grope in the dark, and if he does come back he won't find us. If we can't grope all the way down, we'll build a fire somewhere below and wait for light to show us the rest of the way."

"You were right about me, John," said Miss Annalinda, starting to gabble fast. "You saw all through me, my spell was to get you up here for spite. But it's not spite any more, John, it's love, it's love—I love you, John—"

"You know," I right away changed the subject, "there's one more thing about this soap bubble idea. The soap bubble we live in keeps stretching and swelling. But a soap bubble can't last forever. Some time or other, it stretches and swells so tight, it just bursts."

That did what I was after. It stopped her flood of words. She stared up and away and all around. I saw the whites of her eyes glitter in the last of the fireglow.

"Bursts?" she said slowly. "Then what?"

"Then nothing, Miss Annalinda. When a soap bubble bursts, it's gone."

And we had silence to start our climb down Hark Mountain.

CALL ME FROM THE VALLEY

Down it rained, on hill and hollow, the way you'd think the sky was too heavy to hold it back. It fell so thick and hard fish could have swum in it, all around where we sat holed up under the low wide porch of the country store—five of us. A leather-coated deputy sheriff with a pickup truck. A farmer, who'd sheltered his mule wagon in a shed behind. The old storekeeper, and us two strangers in that part of the hills, a quiet old gentleman and me with my silver-strung guitar.

The storekeeper hung a lantern to the porch rafters as it got dark. The farmer bought us all a bottle of soda, and the storekeeper broke us open a box of cookies. "Gentlemen, you'll all be here for a spell, so sit comfortable," he said. "Friend," he said to me, "did I ask your name?"

"John," I named myself.

"Well, John, do you play that there guitar you're a-toting?"

I played and sang for them, that old song about the hunter's true love:

> Oh, call me sweetheart, call me dear,
> Call me what you will,
> Call me from the valley low,
> Call me from the hill. . . .

Then there was talk about old things and thoughts. I recollect what some of them said:

Such as, you can't win solitaire by cheating just once, you've got to keep cheating; some animals are smarter than folks; who were the ancients who dug mine-holes in the Toe River country, and what were they after, and did they find it; nobody knows what makes the lights come and go like giant fireflies every night on Brown Mountain; you'll never see a man exactly six feet tall, because that was the height of the Lord Jesus.

And the farmer, who next to me was the youngest there, mentioned love and courting, and how when you true-love someone and need your eyes and thoughts clearest, they mist up and maybe make you trouble. That led to how you step down a mullein stalk toward your true love's house, and if it grows up again she loves you; and how the girls used to have dumb suppers, setting plates and knives and forks on the table at night and each girl standing behind a chair put ready, till at midnight the candles blew out and a girl saw, or she thought she saw, a ghosty-looking somebody in the chair before her, that was the appearance of the somebody she'd marry.

"Knew of dumb suppers when I was just a chap," allowed the storekeeper, "but most of the old folks then, they didn't relish the notion. Said it was a devil-made idea, and you might call it something better left outside."

"Ain't no such goings-on in this day and time," nodded the farmer. "I don't take stock in them crazy sayings and doings."

Back where I was born and raised, in the Drowning Creek country, I'd heard tell of dumb suppers but I'd never seen one, so I held my tongue. But the deputy grinned his teeth at the farmer.

"You plant by the moon, don't you?" he asked. "Aboveground things like corn at the full, and underground things like 'taters in the dark?"

"That ain't foolishness, that's the true way," the farmer said back. "Ask anybody's got a lick of sense about farming."

Then a big wiggling three-forked flash of lightning struck, it didn't seem more than arm's-length off, and the thunder was like the falling in of the hills.

"Law me," said the old gentleman, whose name seemed to be Mr. Jay. "That was a hooter."

"Sure God was," the farmer agreed him. "Old Forney Meechum wants us to remember he makes the rain around here."

My ears upped like a rabbit's. "I did hear this is the old Meechum-Donovant feud country," I said. "I've always been wanting to hear the true tale of that. And what about Forney Meechum making the rain—isn't he dead?"

"Deader than hell," the storekeeper told me. "Though folks never thought he could die, thought he'd just ugly away. But him and all the Meechum and Donovant men got killed. Both the names plumb died out, I reckon, yonder in the valley so low where you see the rain a-falling the lavishest. I used to hear about it when I was just a chap."

"Me, too," nodded the deputy. "Way I got it, Forney Meechum went somewheres west when he was young. Was with the James boys or the Younger boys, or maybe somebody not quite that respectable."

"And when he come back," took up the storekeeper again, "he could make it rain whenever it suited him."

"How?" I asked, and old Mr. Jay was listening, too.

"Ain't rightly certain how," said the farmer. "They tell he used to mix up mud in a hole, and sing a certain song. Ever hear such a song as that, John?"

I shook my head *no*, and he went on:

"Forney Meechum done scarier things than that. He witched wells dry. And he raised up dead ghosts to show him where treasure was hid. Even his own kinfolks was scared of him, and all the Meechums took orders from him. So when he fell out with Captain Sam Donovant over a property line, he made them break with all the Donovants."

"Fact," said the storekeeper, who wanted to tell part of the tale. "And them Meechums did what he told them, saving only his cousin's oldest girl, Miss Lute Meechum, and she'd swore eternal love with Captain Ben Donovant's second boy Jeremiah."

Another lightning flash, another thunder growl. Old Mr. Jay hunched his thin shoulders under his jeans coat, and allowed he'd pay for some cheese and crackers if the storekeeper'd fetch it out to us.

"Law me," said the farmer. "I ain't even now wanting to talk against Forney Meechum. But they tell he'd put his eye on Lute himself, and he'd quarreled with his own son Derwood about who'd have her. But next court day at the county seat, was a fight betwixt Jeremiah Donovant and Derwood Meechum, and Jeremiah stuck a knife in Derwood and killed him dead."

Mr. Jay leaned forward in the lantern light. It showed the gray stubble on his gentle old face. "Who drew the first knife?" he asked.

"I've heard tell Derwood drew the knife, and Jeremiah took it away and stuck it into him," said the farmer. "Anyway, Jeremiah Donovant had to run from the law, and down in the valley yonder the Meechums and the Donovants began a-shooting at each other."

"Fact," the storekeeper took it up again as he fetched out the cheese and crackers. "That was 50 years back, the last fight of all. Ary man on both sides was killed, down to boys of ten-twelve years. Old Forney called for rain, but somebody shot him just as he got it started."

"And it falls a right much to this day," said the farmer, gazing at the pour from the porch eaves. "That valley below us is so rainy it's a swamp like. And the widows and orphans that was left alive, both families, they was purely rained out and went other places to live."

"What about Miss Lute Meechum?" I asked next.

"I wondered about her, too," said Mr. Jay.

"Died," said the storekeeper. "Some folks say it was pure down grief killed her, that and lonesomeness for that run-off Jeremiah Donovant. I likewise heard tell old Forney shot her when she said for once and all she wouldn't have him."

The deputy sipped his soda. "All done and past now," he said. "Looks like we're rained in here for all night, gentlemen."

But we weren't. It slacked off while we ate our cheese, and then it was just a drip from the branches. The clouds shredded, and a moon poked through a moment, shy, like a girl at her first play-party. The deputy got up from the slab bench where he'd been sitting.

"Hope my truck'll wallow up that muddy road to town," he said. "Who can I carry with me?"

"I got my mule," added the farmer. "I'll follow along and snake you out when you get stuck in one of them mud holes. John, you better ride with me, you and Mr. Jay."

I shook my head. "I'm not going to town, thank you kindly. I'm going down that valley trail. Swore to an old friend I'd be at his family reunion, up in the hills on the yonder side, by supper time tomorrow."

Mr. Jay said he'd be going that way, too. The storekeeper

offered to let us sleep in his feed shed, but I said I'd better start. "Coming, sir?" I asked old Mr. Jay.

"After while," he told me, so I went on alone. Three minutes down trail between those wet dark trees, and the lantern light under the porch was gone as if it had never shone.

Gentlemen, it was lonesome dark and damp going. I felt my muddy way along, with my brogan shoes squashy-full of water. And yet, sometimes, it wasn't as lonesome as you might call for. There were soft noises, like whispers or crawlings; and once there was a howl, not too far away, like a dog, or a man trying to sound like a dog, or maybe the neither of them. For my own comfort I began to pick the guitar and sing to myself; but the wrong tune had come unbidden:

> In the pines, in the pines,
> Where the sun never shines,
> And I shiver where the wind blows cold! . . .

I stopped when I got that far, it was too much the truth. And it came on to rain again.

I hauled off my old coat to wrap my guitar from it. Not much to see ahead, but I knew I kept going down slope and down slope, and no way of telling how far down it went before it would start up to go to the hills where my friend's kinfolks would gather tomorrow. I told myself I was a gone gump not to stay at the store, the way I was so kindly bid. I hoped that that old Mr. Jay had the sense to stay under cover. But it was too far to go back. And I'd better find some place out of the wet, for my guitar more than me.

Must have been a bend to that trail, because I came all at once in view of the light in the cabin's glass window, before I notioned there was any living place around. The light looked warm yellow through the rain, and I hastened my wet feet. Close enough in, I could judge it was an old-made log house, the corners notch-locked and the logs clay-chinked, and the wide eaves with thick-split shakes on them, but I couldn't really see. "Hello, the house!" I yelled out.

No sound back. Maybe the rain was keeping them from hearing me. I felt my way to the flat door-stone and knocked. No stir inside.

Groping for a knob, I found none, only a leather latch string, old style. And, old style, it was out. In my grandsire's day, a latch string out meant come in. I pulled, and a wooden latch lifted inside and the door swung in before me.

The room was lit from a fireplace full of red coals, and from a candle stuck on a dish on a table middleway of the puncheon floor. That table took my eye as I stepped in. A cloth on it, and a plate of old white china with knife and fork at the sides, and a cup and saucer, yes and a folded napkin. But no food on the table, no coffee in the cup. A chair was set to the plate, and behind the chair, her hands crossed on its back, stood a woman, young and tall and proud-standing.

She didn't move. Nothing moved, except the candle flame in the stir of air from the open door. She might have been cut from wood and put up there to fool folks. I closed the door against the hard drum of the rain, and tracked wet marks on the puncheons as I came toward the table. I took off my old hat, and the water fell from it.

"Good evening, ma'am," I said.

Then her dark eyes moved in her pale face, her sweet, firm-jawed face. Her short, sad mouth opened, slow and shaky.

"You're not—" she started to mumble, half to herself. "I didn't mean—"

There was a copper light moving in her hair as she bent her head and looked down into the empty plate, and then I remembered that talk under the store porch.

"Dumb supper," I said. "I'm right sorry. The rain drove me in here. I reckon this is the only house around, and when nobody answered I walked in. I didn't mean to bother you."

And I couldn't help but look at how she'd set the dumb supper out. Knowing how such things weren't done any more, and hearing that very thing said that night, I was wondered to find it. Through my mind kept running how some scholar-men say it's a way of doing that came over from the Old Country, where dumb suppers were set clear back to the beginning of time. Things that old don't die easy after all, I reckoned.

"He'll still come and sit down," she said to me in her soft voice, like a low-playing flute heard far off. "I've called him and he'll come."

I hung my wet coat by the fireplace, and she saw my guitar.

"Sing to help guide him," she said to me.

I looked at her, so proudly tall behind the chair. She wore a long green dress, and her eyes were darker than her copper hair, that was all in curly ringlets.

"Sing," she said again. "Tole him here."

I felt like doing whatever she told me. I swung the guitar in front of me, and began the song I'd given them at the store:

> *Oh, call me sweetheart, call me dear,*
> *Call me what you will,*
> *Call me from the valley low,*
> *Call me from the hill.*
> *I hear you as the turtle dove*
> *That flies from bough to bough,*
> *And as she softly calls her mate,*
> *You call me softly now. . . .*

One long hand waved me to stop, and I stopped with the silver strings still whispering to both of us. I felt my ears close up tight, the way they feel when you've climbed high, high on a mountain top.

"There's a power working here," I said.

"Yes," she barely made herself heard.

The fire, that had been just coals, found something to blaze up on. Smoke rose dark above the bright flames. The rain outside came barreling down, and there was a rising wind, too, with a whoop and shove to it that made the lock-joints of the cabin's logs creak.

"Sounds like old Forney Meechum's hard at work," I tried to make half a joke, but she didn't take it as such. Her dark-bright eyes lifted their lids to widen, and her hands, on the chair back again, took hold hard.

"Forney doesn't want me to do this," she told me, as if it was my ordinary business.

"He's dead," I reminded her, like to a child.

"No," she shook her copper head. "He's not dead, not all of him. And not all of me, either."

I wondered what she meant, and I stepped away from the fire that was burning bright and hot.

"Are you a Meechum or a Donovant?" I asked.

"A Meechum," she told me. "But my true love's a Donovant."

"Like Lute Meechum and Jeremiah Donovant?"

"You know about that." Her hands trembled a mite, for all they held so hard to the chair. "Who are you?"

"My name's John." I touched the strings to make them whisper again. "Yes, I know the tale about the feud. Old Forney Meechum, who could witch down the rain, said Lute Meechum mustn't have Jeremiah—"

"He's here!" she cried out, with all her loud voice at last.

The wind shook the cabin like a dice-box. The shakes on the roof must have ruffled worse than a hen's feathers. Up jumped the fire, and out winked the candle.

Jumpy myself, I was back against the logs of the wall, my free hand on a shelf-plank that was wedged there. The rain had wetted the clay chinking soft between the logs, and a muddy trickle fell on my fingers. I was watching the fire, and its dirty gray smoke stirred and swelled, and a fat-looking puff of it came crawling out like a live thing.

The smoke stayed in one bunch. It hung there, a sort of egg-shaped chunk of it, hanging above the stones of the hearth. I think the girl must have half fallen, then caught herself; for I heard the legs of the chair scrape on the puncheons. The smoke molded itself, in what light I could make out, and looked solid and shapy, as tall as me but thicker, and two streamy coils waving out in the air like arms.

"Don't!" the girl was begging something. "Don't let him—"

On that shelf at my hand stood a dish and an empty old bottle, the kind of bottle the old glassmakers blew a hundred years ago. I took up the dish in my right fist. I saw that smoke-shape drifting sort of slow and greedy, clear from the hearth, and between those two wavy streamy arm-coils rose up a lumpy thing like a head. There was enough firelight to see that this smoke was thicker

THE LITTLE BLACK TRAIN

There in the High Fork country, with peaks saw-toothing into the sky and hollows diving away down and trees thicketed every which way, you'd think human foot had never stepped. Walking the trail between high pines, I touched my guitar's silver strings for company of the sound. But then a man squandered into sight around a bend—young-like, red-faced, baldy-headed. Gentlemen, he was as drunk as a hoot. I gave him good evening.

"Can you play that thing?" he gobbled at me and, second grab of his shaky hand, he got hold of my hickory shirt sleeve. "Come to the party, friend. Our fiddle band, last moment, they got scared out. We got just only a mouth-harp to play for us."

"What way was the fiddle band scared?" I asked him to tell.

"Party's at Miss Donie Carawan's," he said, without replying me. "Bobbycue pig and chicken, bar'l of good stump-hole whisky."

"Listen," I said, "ever hear tell of the man invited a stranger fiddler, he turned out to be Satan?"

"Shoo," he snickered, "Satan plays the fiddle, you play the guitar, I don't pay your guitar no worry. What's your name, friend?"

"John. What's yours?"

But he'd started up a narrow, grown-over, snaky-turny path you'd not notice. I reckoned the party'd be at a house, where I could sleep the night that was coming, so I followed. He nearly fell back top of me, he was so stone drunk, but we got to a notch on the ridge, and the far side was a valley of trees, dark and secret looking. Going down, I began to hear loud laughing talk. Finally we reached a yard at the bottom. There was a house there, and it looked like enough men and women to swing a primary election.

They whooped at us, so loud it rang my ears. The drunk man waved both his hands. "This here's my friend John," he bawled out, "and he's a-going to play us some music!"

They whooped louder at that, and easiest thing for me to do was start picking "Hell Broke Loose in Georgia"; and, gentlemen, right away they danced up a storm.

Wild-like, they whipped and whirled. Most of them were young folks dressed their best. One side, a great big man called the dance, but you couldn't much hear him, everybody laughed and hollered so loud. It got in my mind that children laugh and yell thataway, passing an old burying-ground where ghosts could be. It was the way they might be trying to dance down the nervouses; I jumped myself, between picks, when something started moaning beside me. But it was just a middling-old fellow with a thin face, playing his mouth-harp along with my guitar.

I looked to the house—it was new and wide and solid, with whitewashed clay chinking between the squared logs of it. Through a dogtrot from front to back I saw clear down valley, west to where the sunball dropped red toward a far string of mountains. The valley-bottom's trees were spaced out with a kind of path or road, the whole length. The house windows began to light up as I played. Somebody was putting a match to lamps, against the night's fall.

End of the tune, everybody clapped me loud and long. "More! More!" they hollered, bunched among the yard trees, still fighting their nervouses.

"Friends," I managed to be heard, "let me make my manners to the one who's giving this party."

"Hi, Miss Donie!" yelled out the drunk man. "Come meet John!"

From the house she walked through the crowded-around folks, stepping so proud she looked taller than she was. A right much stripy skirt swished to her high heels; but she hadn't such a much dress above, and none at all on her round arms and shoulders. The butter yellow of her hair must have come from a bottle, and the doll pink of her face from a box. She smiled up to me, and her perfume tingled my nose. Behind her followed that big dance-caller, with his dead black hair and wide teeth, and his heavy hands swinging like balance weights.

"Glad you came, John," she said, deep in her round throat.

I looked at her robin-egg blue eyes and her butter hair and her red mouth and her bare pink shoulders. She was maybe 35, maybe

40, maybe more and not looking it. "Proud to be here," I said, my politest. "Is this a birthday, Miss Donie Carawan?"

Folks fell quiet, swapping looks. An open cooking fire blazed up as the night sneaked in. Donie Carawan laughed deep.

"Birthday of a curse," and she widened her blue eyes. "End of the curse, too, I reckon. All tonight."

Some mouths came open, but didn't let words out. I reckoned that whatever had scared out the fiddle band was nothing usual. She held out a slim hand, with green-stoned rings on it.

"Come eat and drink, John," she bade me.

"Thanks," I said, for I hadn't eaten ary mouthful since crack of day.

Off she led me, her fingers pressing mine, her eye-corners watching me. The big dance-caller glittered a glare after us. He was purely jealoused up that she'd made me so welcome.

Two dark-faced old men stood at an iron rack over a pit of coals, where lay two halves of a slow-cooking hog. One old man dipped a stick with a rag ball into a kettle of sauce and painted it over the brown roast meat. From a big pot of fat over yet another fire, an old woman forked hush-puppies into pans set ready on a plank table.

"Line up!" called Donie Carawan out, like a bugle. They lined up, talking and hollering again, smiles back on their faces. It was some way like dreams you have, folks carrying on loud and excited, and something bad coming on to happen.

Donie Carawan put her bare arm through my blue-sleeved elbow while an old man sliced chunks of barbecued hog on paper plates for us. The old woman forked on a hush-puppy and a big hobby of cole slaw. Eating, I wondered how they made the bar-becue sauce—wondered, too, if all these folks really wanted to be here for what Donie Carawan called the birthday of a curse.

"John," she said, the way you'd think she read what I won-dered, "don't they say a witch's curse can't work on a pure heart?"

"They say that," I agreed her, and she laughed her laugh. The big dance-caller and the skinny mouth-harp man looked up from their barbecue.

"An old witch cursed me for guilty twenty years back," said Donie Carawan. "The law said I was innocent. Who was right?"

"Don't know how to answer that," I had to say, and again she laughed, and bit into her hush-puppy.

"Look around you, John," she said. "This house is my house, and this valley is my valley, and these folks are my friends, come to help me pleasure myself."

Again I reckoned, she's the only one here that's pleasured, maybe not even her.

"Law me," she laughed, "it's rough on a few folks, holding their breath all these years to see the curse light on me. Since it wouldn't light, I figured how to shoo it away." Her blue eyes looked up. "But what are you doing around High Fork, John?"

The dance-caller listened, and the thin mouth-harp man. "Just passing through," I said. "Looking for songs. I heard about a High Fork song, something about a little black train."

Silence quick stretched all around, the way you'd think I'd been impolite. Yet again she broke the silence with a laugh.

"Why," she said, "I've known that song as long as I've known about the curse, near to. Want me to sing it for you?"

Folks were watching, and, "Please, ma'am," I asked her.

She sang, there in the yellow lamplight and red firelight, among the shady-shadowy trees and the mountain dark, without ary slice of moon overhead. Her voice was a good voice. I put down my plate and, a line or two along, I made out to follow her with the guitar.

> I heard a voice of warning,
> A message from on high,
> "Go put your house in order
> For thou shalt surely die.
> Tell all your friends a long farewell
> And get your business right—
> The little black train is rolling in
> To call for you tonight."

"Miss Donie, that's a tuneful thing," I said. "Sounds right like a train rolling."

"My voice isn't high enough to sound the whistle part," she smiled at me, red-mouthed.

"I might could do that," said the mouth-harp man, coming close and speaking soft. And folks were craning at us, looking sick, embarrassed, purely distasted. I began to wonder why I shouldn't have given a name to that black train song.

But then rose up a big holler near the house, where a barrel was set. The drunk man that'd fetched me was yelling mad at another man near-about as drunk, and they were trying to grab a drinking gourd from each other. Two-three other men on each side hoorawed them on to squabble more.

"Jeth!" called Donie Carawan to the big dance-caller. "Let's stop that before they spill the whisky, Jeth."

Jeth and she headed for the bunch by the barrel, and everybody else was crowding to watch.

"John," said a quiet somebody—the mouth-harp man, with firelight showing lines in his thin face, salty gray in his hair. "What you really doing here?"

"Watching," I said, while big Jeth hauled those two drunk men off from each other, and Donie Carawan scolded them. "And listening," I said. "Wanting to know what way the black train song fits in with this party and the tale about the curse. You know about it?"

"I know," he said.

We carried our food out of the firelight. Folks were crowding to the barrel, laughing and yelling.

"Donie Carawan was to marry Trevis Jones," the mouth-harp man told me. "He owned the High Fork Railroad to freight the timber from this valley. He'd a lavish of money, is how he got to marry her. But," and he swallowed hard, "another young fellow loved her. Cobb Richardson, who ran Trevis Jones's train on the High Fork Railroad. And he killed Trevis Jones."

"For love?" I asked.

"Folks reckoned that Donie Carawan decided against Trevis and love-talked Cobb into the killing; for Trevis had made a will and heired her all his money and property—the railroad and all. But Cobb made confession. Said Donie had no part in it. The law let her go, and killed Cobb in the electric chair, down at the state capital."

"I declare to never," I said.

"Fact. And Cobb's mother—Mrs. Amanda Richardson—spoke the curse."

"Oh," I said, "is she the witch that—"

"She was no witch," he broke me off, "but she cursed Donie Carawan, that the train that Cobb had engine-drove, and Trevis had heired to her, would be her death and destruction. Donie laughed. You've heard her laugh. And folks started the song, the black train song."

"Who made it?" I asked him.

"Reckon I did," he said, looking long at me. He waited to let me feel that news. Then he said, "Maybe it was the song decided Donie Carawan to deal with the Hickory River Railroad, agreeing for an income of money not to run the High Fork train no more."

I'd finished my barbecue. I could have had more; but I didn't feel like it. "I see," I told him. "She reckoned that if no train ran on the High Fork tracks, it couldn't be her death and destruction."

He and I put our paper plates on one of the fires. I didn't look at the other folks, but it seemed to me they were quieting their laughing and talking as the night got darker.

"Only thing is," the mouth-harp man went on, "folks say the train runs on that track. Or it did. A black train runs some nights at midnight, they say, and when it runs a sinner dies."

"You ever see it run?"

"No, John, but I've sure God heard it. And only Donie Carawan laughs about it."

She laughed right then, joking the two men who'd feathered up to fight. Ary man's neck craned at her, and women looked the way you'd figure they didn't relish that. My neck craned some, itself.

"Twenty years back, the height of her bloom," said the mouth-harp man, "law me, you'd never call to look at anything else."

"What does she mean, no more curse?"

"She made another deal, John. She sold off the rails of the High Fork Road, that's stood idle for twenty years. Today the last of them was torn up and carried off. Meanwhile, she's had this house built, across where the right of way used to be. Looky yonder, through the dog-trot. That's where the road ran."

So it was the old road bed made that dark dip amongst the trees. Just now it didn't look so wide a dip.

"No rails," he said. "She figures no black train at midnight. Folks came at her invite—some because they rent her land, some because they owe her money, and some—men folks—because they'll do ary thing she bids them."

"And she never married?" I asked.

"If she done that, she'd lose the money and land she heired from Trevis Jones. It was in his will. She just takes men without marrying, one and then another. I've known men kill theirselves because she'd put her heart back in her pocket on them. Lately, it's been big Jeth. She acts tonight like pick-herself a new beau lover."

She walked back through the lamplight and firelight. "John," she said, "these folks want to dance again."

What I played them was "Many Thousands Gone," with the mouth-harp to help, and they danced and stomped the way you'd think it was a many thousands dancing. In its thick, Donie Carawan promenaded left and right and do-si-doed with a fair-haired young fellow, and Jeth the dance-caller looked pickle-sour. When I'd done, Donie Carawan came swishing back.

"Let the mouth-harp play," she said, "and dance with me."

"Can't dance no shakes," I told her. "Just now, I'd relish to practice the black train song."

Her blue eyes crinkled. "All right. Play, and I'll sing."

She did. The mouth-harp man blew whistle-moanings to my guitar, and folks listened, goggling like frogs.

> A bold young man kept mocking,
> Cared not for the warning word,
> When the wild and lonely whistle
> Of the little black train he heard.
> "Have mercy, Lord, forgive me!
> I'm cut down in my sin!
> O death, will you not spare me?"
> But the little black train rolled in.

When she'd sung that much, Donie Carawan laughed like

before, deep and bantering. Jeth the dance-caller made a funny sound in his bull throat.

"What I don't figure," he said, "was how you all made the train sound like coming in, closer and closer."

"Just by changing the music," I said. "Changing the pitch."

"Fact," said the mouth-harp man. "I played the change with him."

A woman laughed, nervous. "Now I think, that's true. A train whistle sounds higher and higher while it comes up to you. Then it passes and goes off, sounding lower and lower."

"But I didn't hear the train go away in the song," allowed a man beside her. "It just kept coming." He shrugged, maybe he shivered.

"Donie," said the woman, "reckon I'll go along."

"Stay on, Lettie," began Donie Carawan, telling her instead of asking.

"Got a right much walking to do, and no moon," said the woman. "Reuben, you come, too."

She left. The man looked back just once at Donie Carawan, and followed. Another couple, and then another, went with them from the firelight. Maybe more would have gone, but Donie Carawan snorted, like a horse, to stop them.

"Let's drink," she said. "Plenty for all, now those folks I reckoned to be my friends are gone."

Maybe two-three others faded away, between there and the barrel. Donie Carawan dipped herself a drink, watching me over the gourd's edge. Then she dipped more and held it out.

"You drink after a lady," she whispered, "and get a kiss."

I drank. It was good stump-hole whisky. "Tasty," I said.

"The kiss?" she laughed. But the dance-caller didn't laugh, or either the mouth-harp man, or either me.

"Let's dance," said Donie Carawan, and I picked "Sourwood Mountain" and the mouth-harp moaned.

The dancers had got to be few, just in a short while. But the trees they danced through looked bigger, and more of them. It minded me of how I'd heard, when I was a chap, about day-trees and night-trees, they weren't the same things at all; and the night-trees can crowd all round a house they don't like, pound the shingles off the roof, bust in the window glass and the door panels; and that's the sort of night you'd better never set your foot outside. . . .

Not so much clapping at the end of "Sourwood Mountain." Not such a holler of "More!" Folks went to take another drink at the barrel, but the mouth-harp man held me back.

"Tell me," he said, "about that business. The noise sounding higher when the train comes close."

"It was explained out to me by a man I know, place in Tennessee called Oak Ridge," I said. "It's about what they call sound waves, and some way it works with light, too. Don't rightly catch on how, but they can measure how far it is to the stars thataway."

He thought, frowning. "Something like what's called radar?"

I shook my head. "No, no machinery to it. Just what they name a principle. Fellow named Doppler—Christian Doppler, a foreigner—got it up."

"His name was Christian," the mouth-harp man repeated me. "Then I reckon it's no witch stuff."

"Why you worrying it?" I asked him.

"I watched through the dog-trot while we were playing the black train song, changing pitch, making it sound like coming near," he said. "Looky yonder, see for yourself."

I looked. There was a streaky shine down the valley. Two streaky shines, though nary moon. I saw what he meant—it looked like those pulled-up rails were still there, where they hadn't been before.

"That second verse Miss Donie sang," I said. "Was it about—"

"Yes," he said before I'd finished. "That was the verse about Cobb Richardson. How he prayed for God's forgiveness, night before he died."

Donie Carawan came and poked her hand under my arm. I could tell that good strong liquor was feeling its way around her insides. She laughed at almost nothing whatever. "You're not leaving, anyway," she smiled at me.

"Don't have any place special to go," I said.

She upped on her pointed toes. "Stay here tonight," she said in my ear. "The rest of them will be gone by midnight."

"You invite men like that?" I said, looking into her blue eyes. "When you don't know them?"

"I know men well enough," she said. "Knowing men keeps a woman young." Her finger touched my guitar where it hung behind my shoulder, and the strings whispered a reply. "Sing me something, John."

"I still want to learn the black train song."

"I've sung you both verses," she said.

"Then," I told her, "I'll sing a verse I've just made up inside my head." I looked at the mouth-harp man. "Help me with this."

Together we played, raising pitch gradually, and I sang the new verse I'd made, with my eyes on Donie Carawan.

> Go tell that laughing lady
> All filled with worldly pride,
> The little black train is coming,
> Get ready to take a ride.
> With a little black coach and engine
> And a little black baggage car,
> The words and deeds she has said and done
> Must roll to the judgment bar.

When I was through, I looked up at those who'd stayed. They weren't more than half a dozen now, bunched up together like cows in a storm; all but Big Jeth, standing to one side with eyes stabbing at me, and Donie Carawan, leaning tired-like against a tree with hanging branches.

"Jeth," she said, "stomp his guitar to pieces."

I switched the carrying cord off my neck and held the guitar at my side. "Don't try such a thing, Jeth," I warned him.

His big square teeth grinned, with dark spaces between them. He looked twice as wide as me.

"I'll stomp you and your guitar both," he said.

I put the guitar on the ground, glad I'd had but the one drink. Jeth ran and stooped for it, and I put my fist hard under his ear. He hopped two steps away to keep his feet.

Shouldn't anybody name me what he did then, and I hit him twice more, harder yet. His nose flatted out under my knuckles and when he pulled back away, blood trickled.

The mouth-harp man grabbed up my guitar. "This here'll be

a square fight!" he yelled, louder than he'd spoken so far. "Ain't a fair one, seeing Jeth's so big, but it'll be square! Just them two in it, and no more!"

"I'll settle you later," Jeth promised him, mean.

"Settle me first," I said, and got betwixt them.

Jeth ran at me. I stepped sidewise and got him under the ear again as he went shammocking past. He turned, and I dug my fist right into his belly-middle, to stir up all that stump-hole whisky he'd been drinking, then the other fist under the ear yet once more, then on the chin and the mouth, under the ear, on the broken nose—ten licks like that, as fast and hard as I could fetch them in, and eighth or ninth he went slack, and the tenth he just fell flat and loose, like a coat from a nail. I stood waiting, but he didn't move.

"Gentlemen," said the drunk man who'd fetched me, "looky yonder at Jeth laying there! Never figured to see the day! Maybe that stranger-man calls himself John is Satan, after all!"

Donie Carawan walked across, slow, and gouged Jeth's ribs with the pointy toe of her high-heeled shoe. "Get up," she bade him.

He grunted and mumbled and opened his eyes. Then he got up, joint by joint, careful and sore, like a sick bull. He tried to stop the blood from his nose with the back of his big hand. Donie Carawan looked at him and then she looked at me.

"Get out of here, Jeth," she ordered him. "Off my place."

He went, cripply-like, with his knees bent and his hands swinging and his back humped, the way you'd think he carried something heavy.

The drunk man hiccupped. "I reckon to go, too," he said, maybe just to himself.

"Then go!" Donie Carawan yelled at him. "Everybody can go, right now, this minute! I thought you were my friends—now I see I don't have a friend among the whole bunch! Hurry up, get going! Everybody!"

Hands on hips, she blared it out. Folks moved off through the trees, a sight faster than Jeth had gone. But I stood where I was. The mouth-harp man gave me back my guitar, and I touched a chord of its strings. Donie Carawan spun around like on a swivel to set her blue eyes on me.

"You stayed," she said, the way she thought there was something funny about it.

"It's not midnight yet," I told her.

"But near to," added the mouth-harp man. "Just a few minutes off. And it's at midnight the little black train runs."

She lifted her round bare shoulders. She made to laugh again, but didn't.

"That's all gone. If it ever was true, it's not true any more. The rails were taken up—"

"Looky yonder through the dog-trot," the mouth-harp man broke in. "See the two rails in place, streaking along the valley."

Again she swung around and she looked, and seemed to me she swayed in the light of the dying fires. She could see those streaky rails, all right.

"And listen," said the mouth-harp man. "Don't you all hear something?"

I heard it, and so did Donie Carawan, for she flinched. It was a wild and lonely whistle, soft but plain, far down valley.

"Are you doing that, John?" she squealed at me, in a voice gone all of a sudden high and weak and old. Then she ran at the house and into the dog-trot, staring down along what looked like railroad track.

I followed her, and the mouth-harp man followed me. Inside the dog-trot was a floor of dirt, stomped hard as brick. Donie Carawan looked back at us. Lamplight came through a window, to make her face look bright pale, with the painted red of the mouth gone almost black against it.

"John," she said, "you're playing a trick, making it sound like—"

"Not me," I swore to her.

It whistled again, *wooooooeeeee!* And I, too, looked along the two rails, shining plain as plain in the dark moonless night, to curve off around a valley-bend. A second later, the engine itself sounded, *chukchukchukchuk,* and the whistle, *wooooooeeeee!*

"Miss Donie," I said, close behind her, "you'd better go away."

I pushed her gently.

"No!" She lifted her fists, and I saw cordy lines on their backs— they weren't a young woman's fists. "This is my house and my land, and it's my railroad!"

"But—" I started to say.

"If it comes here," she broke me off, "where can I run to from it?"

The mouth-harp man tugged my sleeve. "I'm going," he said. "You and me raised the pitch and brought the black train. Thought I could stay, watch it and glory in it. But I'm not man enough."

Going, he blew a whistle-moan on his mouth-harp, and the other whistle blew back an answer, louder and nearer.

And higher in the pitch.

"That's a real train coming," I told Donie Carawan, but she shook her yellow head.

"No," she said, dead-like. "It's coming, but it's no real train. It's heading right to this dog-trot. Look, John. On the ground."

Rails looked to run there, right through the dog-trot like through a tunnel. Maybe it was some peculiar way of the light. They lay close together, like narrow-gauge rails. I didn't feel like touching them with my toe to make sure of them, but I saw them. Holding my guitar under one arm, I put out my other hand to take Donie Carawan's elbow. "We'd better go," I said again.

"I can't!"

She said it loud and sharp and purely scared. And taking hold of her arm was like grabbing the rail of a fence, it was so stiff and unmoving.

"I own this land," she was saying. "I can't leave it."

I tried to pick her up, and that couldn't be done. You'd have thought she'd grown to the ground inside that dog-trot, sprang between what looked like the rails, the way you'd figure roots had come from her pointy toes and high heels. Out yonder, where the trackmarks curved off, the sound rose louder, higher, *chukchuk-chukchuk—woooooeeeee!* And light was coming from round the curve, like a headlight maybe, only it had some blue to its yellow.

The sound of the coming engine made the notes of the song in my head:

> *Go put your house in order*
> *For thou shalt surely die—*

Getting higher, getting higher, changing pitch as it came close and closer—

I don't know when I began picking the tune on my guitar, but I was playing as I stood there next to Donie Carawan. She couldn't flee. She was rooted there, or frozen there, and the train was going to come in sight in just a second.

The mouth-harp man credited us, him and me, with bringing it, by that pitch-changing. And, whatever anybody deserved, wasn't for me to bring their deservings on them. I thought things like that. Also:

Christian Doppler was the name of the fellow who'd thought out the why and wherefore of how pitch makes the sound closeness. Like what the mouth-harp man said, his name showed it wasn't witch stuff. An honest man could try . . .

I slid my fingers back up the guitar-neck, little by little, as I picked the music, and the pitch sneaked down.

"Here it comes, John," whimpered Donie Carawan, standing solid as a stump.

"No," I said. "It's going—listen!"

I played so soft you could pick up the train-noise with your ear. And the pitch was dropping, like with my guitar, and the whistle sounded *woooooeeeee!* Lower it sounded.

"The light—dimmer—" she said. "Oh, if I could have the chance to live different—"

She moaned and swayed.

Words came for me to sing as I picked.

> *Oh, see her standing helpless,*
> *Oh, hear her shedding tears.*
> *She's counting these last moments*
> *As once she counted years.*
> *She'd turn from proud and wicked ways,*
> *She'd leave her sin, O Lord!*
> *If the little black train would just back up*
> *And not take her aboard.*

For she was weeping, all right. I heard her breath catch and strangle and shake her body, the way you'd look for it to tear her ribs loose from her backbone. I picked on, strummed on, lower and lower.

Just for once, I thought I could glimpse what might have come at us.

It was little, all right, and black under that funny cold-blue light it carried. And the cars weren't any bigger than coffins, and some way the shape of coffins. Or maybe I just sort of imagined that, dreamed it up while I stood there. Anyway, the light grew dim, and the *chukchukchukchuk* went softer and lower, and you'd guess the train was backing off, out of hearing.

I stopped my hand on the silver strings. We stood there in a silence like what there must be in some lifeless, airless place like on the moon.

Then Donie Carawan gave out one big, broken sob, and I caught her with my free arm as she fell.

She was soft enough then. All the tight was gone from her. She lifted one weak, round, bare arm around my neck, and her tears wet my hickory shirt.

"You saved me, John," she kept saying. "You turned the curse away."

"Reckon I did," I said, though that sounded like bragging. I looked down at the rails, and they weren't there, in the dog-trot or beyond. Just the dark of the valley. The cooking fires had burned out, and the lamps in the house were low.

Her arm tightened around my neck. "Come in," she said. "Come in, John. You and me, alone in there."

"It's time for me to head off away," I said.

Her arm dropped from me. "What's the matter? Don't you like me?" she asked.

I didn't even answer that one, she sounded so pitiful. "Miss Donie," I said, "you told a true thing. I turned the curse from you. It hadn't died. You can't kill it by laughing at it, or saying there aren't such things, or pulling up rails. If it held off tonight, it might come back."

"Oh!" She half raised her arms to me again, then put them down.

"What must I do?" she begged me.

"Stop being a sinner."

Her blue eyes got round in her pale face.

"You want me to live," she said, hopeful.

"It's better for you to live. You told me that folks owe you money, rent land from you and such. How'd they get along if you got carried off?"

She could see what I meant, maybe the first time in her life.

"You'd be gone," I minded her, "but the folks would stay behind, needing your help. Well, you're still here, Miss Donie. Try to help the folks. There's a thousand ways to do it. I don't have to name them to you. And you act right, you won't be so apt to hear that whistle at midnight."

I started out of the dog-trot.

"John!" My name sounded like a wail in her mouth. "Stay here tonight, John," she begged me. "Stay with me! I want you here, John, I need you here!"

"No, you don't need me, Miss Donie," I said. "You've got a right much of thinking and planning to do. Around about the up of sun, you'll have done enough, maybe, to start living different from this on."

She started to cry. As I walked away I noticed how, farther I got, lower her voice-pitch sounded.

I sort of stumbled on the trail. The mouth-harp man sat on a chopped-down old log.

"I listened, John," he said. "Think you done right?"

"Did the closest I could to right. Maybe the black train was bound to roll, on orders from whatever station it starts from; maybe it was you and me, raising the pitch the way we did, brought it here tonight."

"I left when I did, dreading that thought," he nodded.

"The same thought made me back it out again," I said. "Anyway, I kind of glimmer the idea you all can look for a new Donie Carawan hereabouts, from now forward."

He got up and turned to go up trail. "I never said who I was."

"No, sir," I agreed him. "And I never asked."

"I'm Cobb Richardson's brother. Wyatt Richardson. Dying, my mother swore me to even things with Donie Carawan for what happened to Cobb. Doubt if she meant this sort of turn-out, but I reckon it would suit her fine."

We walked into the dark together.

"Come stay at my house tonight, John," he made the offer. "Ain't much there, but you're welcome to what there is."

"Thank you kindly," I said. "I'd be proud to stay."

SHIVER IN THE PINES

We sat along the edge of Mr. Hoje Cowand's porch, up the high hills of the Rebel Creek country. Mr. Hoje himself, and his neighbor Mr. Eddy Herron who was a widowman like Mr. Hoje, and Mr. Eddy's son Clay who was a long tall fellow like his daddy, and Mr. Hoje's pretty-cheeked daughter Sarah Ann, who was courting with Clay. And me. I'd stopped off to hand-help Mr. Hoje build him a new pole fence, and nothing would do him but I'd stay two-three days. Supper had been pork and fried apples and pone and snap beans. The sun made to set, and they all asked me to sing.

So I picked the silver strings on my guitar and began the old tuneful one:

> *Choose your partner as you go,*
> *Choose your partner as you go.*

"Yippeehoo!" hollered old Mr. Eddy. "You sure enough can play that, John! Come on, choose partners and dance!"

Up hopped Clay and Sarah Ann, on the level-stamped front yard, and I played it up loud and sang, and Mr. Eddy called figures for them to step to:

"Honor your partner! . . . Swing your partner! . . . Do-si-do! . . . Allemand right!" Till I got to one last chorus and I sang out loudly:

> *Fare thee well, my charming gal,*
> *Fare thee well, I'm gone!*
> *Fare thee well, my charming gal,*
> *With golden slippers on!*

"Kiss your partner and turn her loose!" whooped out Mr. Eddy as I stopped. Clay kissed Sarah Ann the way you'd think it was his whole business in life, and Sarah Ann, up on her little toes, kissed him back.

"Won't be no better singing and dancing the day these young ones marry up," said Mr. Hoje. "And no fare thee wells then."

"And I purely wish I could buy you golden slippers, Sarah Ann," said Clay as the two sat down together again.

"Gold's where you find it," quoted Mr. Eddy from the Book. "Clay, you might ransack round them old lost mines the Ancients dug, that nobody knows about. John, you remember the song about them?"

I remembered, for Mr. Eddy and Mr. Hoje talked a right much about the Ancients and their mines. I sang it:

> *Where were they, where were they,*
> *On that gone and vanished day*
> *When they shoveled for their treasure of gold?*
> *In the pines, in the pines,*
> *Where the sun never shines,*
> *And I shiver when the wind blows cold. . . .*

As I stopped, a throat rasped, loud. "Odd," said somebody, walking into the yard, "to hear that song just now."

We didn't know the somebody. He was blocky-made, not young nor either old, with a store suit and a black hat, like a man running for district judge. His square face looked flat and white, like a face drawn on paper.

"Might I sit for a minute?" he asked, mannerly. "I've come a long, long way."

"Take the door-log, and welcome," Mr. Hoje bade him. "My name's Hoje Cowand, and this is my daughter Sarah Ann, and these are the Herrons, and this here's John, who's a-visiting me. Come a long way, you said? Where from, sir?"

"From going to and fro in the world," said the stranger, lifting the hat from his smoke-gray hair, "and from walking up and down in it."

Another quotation from the Book; and if you've read Job's first chapter, you know who's supposed to have said it. The man saw how we gopped, for he smiled as he sat down and stuck out his dusty shoes.

"My name's Reed Barnitt," he said. "Odd, to hear talk of the Ancients and their mines. For I've roved around after talk of them."

"Why," said Mr. Hoje, "folks say the Ancients came into these mountains before the settlers. Close to four hundred years back."

"That long, Mr. Hoje?" asked young Clay.

"Well, a tree was cut that growed in the mouth of an Ancients' mine, near Horse Stomp," Mr. Hoje allowed. "Schooled folks counted the rings in the wood, and there was full three hundred. It was before the Yankee war they done that, so the tree seeded itself in the mine-hole four hundred years back, or near about."

"The time of the Spaniards," nodded Reed Barnitt. "Maybe about when de Soto and his Spanish soldiers crossed these mountains."

"I've heard tell the Ancients was here around that time," put in Mr. Eddy, "but I've likewise heard tell they wasn't Spanish folks, nor either Indians."

"Did they get what they sought?" wondered Reed Barnitt.

"My daddy went into that Horse Stomp heading once," said Mr. Eddy. "He said it run back about seven hundred foot as he stepped it, and a deep shaft went down at the end. Well, he figured no mortal soul would dig so far, saving he found what he was after." He had hold of Mr. Hoje's jug, and now he pushed it toward Mr. Barnitt. "Have a drink?"

"Thank you kindly, I don't use it. What did the Ancients want?"

"I've seen only one of their mines, over the ridge yonder," and Mr. Hoje nodded through the dusk. "Where they call it Black Pine Hollow—"

"Where the sun never shines," put in Mr. Barnitt, "and I shiver when the wind blows cold." His smile at me was tight.

"I was there three-four times when I was a chap, but not lately, for folks allows there's haunts there. I saw a right much quartz laying around, and I hear tell gold comes from quartz rock."

"Gold," nodded Reed Barnitt. He put his hand inside his coat. "You folks are treating me clever," he said, "and I hope you let me make a gift. Miss Sarah Ann, I myself don't have use for these, so if you'd accept—"

What he held out was golden slippers, that shone in the down-going sun's last suspicions.

Gentlemen, you should have heard Sarah Ann cry out her pleasure, you should have seen the gold shine in her eyes. But she drew back the hand she put out.

"I couldn't," she said. "Wouldn't be fitting to."

"Then I'll give them to this young man." Reed Barnitt set the slippers in Clay's lap. "Young sir, I misdoubt if Miss Sarah Ann would refuse a gift at your hands."

The slippers had high heels and pointy toes, and they shone like glory. Clay smiled at Sarah Ann and gave them to her. To see her smile back, you'd think it was Clay, and not Reed Barnitt, had taken them from nowhere for her.

"I do thank you kindly," said Sarah Ann. She shucked off her scuffy old shoes, and the golden slippers fitted her like slippers made to the measure of her feet. "John," she said, "was just singing about things like this."

"Heard him as I came up trail from Rebel Creek," said Reed Barnitt. "And likewise heard him sing of the Ancients in Black Pine Hollow." His square face looked at us around. "Gentlemen," he said, "I wonder if there's heart in you all to go there with me."

We gopped again. Finally Clay said, "For gold?"

"For what else?" said Reed Barnitt. "Nobody's found it there, because nobody had the special way to look for it."

Nary one of us was really surprised to hear what the man said. There'd been such a story as long as anybody had lived around Rebel Creek. Mr. Hoje drank from the jug. Finally he said, "In what respect a special way, Mr. Barnitt?"

"I said I'd roved a far piece. I went to fetch a spell that would show the treasure. But I can't do it alone." Again the white face traveled its look over us. "It takes five folks—men, because a woman mustn't go into a mine."

We knew about that. If lady-folks go down a mine, there'll be something bad befall, maybe a miner killed.

"You've been kindly to me," said Reed Barnitt. "I feel like asking you, will you all come help me? Mr. Cowand, and Mr. Herron, and you his son, and you, John. Five we'd seek the treasure of the Ancients and five ways we'd divide it."

Sarah Ann had her manners with her. "I'll just go do the dishes," she said to us. "No, Clay, don't come help. Stay and talk here."

Reed Barnitt watched her go into the house. She left the door open, and the shine from the hearth gave us red light after sundown.

"You're a lucky young rooster," Reed Barnitt said to Clay. "A fifth chunk of the Ancients' treasure would sure enough pleasure that girl."

"Mr. Barnitt, I'm with you," Clay told him quick.

"So am I," said Mr. Eddy, because his son had spoken.

"I don't lag back when others go forward," I added on.

"Count on me," finished Mr. Hoje for us. "That makes five, like you want it, sir. But you studied the thing out and got the spell. You should have more than a fifth of whatever we find."

But the white square face shook sideways. "No. Part of the business is that each of the five takes his equal part, of the doing and of the sharing. That's how it must be. Now—we begin."

"Right this instant?" asked Clay.

"Yes," said Reed Barnitt. "Stand round, you all."

He got up from the door-log and stepped into the yard, and the rest of us with him. "The first part of the spell," he said. "To learn if the Ancients truly left a treasure."

Where the hearth's red glimmer showed on the ground in front of the door, he knelt down. He picked up a stick. He marked in the dirt.

"Five-pointed star," he said. It was maybe four feet across. "Stand at the points, gentlemen. Yes, like that."

Rising, he took his place at the fifth point. He flung away the stick, and put a white hand into the side pocket of his coat. "Silence," he warned us, though he didn't need to.

He stooped and flung something down at the star's center. Maybe it was powder, though I'm not sure, for it broke out into fire quick, and shone like pure white heat yanked in a chunk from the heart of a furnace. I saw it shine sickly on the hairy faces of Mr. Hoje and Mr. Eddy, and Clay's young jaws and cheeks seemed dull and drawn. Reed Barnitt needed no special light to be pale.

He began to speak. "Moloch, Lucifer," he said in a voice like praying. "Anector, Somiator, sleep ye not, awake. The strong hero Holoba, the powerful Ischiros, the mighty Manus Erohye—show us the truth! Amen."

Again his hand in his pocket, and he brought out a slip of paper the size of a postcard, whiter than white in the glow. He handed it to Clay, who was nearest him. "Breathe on it," said Reed Barnitt, "and the others do likewise."

Clay breathed on it, and passed it to Mr. Hoje. Then it came to me, and to Mr. Eddy, and back to Reed Barnitt. He stooped again, and held it above that sick-white heat. Back he jumped, quick, and yelled out loud, "Earth on the fire! Smother it before we lose the true word!"

Clay and his father flung on dirt. Mr. Hoje and Reed Barnitt walked side by side to the porch, whispering together. Then Mr. Hoje called in to Sarah Ann, "Fetch out the lamp, honey."

She did so. We gathered round to look at the paper. Writing was on it, spidery-looking and rough, the way you'd think it was written in mud instead of ink. Reed Barnitt gave it to Sarah Ann.

"Your heart is good," he said. "Read out what it says for us."

She held the lamp in one hand, the paper in the other.

"Do right, and prosper," she read, soft and shaky, "and what you seek is yours. Great treasure. Obey orders. To open the way, burn the light—"

"We put out the light," said Clay, but Reed Barnitt waved him quiet.

"Turn the paper over, Miss Sarah Ann," said Reed Barnitt. "Looks like more to read on the other side."

She looked at more muddy-looking scrawl on the back. She went on:

"Aram Harnam has the light. Buy it from him, but don't tell him why. He is wicked. Pay what he asks. The power is dear and scarce."

She looked up. "That's all it says," she told us, and gave the paper back to Reed Barnitt.

We all sat down, the lamp on the porch floor among us. "Anybody know that man, what's-his-name?" asked Reed Barnitt.

"Yes," answered Mr. Hoje. "We know Aram Harnam."

At least, I'd heard what others along Rebel Creek said about Aram Harnam, and it wasn't good.

Seems he'd gone to a college to be a preacher. But that college sent him to be tried, with a sermon to some folks in another county. His teachers went to hear. When he had done, as I heard it told, those teachers told Aram Harnam that from what he'd said under name of a sermon they wanted him to pack his things and leave the college before even another sun rose.

So he came back to Rebel Creek. One night he went up on a bald hill most folks stayed away from, and put his hand on his head and said that all beneath his hand could be Satan's property. After that, he did witch-doctoring. Nobody liked him but ary man, woman and child in the Rebel Creek county feared him.

"I take it that Aram Harnam's a bad man," Reed Barnitt suggested.

"You take it right, sir," allowed Mr. Eddy. "So does whoever wrote on that paper."

"Wrote on the paper?" Reed Barnitt said after him, and held it out to the light. It was white and empty; so was the other side when he turned that up.

"The writing's been taken back," he said, nodding his pale face above it. "But we all remember what it said. We must buy the light, and not let Aram Harnam know why we want it."

"When do we go see him?" asked Mr. Hoje.

"Why not now?" said Reed Barnitt, but Mr. Hoje and Mr. Eddy spoke against that. Neither of them wanted to be trucking round Aram Harnam's place in the dark of night. We made it up to meet tomorrow morning for breakfast at Mr. Eddy's, then go.

Mr. Eddy and Clay left. Mr. Hoje and Sarah Ann made up pallets for Reed Barnitt and me just inside the front door. Reed Barnitt slept right off quick, but I lay awake a good spell. There was a sight of hoot owls hooting in the trees round the cabin, and a sight of thoughts in my head.

Way I've told it so far, you might wonder why we came in so quick on Reed Barnitt's spell and scheme. Lying there, I was wondering the same thing. It came to mind that Clay had first said he'd join. That was for Sarah Ann, and Clay without land or money, wanting to marry her and have enough to make her happy. After Clay spoke, Mr. Eddy and Mr. Hoje felt bound to do the same, for with them the kingdom and the power and the glory tied up to their young ones, and they wanted to see them wed and happy. Mr. Hoje special. He worked hard on a little place, with corn patches on terraces up slope you had to hang on with one hand while you chopped weeds with the other, and just one cow and two hogs in his pens.

I reckoned it was hope, more than belief, that caused them to say yes to Reed Barnitt. And me—well, I'd gone a many miles and seen a right much more things than any of my friends, and some of the things not what you'd call everyday things. I reckon I was hoping, too, for a good piece of luck for Clay and Sarah Ann. Never having had anything myself, or expecting to, I could anyhow see how he and she wanted something. So why not help out? Maybe, one or two things I'd watched happen, I could know to help out more than either of their fathers.

Figuring like that, I slept at last, and at the dawn gray we up to meet at Mr. Eddy's.

My first look at Aram Harnam, sitting in front of his low-built little shanty, I reckoned I'd never seen a hairier man, and mighty few hairier creatures. He had a juniper-bark basket betwixt his patched knees, and he was picking over a mess of narrow-leafed plants in it. His hands crawled in the basket like black-furred spiders. Out between his shaggy hair and his shaggy beard looked only his bright eyes and his thin brown nose, and if he smiled or frowned at us, none could say. He spoke up with a boom, and I recollected how once he'd studied to preach.

"Hoje Cowand," he said, "you're welcome, and your friends, too. I knew you all was coming."

"Who done told you that?" asked Mr. Hoje.

"Little bird done told me," said Aram Harnam. "Little black bird with green eyes, that tells me a many things."

It minded me of the Ugly Bird, that once I killed and freed a whole district of folks from the scare of it.

"Maybe your little bird told you what we want," said Mr. Eddy, standing close to Clay, but Aram Harnam shook his head.

"No sir, didn't say that." He set down the basket. "I'm a-waiting to hear."

Mr. Hoje introduced Reed Barnitt and me, and neither of us nor yet Aram Harnam made offer to shake hands.

"It's a light we want of you, Aram Harnam," said Mr. Hoje then. "A special kind of light."

"Oh." Aram Harnam leaned back against the logs of his shanty. "The light that shows you what you'd miss else? I can fix you such a light."

"How much?" asked Clay.

Aram Harnam's furry hand fiddled in his beard. "It's a scarce thing, that light. Cost you five hundred dollars."

"Five hundred dollars!" whooped out Mr. Eddy.

The eyes among all Aram Harnam's hair came to me. "Hear that echo, son?" he asked me. "Right clear today—these hills and mountains sure enough give you back echoes." Then, to Mr. Eddy. "Yes, sir. Five hundred dollars."

Mr. Hoje gulped. "We ain't got that kind of money."

"Got to have that kind of money for that kind of light," said Aram Harnam.

"Step aside with me, gentlemen," said Reed Barnitt, and Aram Harnam sat and watched us pull back a dozen or twenty steps to talk with our heads together.

"He knows something," Reed Barnitt whispered, "but not everything, or I judge he'd put his price higher still. Anyway, our spell last night told us there's treasure, and we need the light to find it."

"I ain't got but forty dollars," said Mr. Eddy. "Anybody else got enough to put with my forty dollars to make five hundred?"

"Twenty's all I have," Reed Barnitt told us, and breathed long and worried. "That's sixty so far. John?"

"Maybe the change in my pockets would add up to a dollar," I said. "I'm not right sure."

Aram Harnam laughed, or coughed, one. "You all make a big thing out of five hundred dollars," he called to us.

Mr. Hoje faced around and walked back toward him. "We don't have it."

"Cash," said Aram Harnam after him. "I might credit you, Hoje Cowand."

"Five hundred dollars' worth?" asked Mr. Hoje. "What on?"

"We-ell . . ." The word came slow out of the hair and whiskers.

"You've got a piece of land, and a house, and a cow and a pig or two . . ."

"I can't give you those," Mr. Hoje put in.

"You could put them up. And Mr. Eddy could put up his place, too."

"The two places are worth plenty more than five hundred dollars," Mr. Eddy started to argue.

"Not on the tax bills, the way I hear from my little green-eyed black bird."

Reed Barnitt beckoned us round him again. "Isn't there any way to raise the money?" he whispered. "We're just before finding a fortune."

Mr. Hoje and Mr. Eddy shook their heads.

"Gentlemen, we've as good as got that Ancients' treasure," Reed Barnitt said, and rummaged money from his pocket—a wadded ten, a five and some ones. "I'll risk my last cent, and take it back from off the top of whatever find. You others can do the same."

"Wait," said Mr. Hoje.

He put his arm around Mr. Eddy's neck, and the two of them mumbled together a while, and we others watched. Then they turned, both of them, and went back to Aram Harnam.

"We'd want a guarantee," said Mr. Hoje.

"Guarantee?" repeated Aram Harnam. "Oh, I'll guarantee the light. Put it in writing that it'll show you what you seek."

"Draw us up some loan papers," said Mr. Eddy. "Two hundred and fifty dollars credit to each of us, against our places, and a guarantee the light will work, and sixty days of time."

Mr. Eddy spoke sharp and deeply. Aram Harnam looked at him, then went into the shanty. He brought out a tablet of paper and an ink bottle and an old stump of a pen. He wrote two pages, and when Mr. Hoje and Mr. Eddy read them over they signed their names.

Then Aram Harnam bade us wait. He carried the papers back inside. What he did in there took time, and I watched part of it through the open door. He mixed stuff in a pot—I thought I smelled burning sulphur, and once something sweet and spicy, like what incense must smell like. There was other stuff. He heated it

so it smoked, then worked it with those furry hands. After while
he fetched out what he'd made. It was a big rough candle, as big
around as your wrist and as long as your arm to the elbow. Its wick
looked like gray yarn, and the candle wax was dirty black.

"Light it at midnight," he said, "and carry it forward. It'll go
out at the place where you'll find your wish. Understand?"

We said we understood.

"Then good day to you all," said Aram Harnam.

Nobody felt the need of sleep that night. At eleven o'clock
by Mr. Hoje's big silver turnip watch, we started out to cross the
ridge to Black Pine Hollow. Clay went first, with a lantern. Reed
Barnitt followed, with the candle. Then me, with my guitar slung
on my back because I had a notion to carry it along, and a grubbing hoe in my hand. Then Mr. Hoje with a spade, and Mr. Eddy
last of all with a crowbar. Sarah Ann watched us from the door,
until we got out of her sight.

Not much of a trail led to Black Pine Hollow, for folks don't go
there much. Last night's hoot owls were at it again, and once or
twice we heard rattlings to right and left, like things keeping pace
with us among the bushes. Down into the hollow we went, while
a breeze blew down on us, chill for that time of year. I thought,
but didn't sing out loud:

> In the pines, in the pines,
> Where the sun never shines,
> And I shiver when the wind blows cold. . . .

"Where's this mine?" asked Reed Barnitt.

"I can find it better than Clay," called Mr. Hoje. He pushed
ahead and took the lantern. The light showed duller and duller,
the deeper we went into the hollow; it showed a sort of dim
brown, the way you'd think that moonless night was trying to
smother it. Around us crowded the black pines the hollow was
named after. For my own comfort I reached back and tweaked a
silver guitar-string, and it rang so loud we all jumped.

"Now," said Mr. Hoje, after a long, long while, "I think this
must be it."

He turned off among a thick bunch of the blackest-looking pines, and held the lantern high. Hidden there behind the trees rose a rock face like a wall, and in the rock was a hole the size of a door, but uneven. Vines hung down around it, but they looked dead and burnt out. As we stood still and looked, there was a little timid foot-patter inside.

"Let's pray that's no rat," said Clay. "Rats in mines are plumb bad luck."

"Shoo," said his daddy, "let's hope it's nothing worse than just a rat."

Reed Barnitt shoved forward. "I'm going in," he said through his teeth, "and I sure enough don't want to go in alone."

We went in together. Gentlemen, it was so black in that mine, you'd think a hunk of coal would show white. Maybe the lantern was smoking; it made just a pool of dim glow for us. Reed Barnitt struck a match on the seat of his pants and set it to the yarny wick of that five hundred dollar candle. It blazed up clean and strong, like the light Reed Barnitt had made in the middle of the star when it cast the spell. We saw where we were.

Seemed as if once there'd been a long hallway cut in the brown rock, but rocks had fallen down. They lay one on top of the other before us, shutting us away from the hall, so that we stood in a little space not much bigger than Mr. Hoje's front room. To either side the walls were of brown stone, marked by cutting tools—those Ancients had made their way through solid rock—and underfoot were pebbles. Some were quartz, like Mr. Hoje had said. Everything was quiet as the inside of a coffin the night before judgment.

"The flame's pointing," Reed Barnitt called to us. It did point, like a burning finger, straight into the place. He stepped toward those piled rocks, that made something like steps to go up, and we moved with him. I don't think anybody wanted to go over the rocks and beyond. The blackness there made you feel that not only nobody had ever been in there, but likewise nobody could ever go; the blackness would shove him back like a hand.

I moved behind Reed Barnitt with the others. The light of the candle shone past his blocky body and wide hat, making him look like something cut out of black cloth. Two-three steps, and he stopped, so quick we almost bumped him. "The light flutters," he said.

It did flutter, and it didn't point to the piled rocks, but to the wall at their right. When Reed Barnitt made a pace that way, it winked out. We all stood close together in the dim lantern light.

Reed Barnitt put his hand on the rock wall. It showed ghost white on the brown. His finger crawled along a seamy crack.

"Dig there," he said to us.

By what light the lantern showed, I shoved the pick end of the grubbing hoe into the crack and gouged. Seemed to me the whole wall fought me, but I heaved hard and the crack widened. It made a heavy spiteful noise somewhere. Mr. Eddy drove in the point of his bar and pulled down.

"Come help me, Clay," he called. "Put your man on this."

The two pulled down with their long tall bodies, then together they pushed up. My heart jumped inside me, for a piece of rock the size of a table top was moving. I shoved on the hoe handle. Reed Barnitt grabbed the free edge of the moving piece, and we laid into it—then jumped back just in time.

The big loose chunk dropped like the lid of a box. Underneath was dark dirt. Mr. Eddy drove the bar point into it.

"Light that candle thing again," he asked Reed Barnitt.

Reed Barnitt struck another match and tried. "Won't light," he said. "We've got our hand right on the treasure."

I reckoned that's the moment we all believed we had it. So far we'd worried and bothered, but now we stopped, and just worked. Clay took the spade from Mr. Hoje, and I swung my hoe. He scooped out the dirt I loosened. We breathed hard, watching or working. Suddenly:

"John," said Clay, "didn't I hear that hoe-blade hit metal?"

I slammed it into the dirt again, hard as I could. Clay scooped out a big spadeful. Bright yellow glimmered up out of the dark dirt. Clay grabbed into it, and so did his daddy. I had my mouth open to yell, but Reed Barnitt yelled first.

"God in the bushes! Look up there!"

We looked. Reed Barnitt had turned away from our work, and he pointed up those step-piled rocks. On the top rock of them stood something against the choking blackness.

It stood up the height of a man, that thing, but you couldn't make sure of its shape. Because it was strung and swaddled over with webby rags. They stirred and fluttered around it like gray smoke. And it had a hand, and the hand held a skull, with white grinning teeth and eyes that shone.

"It's an Ancient!" Reed Barnitt yelled, and the thing growled, deep and hungry and ugly.

Clay dropped his spade. I heard the clink and jangle of metal pieces on the floor pebbles. He gave back, and Mr. Hoje and Mr. Eddy gave back with him. I stood where I was, putting down my hoe. Reed Barnitt was the only one that moved forward.

"Stay away from us," he sort of breathed out at the ragged-gray thing.

It just pushed out the skull at him, and the skull's eye-lights blinked and glared. Reed Barnitt backed up.

"Let's get out of here," he choked, "before that Ancient—"

He didn't know we'd found the treasure, his eyes had been on whatever the thing was. He was for running, but I wasn't.

In my mind I saw the peculiar things I'd faced before this. The Ugly Bird ... One Other ... Mr. Loden who might have lived three hundred years but for me ... Forney Meechum whose dead ghost had fled from me. I'd even seen the Behinder that nobody's ever reckoned to see, and I'd come back to tell of it. I wouldn't run from that gray-raggedy thing that held a skull like a lantern.

I shrugged my guitar in front of me. My left hand grabbed its neck and my right spread on the silver strings, the silver that's sure sudden death to witch-stuff. I dragged a chord of music from them, and it echoed in there like a whole houseful of guitar-men helping me. And I thought the thing up there above shuddered, and the skull it held wabbled from side to side, trying maybe to say no to me.

"You don't like my music?" I said to it, and swept out another chord and got my foot on the bottom step-stone.

"John!" came Reed Barnitt's sick voice. "Take care—"

"Let that thing take care!" I told him and moved up on the rocks.

The gray thing flung the skull at me. I dodged, and felt the wind of the skull as it sailed grinning past, and I heard it smash like a bottle on the floor behind me. For a moment that flinging hand stuck out of the gray rags.

I knew whose hand it was, black-furry like a spider.

"Aram Harnam!" I yelled out, and let my guitar fall to hang by its string, and I charged up those stairs of stones.

Reed Barnitt was after me as I got to the top.

"It's a put-up show!" I was shouting, and grabbed my hands full of rags. Reed Barnitt clamped onto my arm and flung me down the step-stones so I almost fell flat on the floor. But rags had torn away in my grip, and you could see Aram Harnam's face, all a thicket of hair and beard, with hooked nose and shining eyes.

"What's up?" hooted out Mr. Eddy.

"Aram Harnam's up!" I yelled to him and the others. "Sold us that candle-thing, then came here to scare us out!" I pointed. "And Reed Barnitt's in it with him!"

Reed Barnitt, on the top stone beside Aram Harnam, turned around, his eyes big in his white face. I got my feet under me to charge back up at those two.

But then I stopped, the way you'd think roots had sprung from my toes into the rock. There were three up there, not two.

That third one looked at first glimpse like a big, big man wearing a fur coat; until you saw the fur was on his skin, with warty muscles bunching through. His head was more like a frog's than anything else, wide in the mouth and big in the eye and no nose. He spread his arms and put them quiet-like round the shoulders of Reed Barnitt and Aram Harnam, and took hold with his hands that had both webs and claws.

The two men he touched screamed out like animals in a snap-trap. I sort of reckon they tried to pull free, but those two big shaggy arms just hugged them close and hiked them off their feet. And what had come to fetch them, it fetched them away, all in a blink of time, back into that darkness no sensible soul would dare.

That's when we four others up and ran like rabbits, dropping the lantern.

We got back to Mr. Hoje's, and lighted a lamp there, and looked at those two handfuls of metal pieces Clay and Mr. Eddy had grabbed and never turned loose.

"I reckon they're money," said Mr. Hoje, "but I never seen the like."

None of us had. They weren't even round. Just limpy-edged and flattened out. You could figure how they'd been made, a lump of soft gold put between two jaws of a die and stamped out. The smallest was bigger and thicker than a four-bit piece. They had figures, like men with horned heads and snaky tails, and there were what might be letters or numbers, but nothing any of us could name in any language we'd ever heard tell of.

We put all those coins into an old salt-bag, and sat up the rest of the night, not talking much but pure down glad of each other's company. We had breakfast together, cooked by Sarah Ann, who had the good sense not to question. And after that, came up a young man who was sheriff's deputy.

"Gentlemen," he said to us, "has ary one of you seen a fellow with a white face and a broad build?"

"What's up with such a one?" asked Mr. Hoje.

"Why, Mr. Hoje," said the sheriff's deputy, "they want him bad at the state prison. He was a show-fellow, doing play-magic tricks, but he took to swindling folks and got in jail and then got out again, and the law's after him."

"We've seen such a man," allowed Mr. Eddy, "but he's gone from here now."

When we were left alone again, we told each other we could see how it was. Reed Barnitt did his false magic tricks, like setting the light on the star and making words show on the white paper by heating it. And he'd planned it with Aram Harnam to furnish us that black candle, to get hold of the property of Mr. Hoje and Mr. Eddy—scaring them afterward, so bad they'd never dare look again, and forfeit their home places.

Only: There *was* treasure there, the way those two swindlers never guessed. And there was something left to watch and see it wasn't robbed away.

I don't call to mind which of us said that all we could do was take back the gold pieces, because such things could never do anybody good. We went back that noon to Black Pine Hollow, where the sun sure enough didn't shine. We shivered without ary wind blowing.

Inside the mine-mouth, we picked up the lantern and lighted it. Clay had the nerve to pick up the broken skull Aram Harnam had flung, and we saw why the eyes had shone—pieces of tin in them. We found our spade and hoe. Into the hole we flung the gold pieces, on top of what seemed a heap more lying there. Then we put back the dirt, tamped it down hard, and we all heaved and sweated till we put the piece of rock in place again.

"There, the Ancients got their treasure back," said Mr. Hoje, breathing hard.

Then, noise up on those stepstones. I held up the lantern.

Huddled and bent they stood up there, Reed Barnitt and Aram Harnam.

They sort of leaned together, like tired horses in plow harness, not quite touching shoulders. Their hands—Reed Barnitt's white ones, Aram Harnam's shaggy ones—hung with the fingers bent and limp. They looked down at us with tired eyes and mouths drooped open, the way you'd think they had some hope about us, but not much.

"Look," said Clay, just behind my neck. "We gave back the gold. They're giving back those two that they dragged away last night."

But they looked as if they'd been gone more than a night.

The hair on Reed Barnitt's hatless head was as white as his face. And Aram Harnam's beard, and the fur on his hands—black no more, but a dirty, steamy gray. Maybe it had changed from fear, the way folks say can happen. Or maybe there'd been *time* for it to change, where they were.

"Go fetch them, John," Mr. Hoje asked me. "And we'll get a doctor for them when we get them to my house."

I started up over the stones with the lantern.

Their eyes picked up the lantern light and shone green, like the eyes of dogs. One of them, I don't know which, made a little whimpering cry with no words in it. They ran from me into the dark, and I saw their backs, bent more than I'd thought possible.

I ran up to the top stone, holding out the lantern.

As I watched they sort of fell forward and ran on hands and feet. Like animals. Not quite sure of how to run that way on all fours; but something told me, mighty positive, that they'd learn better as time went by. I backed down again, without watching any more.

"They won't come out," I said.

Mr. Hoje spit on the pebbles. "From what I saw, maybe it's just as well. They can live in there with the Ancients."

"Live?" repeated Clay. "The Ancients are dead. Way I figure, what's in there isn't Ancients—just something Ancients left behind. I don't want any part of it."

From Black Pine Hollow we went to Aram Harnam's empty shanty and there we found the papers he'd tricked Mr. Hoje and Mr. Eddy into signing, and we burned them up. On the way back, the two old men made it up between themselves to spare Clay and Sarah Ann a few acres from both places. As to the cabin, neighbors would be proud to help build it.

"One thing wonders me," said Clay. "John, you didn't have any notion night before last of singing about the girl with golden slippers?"

"Not till I struck the strings and piped up," I told him.

"Then how did Reed Barnitt just happen to take them from under his coat for Sarah Ann?" Clay asked us. "Stage-show magician or not, how did he just happen to do that?"

None of us could guess.

But Sarah Ann kept the golden slippers, and nobody could see any reason why not. She wore them to marry up with Clay, and danced in them while I played song after song—"Pretty Fair Maid," and "Willie From the Western States," and "I Dreamed Last Night of My True Love, All In My Arms I Had Her." Preacher Miller said the service, what God hath joined together let no man put asunder. I kissed the pretty-cheeked bride, and so did many a kind friend, but the only man of us she kissed back was long tall Clay Herron.

WALK LIKE A MOUNTAIN

Once at Sky Notch, I never grudged the trouble getting there. It was so purely pretty, I was glad outlanders weren't apt to crowd in and spoil all.

The Notch cut through a tall peak that stood against a higher cliff. Steep brushy faces each side, and a falls at the back that made a trickly branch, with five pole cabins along the waterside. Corn patches, a few pigs in pens, chickens running round, a cow tied up one place. It wondered me how they ever got a cow up there. Laurels grew, and viney climbers, and mountain flowers in bunches and sprawls. The water made a happy noise. Nobody moved in the yards or at the doors, so I stopped by a tree and hollered the first house.

"Hello the house!" I called. "Hello to the man of the house and all inside!"

A plank door opened about an inch. "Hello to yourself," a gritty voice replied me. "Who's that out there with the guitar?"

I moved from under the tree. "My name's John. Does Mr. Lane Jarrett live up here? Got word for him, from his old place on Drowning Creek."

The door opened wider, and there stood a skimpy little man with gray whiskers. "That's funny," he said.

The funnyness I didn't see. I'd known Mr. Lane Jarrett years back, before he and his daughter Page moved to Sky Notch. When his uncle Jeb died and heired him some money, I'd agreed to carry it to Sky Notch, and, gentlemen, it was a long, weary way getting there.

First a bus, up and down and through mountains, stop at every pig trough for passengers. I got off at Charlie's Jump—who Charlie was, nor why or when he jumped, nobody there can rightly say. Climbed a high ridge, got down the far side, then a twenty-devil way along a deep valley river. Up another height, another beyond that. Then it was night, and nobody would want to climb the steep face above, because it was grown up with the kind of trees that the dark melts in around you. I made a fire and took my supper rations from my pocket. Woke at dawn and climbed up and up and up, and here I was.

"Funny, about Lane Jarrett," gritted the little man out. "Sure you ain't come about that business?"

I looked up the walls of the Notch. Their tops were toothy rocks, the way you'd think those walls were two jaws, near about to close on what they'd caught inside them. Right then the Notch didn't look so pretty.

"Can't say, sir," I told him, "till I know what business you mean."

"Rafe Enoch!" he boomed out the name, like firing two barrels of a gun. "That's what I mean!" Then he appeared to remember his manners, and came out, puny in his jeans and no shoes on his feet. "I'm Oakman Dillon," he named himself. "John—that's your name, huh? Why you got that guitar?"

"I pick it some," I replied him. "I sing." Tweaking the silver strings, I sang a few lines:

> By the shore of Lonesome River
> Where the waters ebb and flow,
> Where the wild red rose is budding
> And the pleasant breezes blow,
>
> It was there I spied the lady
> That forever I adore,
> As she was a-lonesome walking
> By the Lonesome River shore. . . .

"Rafe Enoch!" he grit-grated out again. "Carried off Miss Page Jarrett the way you'd think she was a banty chicken!"

Slap, I quieted the strings with my palm. "Mr. Lane's little daughter Page was stolen away?"

He sat down on the door-log. "She ain't suchy little daughter. She's six foot maybe three inches—taller'n you, even. Best-looking big woman I ever seen, brown hair like a wagonful of home-cured tobacco, eyes green and bright as a fresh-squoze grape pulp."

"Fact?" I said, thinking Page must have changed a right much from the long-leggy little girl I'd known, must have grown tall like her daddy and her dead mammy, only taller. "Is this Rafe Enoch so big, a girl like that is right for him?"

"She's puny for him. He's near about eight foot tall, best I judge." Oakman Dillon's gray whiskers stuck out like a mad cat's. "He just grabbed her last evening, where she walked near the fall, and up them rocks he went like a possum up a jack oak."

I sat down on a stump. "Mr. Lane's a friend of mine. How can I help?"

"Nobody can't help, John. It's right hard to think you ain't knowing all this stuff. Don't many strangers come up here. Ain't room for many to live in the Notch."

"Five homes," I counted them with my eyes.

"Six. Rafe Enoch lives up at the top." He jerked his head toward the falls. "Been there a long spell—years, I reckon, since when he run off from somewhere. Heard tell he broke a circus man's neck for offering him a job with a show. He built up top the falls, and he used to get along with us. Thanked us kindly for a mess of beans or roasting ears. Lately, he's been mean-talking."

"Nobody mean-talked him back? Five houses in the Notch mean five grown men—couldn't they handle one giant?"

"Giant size ain't all Rafe Enoch's got." Again the whiskers bristled up. "Why! He's got powers, like he can make rain fall—"

"No," I put in quick. "Can't even science men do that for sure."

"I ain't studying science men. Rafe Enoch says for rain to fall, down it comes, ary hour day or night he speaks. Could drown us out of this Notch if he had the mind."

"And he carried off Page Jarrett," I went back to what he'd said.

"That's the whole truth, John. Up he went with her in the evening, daring us to follow him."

I asked, "Where are the other Notch folks?"

"Up yonder by the falls. Since dawn we've been talking Lane Jarrett back from climbing up and getting himself neck-twisted. I came to feed my pigs, now I'm heading back."

"I'll go with you," I said, and since he didn't deny me I went.

The falls dropped down a height as straight up as a chimney, and a many times taller, and their water boiled off down the branch. Either side of the falls, the big boulder rocks piled on top of each other like stones in an almighty big wall. Looking up, I saw clouds boiling in the sky, dark and heavy and wet-looking, and I remembered what Oakman Dillon had said about big Rafe Enoch's rain-making.

A bunch of folks were there, and I made out Mr. Lane Jarrett, bald on top and bigger than the rest. I touched his arm, and he turned.

"John! Ain't seen you a way-back time. Let me make you known to these here folks."

He called them their first names—Yoot, Ollie, Bill, Duff, Miss Lulie, Miss Sara May and so on. I said I had a pocketful of money for him, but he just nodded and wanted to know did I know what was going on.

"Looky up against them clouds, John. That pointy rock. My girl Page is on it."

The rock stuck out like a spur on a rooster's leg. Somebody was scrouched down on it, with the clouds getting blacker above, and a long, long drop below.

"I see her blue dress," allowed Mr. Oakman, squinting up. "How long she been there, Lane?"

"I spotted her at sunup," said Mr. Lane. "She must have got away from Rafe Enoch and crope out there during the night. I'm going to climb."

He started to shinny up a rock, up clear of the brush around us. And, Lord, the laugh that came down on us! Like a big splash of water, it was clear and strong, and like water it made us shiver. Mr. Oakman caught onto Mr. Lane's ankle and dragged him down.

"Ain't a God's thing ary man or woman can do, with him waiting up there," Mr. Oakman argued.

"But he's got Page," said Mr. Lane busting loose again. I grabbed his elbow.

"Let me," I said.

"You, John? You're a stranger, you ain't got no pick in this."

"This big Rafe Enoch would know if it was you or Mr. Oakman

or one of these others climbing, he might fling down a rock or the like. But I'm strange to him. I might wonder him, and he might let me climb all the way up."

"Then?" Mr. Page said, frowning.

"Once up, I might could do something."

"Leave him try it," said Mr. Oakman to that.

"Yes," said one of the ladyfolks.

I slung my guitar behind my shoulder and took to the rocks. No peep of noise from anywhere for maybe a minute of climbing. I got on about the third or fourth rock from the bottom, and that clear, sky-ripping laugh came from over my head.

"Name yourself!" roared down the voice that had laughed.

I looked up. How high was the top I can't say, but I made out a head and shoulders looking down, and knew they were another sight bigger head and shoulders than ever I'd seen on ary mortal man.

"Name yourself!" he yelled again, and in the black clouds a lightning flash wiggled, like a snake caught fire.

"John!" I bawled back.

"What you aiming to do, John?"

Another crack of lightning, that for a second seemed to peel off the clouds right and left. I looked this way and that. Nowhere to get out of the way should lightning strike, or a rock or anything. On notion, I pulled my guitar to me and picked and sang:

> Went to the rock to hide my face,
> The rock cried out,
> "No hiding place!". . . .

Gentlemen, the laugh was like thunder after the lightning.

"Better climb quick, John!" he hollered me. "I'm a-waiting on you up here!"

I swarmed and swarved and scrabbled my way up, not looking down. Over my head that rock-spur got bigger, I figured it for maybe twelve-fifteen feet long, and on it I made out Page Jarrett in her blue dress. Mr. Oakman was right, she was purely big and she was purely good-looking. She hung to the pointy rock with her both long hands.

"Page," I said to her, with what breath I had left, and she stared with her green eyes and gave me an inch of smile. She looked to have a right much of her daddy's natural sand in her craw.

"John," boomed the thunder-voice, close over me now. "I asked you a while back, why you coming up?"

"Just to see how you make the rain fall," I said, under the overhang of the ledge. "Help me up."

Down came a bare brown honey-hairy arm, and a hand the size of a scoop shovel. It got my wrist and snatched me away like a turnip coming out of a patch, and I landed my feet on broad flat stones.

Below me yawned up those rock-toothed tops of the Notch's jaws. Inside them the brush and trees looked mossy and puny. The cabins were like baskets, the pigs and the cow like play-toys, and the branch looked to run so narrow you might bridge it with your shoe. Shadow fell on the Notch from the fattening dark clouds.

Then I looked at Rafe Enoch. He stood over me like a sycamore tree over a wood shed. He was the almightiest big thing I'd ever seen on two legs.

Eight foot high, Oakman Dillon had said truly, and he was thick-made in keeping. Shoulders wide enough to fill a barn door, and legs like tree trunks with fringe-sided buckskin pants on them, and his big feet wore moccasin shoes of bear's hide with the fur still on. His shirt, sewed together of pelts—fox, coon, the like of that—hadn't any sleeves, and hung open from that big chest of his that was like a cotton bale. Topping all, his face put you in mind of the full moon with a yellow beard, but healthy-looking brown, not pale like the moon. Big and dark eyes, and through the yellow beard his teeth grinned like big white sugar lumps.

"Maybe I ought to charge you to look at me," he said.

I remembered how he'd struck a man dead for wanting him in a show, and I looked elsewhere. First, naturally, at Page Jarrett on the rock spur. The wind from the clouds waved her brown hair like a flag, and fluttered her blue skirt around her drawn-up feet. Then I turned and looked at the broad space above the falls.

From there I could see there was a right much of higher country, and just where I stood with Rafe Enoch was a big shelf, like a lap, with slopes behind it. In the middle of the flat space showed a pond of water, running out past us to make the falls. On its edge stood Rafe Enoch's house, built wigwam-style of big old logs leaned together and chinked between with clay over twigs. No trees to amount to anything on the shelf—just one behind the wigwam-house, and to its branches hung joints that looked like smoke meat.

"You hadn't played that guitar so clever, maybe I mightn't have saved you," said Rafe Enoch's thunder-voice.

"Saved?" I repeated him.

"Look." His big club of a finger pointed to the falls, then to those down-hugged clouds. "When they get together, what happens?"

Just at the ledge lip, where the falls went over, stones looked halfway washed out. A big shove of water would take them out the other half, and the whole thing pour down on the Notch.

"Why you doing this to the folks?" I asked.

He shook his head. "John, this is one rain I never called for." He put one big pumpkin-sized fist into the palm of his other hand. "I can call for rain, sure, but some of it comes without me. I can't start it or either stop it, I just know it's coming. I've known about this for days. It'll drown out Sky Notch like a rat nest."

"Why didn't you try to tell them?"

"I tried to tell her." His eyes cut around to where Page Jarrett hung to the pointy rock, and his stool-leg fingers raked his yellow beard. "She was walking off by herself, alone. I know how it feels to be alone. But when I told her, she called me a liar. I brought her up here to save her, and she cried and fought me." A grin. "She fought me better than ary living human I know. But she can't fight me hard enough."

"Can't you do anything about the storm?" I asked him to tell.

"Can do this." He snapped his big fingers, and lightning crawled through the clouds over us. It made me turtle my neck inside my shirt collar. Rafe Enoch never twitched his eyebrow.

"Rafe," I said, "you might could persuade the folks. They're not your size, but they're human like you."

"Them?" He roared his laugh. "They're not like me, nor you

aren't like me, either, though you're longer-made than common. Page yonder, she looks to have some of the old Genesis giant blood in her. That's why I saved her alive."

"Genesis giant blood," I repeated him, remembering the Book, sixth chapter of Genesis. " 'There were giants in the earth in those days.' "

"That's the whole truth," said Rafe. "When the sons of God took wives of the daughters of men—their children were the mighty men of old, the men of renown. That's not exact quote, but it's near enough."

He sat down on a rock, near about as tall sitting as I was standing. "Ary giant knows he was born from the sons of the gods," he said. "My name tells it, John."

I nodded, figuring it. "Rafe—Raphah, the giant whose son was Goliath, Enoch—"

"Or Anak," he put in. "Remember the sons of Anak, and them scared-out spies sent into Canaan? They was grasshoppers in the sight of the sons of Anak, and more ways than just size, John." He sniffed. "They got scared back into the wilderness for forty years. And Goliath!"

"David killed him," I dared remind Rafe.

"By a trick. A slingshot stone. Else he'd not lasted any longer than that."

A finger-snap, and lightning winged over us like a hawk over a chicken run. I tried not to scrouch down.

"What use to fight little old human men," he said, "when you got the sons of the gods in your blood?"

I allowed he minded me of Strap Buckner with that talk.

"Who's Strap Buckner? Why do I mind you of him?"

I picked the guitar, I sang the song:

Strap Buckner he was called, he was more than eight foot tall,
And he walked like a mountain among men.
He was good and he was great, and the glorious Lone Star State
Will never look upon his like again.

"Strap Buckner had the strength of ten lions," I said, "and he used it as ten lions. Scorned to fight ordinary folks, so he challenged old Satan himself, skin for skin, on the banks of the Brazos, and if Satan hadn't fought foul—"

"Another dirty fighter!" Rafe got up from where he sat, quick as quick for all his size. "Foul or not, Satan couldn't whup me!"

"Might be he couldn't," I judged, looking at Rafe. "But anyway, the Notch folks never hurt you. Used to give you stuff to eat."

"Don't need their stuff to eat," he said, the way you'd think that was the only argument. He waved his hand past his wigwam-house. "Down yonder is a bunch of hollows, where ain't no human man been, except maybe once the Indians. I hoe some corn there, some potatoes. I pick wild salad greens here and yonder. I kill me a deer, a bear, a wild hog—ain't no human man got nerve to face them big wild hogs, but I chunk them with a rock or I fling a sharp ash sapling, and what I fling at I bring down. In the pond here I spear me fish. Don't need their stuff to eat, I tell you."

"Need it or not, why let them drown out?"

His face turned dark, the way you'd think smoke drifted over it.

"I can't abide little folks' little eyes looking at me, wondering themselves about me, thinking I'm not rightly natural."

He waited for what I had to say, and it took nerve to say it.

"But you're not a natural man, Rafe. You've allowed that yourself, you say you come from different blood. Paul Bunyan thought the same thing."

He grinned his big sugar-lump teeth at me. Then: "Page Jarrett," he called, "better come off that rock before the rain makes it slippy and you fall off. I'll help you—"

"You stay where you are," she called back. "Let John help."

I went to the edge of that long drop down. The wind blew from some place—maybe below, maybe above or behind or before. I reached out my guitar, and Page Jarrett crawled to where she could lay hold, and that way I helped her to the solid standing. She stood beside me, inches taller, and she put a burning mean look on Rafe Enoch. He made out he didn't notice.

"Paul Bunyan," he said, after what I'd been saying. "I've heard tell his name—champion logger in the northern states, wasn't he?"

"Champion logger," I said. "Bigger than you, I reckon—"

"Not bigger!" thundered Rafe Enoch.

"Well, as big."

"Know ary song about him?"

"Can't say there's been one made. Rafe, you say you despise to be looked on by folks."

"Just by little folks, John. Page Jarrett can look on me if she relishes to."

Quick she looked off, and drew herself up proud. Right then she appeared to be taller than what Mr. Oakman Dillon had reckoned her, and a beauty-looking thing she was, you hear what I say, gentlemen. I cut my eyes up to the clouds; they hung down over us, loose and close, like the roof of a tent. I could feel the closeness around me, the way you feel water when you've waded up to the line of your mouth.

"How soon does the rain start falling?" I asked Rafe.

"Can fall ary time now," said Rafe, pulling a grass-stalk to bite in his big teeth. "Page's safe off that rock point, it don't differ me a shuck when that rain falls."

"But when?" I asked again. "You know."

"Sure I know." He walked toward the pond, and me with him. I felt Page Jarrett's grape-green eyes digging our backs. The pond water was shiny tarry black from reflecting the clouds. "Sure," he said, "I know a right much. You natural human folks, you know so pitiful little I'm sorry for you."

"Why not teach us?" I wondered him, and he snorted like a big mean horse.

"Ain't the way it's reckoned to be, John. Giants are figured stupid. Remember the tales? Your name's John—do you call to mind a tale about a man named Jack, long back in time?"

"Jack the Giant Killer," I nodded. "He trapped a giant in a hole—"

"Cormoran," said Rafe. "Jack dug a pit in front of his door. And Blunderbore he tricked into stabbing himself open with a knife. But how did them things happen? He blew a trumpet to tole Cormoran out, and he sat and ate at Blunderbore's table like a friend before tricking him to death." A louder snort. "More foul fighting, John. Did you come up here to be Jack the Giant Killer?

Got some dirty tricks? If that's how it is, you done drove your ducks to the wrong puddle."

"More than a puddle here," I said, looking at the clouds and then across the pond. "See yonder, Rafe, where the water edge comes above that little slanty slope. If it was open, enough water could run off to keep the Notch from flooding."

"Could be done," he nodded his big head, "if you had machinery to pull the rocks out. But they're bigger than them fall rocks, they ain't half washed away to begin with. And there ain't no machinery, so just forget it. The Notch washes out, with most of the folks living in it—all of them, if the devil bids high enough. Sing me a song."

I swept the strings with my thumb. "Thinking about John Henry," I said, half to myself. "He wouldn't need a machine to open up a drain-off place yonder."

"How'd he do it?" asked Rafe.

"He had a hammer twice the size ary other man swung," I said. "He drove steel when they cut the Big Bend Tunnel through Cruze Mountain. Out-drove the steam drill they brought to compete him out of his job."

"Steam drill," Rafe repeated me, the way you'd think he was faintly recollecting the tale. "They'd do that—ordinary size folks, trying to work against a giant. How big was John Henry?"

"Heard tell he was the biggest man ever in Virginia."

"Big as me?"

"Maybe not quite. Maybe just stronger."

"Stronger!"

I had my work cut out not to run from the anger in Rafe Enoch's face.

"Well," I said, "he beat the steam drill. . . ."

> John Henry said to his captain,
> "A man ain't nothing but a man,
> But before I let that steam drill run me down,
> I'll die with this hammer in my hand. . . ."

"He'd die trying," said Rafe, and his ears were sort of cocked forward, the way you hear elephants do to listen.

"He'd die winning," I said, and sang the next verse:

> *John Henry drove steel that long day through,*
> *The steam drill failed by his side.*
> *The mountain was high, the sun was low,*
> *John he laid down his hammer and he died. . . .*

"Killed himself beating the drill!" and Rafe's pumpkin fist banged into his other palm. "Reckon I could have beat it and lived!"

I was looking at the place where the pond could have a drain-off.

"No," said Rafe. "Even if I wanted to, I don't have no hammer twice the size of other folks' hammers."

A drop of rain fell on me. I started around the pond.

"Where you going?" Rafe called, but I didn't look back. Stopped beside the wigwam-house and put my guitar inside. It was gloomy in there, but I saw his home-made stool as high as a table, his table almost chin high to a natural man, a bed woven of hickory splits and spread with bear and deer skins to be the right bed for Og, King of Bashan, in the Book of Joshua. Next to the door I grabbed up a big pole of hickory, off some stacked firewood.

"Where you going?" he called again.

I went to where the slope started. I poked my hickory between two rocks and started to pry. He laughed, and rain sprinkled down.

"Go on, John," he granted me. "Grub out a sluiceway there. I like to watch little scrabbly men work. Come in the house, Page, we'll watch him from in there."

I couldn't budge the rocks from each other. They were big— like trunks or grain sacks, and must have weighed in the half-tons. They were set in there, one next to the other, four-five of them holding the water back from pouring down that slope. I heaved on my hickory till it bent like a bow.

"Come on," said Rafe again, and I looked around in time to see him put out his shovel hand and take her by the wrist. Gentlemen, the way she slapped him with her other hand it made me jump with the crack.

I watched, knee deep in water. He put his hand to his gold-bearded cheek and his eye-whites glittered in the rain.

"If you was a man," he boomed down at Page, "I'd slap you dead."

"Do it!" she blazed him back. "I'm a woman, and I don't fear you or ary overgrown, sorry-for-himself giant ever drew breath!"

With me standing far enough off to forget how little I was by them, they didn't seem too far apart in size. Page was like a small-made woman facing up to a sizable man, that was all.

"If you was a man—" he began again.

"I'm no man, nor neither ain't you a man!" she cut off. "Don't know if you're an ape or a bull-brute or what, but you're no man! John's the only man here, and I'm helping him! Stop me if you dare!"

She ran to where I was. Rain battered her hair into a brown tumble and soaked her dress snug against her line proud strong body. Into the water she splashed.

"Let me pry," and she grabbed the hickory pole. "I'll pry up and you tug up, and maybe—"

I bent to grab the rock with my hands. Together we tried. Seemed to me the rock stirred a little, like the drowsy sleeper in the old song. Dragging at it, I felt the muscles strain and crackle in my shoulders and arms.

"Look out!" squealed Page. "Here he comes!"

Up on the bank she jumped again, with the hickory ready to club at him. He paid her no mind, she stooped down toward where I was.

"Get on out of there!" he bellowed, the way I've always reckoned a buffalo bull might do. "Get out!"

"But—but—" I was wheezing. "Somebody's got to move this rock—"

"You ain't budging it ary mite!" he almost deafened me in the ear. "Get out and let somebody there can do something!"

He grabbed my arm and snatched me out of the water, so sudden I almost sprained my fingers letting go the rock. Next second he jumped in, with a splash like a jolt-wagon going off a bridge. His big shovelly hands clamped the sides of the rock, and through the falling rain I saw him heave.

He swole up like a mad toad-frog. His patchy fur shirt split down the middle of his back while those muscles humped under his skin. His teeth flashed out in his beard, set hard together.

Then, just when I thought he'd bust open, that rock came out of its bed, came up in the air, landing on the bank away from where it'd been.

"I swear, Rafe—" I began to say.

"Help him," Page put in. "Let's both help."

We scrabbled for a hold on the rock, but Rafe hollered us away, so loud and sharp we jumped back like scared dogs. I saw that rock quiver, and cracks ran through the rain-soaked dirt around it. Then it came up on end, the way you'd think it had hinges, and Rafe got both arms around it and heaved it clear. He laughed, with the rain wet in his beard.

Standing clear where he'd told her to stand, Page pointed to the falls' end.

Looked as if the rain hadn't had to put down but just a little bit. Those loose rocks trembled and shifted in their places. They were ready to go. Then Rafe saw what we saw.

"Run, you two!" he howled above that racketty storm. "Run, run—quick!"

I didn't tarry to ask the reason. I grabbed Page's arm and we ran toward the falls. Running, I looked back past my elbow.

Rafe had straightened up, straddling among the rocks by the slope. He looked into the clouds, that were almost resting on his shaggy head, and both his big arms lifted and his hands spread and then their fingers snapped. I could hear the snaps—*Whop! Whop!* like two pistol shots.

He got what he called for, a forked stroke of lightning, straight and hard down on him like a fish-gig in the hands of the Lord's top angel. It slammed down on Rafe and over and around him, and it shook itself all the way from rock to clouds. Rafe Enoch in its grip lit up and glowed, the way you'd think he'd been forge-hammered out of iron and heated red in a furnace to temper him.

I heard the almightiest tearing noise I ever could call for. I felt the rock shelf quiver all the way to where we'd stopped dead to watch. My thought was, the falls had torn open and the Notch was drowning.

But the lightning yanked back to where it had come from. It had opened the sluiceway, and water flooded through and down slope, and Rafe had fallen down while it poured and puddled over him.

"He's struck dead!" I heard Page say over the rain.

"No," I said back.

For Rafe Enoch was on his knees, on his feet, and out of that drain-off rush, somehow staggering up from the flat sprawl where the lightning had flung him. His knees wobbled and bucked, but he drew them up straight and mopped a big muddy hand across his big muddy face.

He came walking toward us, slow and dreamy-moving, and by now the rain rushed down instead of fell down. It was like what my old folks used to call raining tomcats and hoe handles. I bowed my head to it, and made to pull Page toward Rafe's wigwam; but she wouldn't pull, she held where she was, till Rafe came up with us. Then, all three, we went together and got into the tight, dark shelter of the wigwam-house, with the rain and wind battering the outside of it.

Rafe and I sat on the big bed, and Page on a stool, looking small there. She wrung the water out of her hair.

"You all right?" she inquired Rafe.

I looked at him. Between the drain-off and the wigwam, rain had washed off that mud that gaumed all over him. He was wet and clean, with his patch-pelt shirt hanging away from his big chest and shoulders in soggy rags.

The lightning had singed off part of his beard. He lifted big fingers to wipe off the wet, fluffy ash, and I saw the stripe on his naked arm, on the broad back of his hand, and I made out another stripe just like it on the other. Lightning had slammed down both hands and arms, and clear down his flanks and legs—I saw the burnt lines on his fringed leggings. It was like a double lash of God's whip.

Page got off the stool and came close to him. Just then he didn't look so out-and-out much bigger than she was. She put a long gentle finger on that lightning lash where it ran along his shoulder.

"Does it hurt?" she asked. "You got some grease I could put on it?"

He lifted his head, heavy, but didn't look at her. He looked at me. "I lied to you all," he said.

"Lied to us?" I asked him.

"I did call for the rain. Called for the biggest rain I ever thought of. Didn't pure down want to kill off the folks in the Notch, but to my reckoning, if I made it rain, and saved Page up here—"

At last he looked at her, with a shamed face.

"The others would be gone and forgotten. There'd be Page and me." His dark eyes grabbed her green ones. "But I didn't rightly know how she disgusts the sight of me." His head dropped again. "I feel the nearest to nothing I ever did."

"You opened the drain-off and saved the Notch from your rain," put in Page, her voice so gentle you'd never think it. "Called down the lightning to help you."

"Called down the lightning to kill me," said Rafe. "I never reckoned it wouldn't. I wanted to die. I want to die now."

"Live," she bade him.

He got up at that, standing tall over her.

"Don't worry when folks look on you," she said, her voice still ever so gentle. "They're just wondered at you, Rafe. Folks were wondered that same way at Saint Christopher, the giant who carried Lord Jesus across the river."

"I was too proud," he mumbled in his big bull throat. "Proud of my Genesis giant blood, of being one of the sons of God—"

"Shoo, Rafe," and her voice was gentler still, "the least man in size you'd call for, when he speaks to God, he says, 'Our Father.'"

Rafe turned from her.

"You said I could look on you if I wanted," said Page Jarrett. "And I want."

Back he turned, and bent down, and she rose on her toetips so their faces came together.

The rain stopped, the way you'd think that stopped it. But they never seemed to know it, and I picked up my guitar and went out toward the lip of the cliff.

The falls were going strong, but the drain-off handled enough water so there'd be no washout to drown the folks below. I reckoned the rocks would be the outdoingist slippery rocks ever climbed down by mortal man, and it would take me a long time.

Long enough, maybe so, for me to think out the right way to tell Mr. Lane Jarrett he was just before having himself a son-in-law of the Genesis giant blood, and pretty soon after while, grandchildren of the same strain.

The sun came stabbing through the clouds and flung them away in chunks to right and left, across the bright blue sky.

ON THE HILLS AND EVERYWHERE

"John, the children have opened their presents, and I want them to have some hot rations inside them before they start in on that store-bought candy you fetched them. So why don't you tell us a Christmas story while Mother's putting dinner on the table?"

"Be proud to do so. And this won't be any far-away tale—it happened to neighbor-folks you know."

You all and I and everybody worried our minds about Mr. Absalom Cowand and his fall-out with Mr. Troy Holcomb who neighbors with him in the hills above Rebel Creek. Too bad when old friends aren't friends any more. Especially the kind of friend Mr. Absalom can be.

You've been up to his place, I reckon. Only a man with thought in his head and bone in his back would build and work where Mr. Absalom Cowand does, in those high hills up the winding road beyond those lazy creek-bottom patches. He's terraced his fields up and up behind his house on the slope, growing some of the best-looking corn in this day and time. And nice cow-brutes in his barns, and good hogs and chickens in his pens, and money in the bank down yonder at the county seat. Mr. Absalom will feed ary hungry neighbor, or tend ary sick one, saving he's had a quarrel with them, like the quarrel with Mr. Troy Holcomb.

"What for did they quarrel, John?"

"Over something Mr. Troy said wasn't so, and Mr. Absalom said was. I'll come to that."

That farm is Mr. Absalom's pride and delight. Mr. Troy's place next door isn't so good, though good enough. Mr. Absalom looked over to Mr. Troy's, the day I mention, and grinned in his big thicketty beard, like a king's beard in a history-book picture.

If it sorrowed him to be out with Mr. Troy, he didn't show it. All that sorrowed him, maybe, was his boy, Little Anse—crippled ever since he'd fallen off the jolt-wagon and it ran over his legs so he couldn't walk, couldn't crawl hardly without the crutches his daddy had made for him.

It was around noon when Mr. Absalom grinned his tiger grin from his front yard over toward Mr. Troy's, then looked up to study if maybe a few clouds didn't mean weather coming. He needed rain from heaven. It wondered him if a certain somebody wasn't witching it off from his place. Witch-men are the meanest folks God ever forgot. Looking up thataway, Mr. Absalom wasn't aware of a man coming till he saw him close in sight above the road's curve, a stranger-fellow with a tool chest on his shoulder. The stranger stopped at Mr. Absalom's mail box and gave him a good day.

"And good day to you," Mr. Absalom said, stroking his beard where it bannered onto his chest. "What can I do for you?"

"It's what can I do for you," the stranger replied him back. "I had in mind that maybe there's some work here for me."

"Well," said Mr. Absalom, relishing the way the stranger looked.

He was near about as tall as Mr. Absalom's own self, but no way as thick built, nor as old. Maybe in his thirties, and neat dressed in work clothes, with brown hair combed back. He had a knowledge look in his face, but nothing secret. The shoulder that carried the tool chest was a square, strong shoulder.

"You ain't some jack-leg carpenter?" said Mr. Absalom.

"No. I learned my trade young, and I learned it right."

"That's bold spoken, friend."

"I just say that I'm skilled."

Those words sounded right and true.

"I like to get out in the country to work," the carpenter-man said on. "No job too big or too small for me to try."

"Well," said Mr. Absalom again, "so happens I've got a strange-like job needs doing."

"And no job too strange," the carpenter added.

Mr. Absalom led him around back, past the chicken run and the hog lot. A path ran there, worn years deep by folks' feet. But, some way past the house, the path was chopped off short.

ON THE HILLS AND EVERYWHERE

Between Mr. Absalom's side yard and the next place was a ditch, not wide but deep and strong, with water tumbling down from the heights behind. Nobody could call for any plainer mark betwixt two men's places.

"See that house yonder?" Mr. Absalom pointed with his bearded chin.

"The square-log place with the shake roof? Yes, I see it."

"That's Troy Holcomb's place."

"Yes."

"My land," and Mr. Absalom waved a thick arm to show, "terraces back off thataway, and his land terraces off the other direction. We helped each other do the terracing. We were friends."

"The path shows you were friends," said the carpenter. "The ditch shows you aren't friends any more."

"You just bet your neck we ain't friends any more," said Mr. Absalom, and his beard crawled on his jaw as he set his mouth.

"What's wrong with Troy Holcomb?" asked the carpenter.

"Oh, nothing. Nothing that a silver bullet might not fix." Mr. Absalom pointed downhill. "Look at the field below the road."

The carpenter looked. "Seems like a good piece of land. Ought to be a crop growing there."

Now Mr. Absalom's teeth twinkled through his beard, like stars through storm clouds. "A court of law gave me that field. Troy Holcomb and I both laid claim to it, but the court said I was in the right. The corn I planted was blighted to death."

"Been quite a much of blight this season," said the carpenter.

"Yes, down valley, but not up here." Mr. Absalom glittered his eyes toward the house across the ditch. "A curse was put on my field. And who'd have reason to put a curse on, from some hateful old witch-book or other, but Troy Holcomb? I told him to his face. He denied the truth of that."

"Of course he'd deny it," said the carpenter.

"Shoo, John, is Mr. Troy Holcomb a witch-man? I never heard that."
"I'm just telling what Mr. Absalom said. Well:"

"If he was a foot higher, I'd have hit him on top of his head," grumbled Mr. Absalom. "We haven't spoken since. And you know what he's done?"

"He dug this ditch." The carpenter looked into the running water. "To show he doesn't want the path to join your place to his any more."

"You hit it right," snorted Mr. Absalom, like a mean horse. "Did he reckon I'd go there to beg his pardon or something? Do I look like that kind of a puppy-man?"

"Are you glad not to be friends with him?" the carpenter inquired his own question, looking at the squared-log house.

"Ain't studying about that," said Mr. Absalom. "I'm studying to match this dig-ditch job he did against me. Look yonder at that lumber."

The carpenter looked at a stack of posts, a pile of boards.

"He cut me off with a ditch. If you want work, build me a fence along this side of his ditch, from the road down there up to where my back-yard line runs." Mr. Absalom pointed up slope. "How long will that take you?"

The carpenter set down his tool chest and figured in his head. Then: "I could do you something to pleasure you by supper time."

"Quick as that?" Mr. Absalom looked at him sharp, for he'd reckoned the fence job might take two-three days. "You got it thought out to be a little old small piece of work, huh?"

"Nothing too big or too small for me to try," said the carpenter again. "You can say whether it suits you."

"Do what I want, and I'll pay you worth your while," Mr. Absalom granted him. "I'm heading up to my far corn patch. Before sundown I'll come look." He started away. "But it's got to suit me."

"It will," the carpenter made promise, and opened his chest.

Like any lone working man, he started out to whistle.

His whistling carried all the way to Mr. Absalom's house. And inside, on the front room couch, lay Little Anse.

You all know how Little Anse couldn't hardly stand on his poor swunk up legs, even with crutches. It was pitiful to see him scuff a crutch out, then the other, then lean on them and swing his little feet between. He'd scuff and swing again, inching along. But Little Anse didn't pity himself. He was cheerful-minded, laughing at what trifles he could find. Mr. Absalom had had him to one doctor after another, and none could bid him hope. Said Little Anse was crippled for life.

When Little Anse heard the whistling, he upped his ears to hear more. He worked his legs off the couch, and sat up and hoisted himself on his crutches. He crutched and scuffed to the door, and out in the yard, and along the path, following that tune.

It took him a time to get to where the carpenter was working. But when he got there he smiled, and the carpenter smiled back.

"Can I watch?" Little Anse asked.

"You're welcome to watch. I'm doing something here to help your daddy."

"How tall are you?" Little Anse inquired him next.

"Just exactly six feet," the carpenter replied.

"Now wait, John, that's just foolish for the lack of sense. Ain't no mortal man on this earth exactly six feet tall."

"I'm saying what the stranger said."

"But the only one who was exactly *six feet—"*

"Hold your tater while I tell about it."

"I relish that song you were whistling, Mr. Carpenter," said Little Anse. "I know the words, some of them." And he sang a verse of it:

> *I was a powerful sinner,*
> *I sinned both night and day,*
> *Until I heard the preacher,*
> *And he taught me how to pray:*

Little Anse went on with part of the chorus:

> *Go tell it on the mountain,*
> *Tell it on the hills and everywhere—*

"Can I help you?"

"You could hand me my tools."

"I'll be proud to."

By then they felt as good friends as if they'd been knowing each other long years. Little Anse sat by the tool chest and searched out the tools as the carpenter wanted them. There was a tale to go with each one.

Like this: "Let me have the saw."

As he used it, the carpenter would explain how, before ary man knew a saw's use there was a sawshape in the shark's mouth down in the ocean sea, with teeth lined up like a saw's teeth; which may help show why some folks claim animals were wise before folks were.

"Now give me the hammer, Little Anse."

While he pounded, the carpenter told of a nation of folks in Europe, that used to believe in somebody named Thor, who could throw his hammer across mountains and knock out thunder and lightning.

And he talked about what folks believe about wood. How some of them knock on wood, to keep off bad luck. How the ancient folks, lifetimes back, thought spirits lived in trees, good spirits in one tree and bad spirits in another. And a staff of white thorn is supposed to scare out evil.

"Are those things true, Mr. Carpenter?"

"Well, folks took them for truth once. There must be some truth in every belief, to get it started."

"An outlander stopped here once, with a prayer book. He read to me from it, about how Satan overcame because of the wood. What did he mean, Mr. Carpenter?"

"He must have meant the Tree of Knowledge in the Garden of Eden," said the carpenter. "You know how Adam and Eve ate of the tree when Satan tempted them?"

"Reckon I do," Little Anse replied him, for, with not much else to do, he'd read the Book a many times.

"There's more to that outlander's prayer," the carpenter added on. "If Satan overcame by the wood, he can also be overcome by the wood."

"That must mean another kind of tree, Mr. Carpenter."

"Yes, of course. Another kind."

Little Anse was as happy as a dog at a fish fry. It was like school, only in school you get wishing the bell would ring and turn you loose. Little Anse didn't want to be anywhere but just there, handing the tools and hearing the talk.

"How come you know so much?" he asked the carpenter.

"I travel lots in my work, Little Anse. That's a nice thing about it."

Little Anse looked over to Mr. Troy Holcomb's. "You know," he said, "I don't agree in my mind that Mr. Troy's a witch." He looked again. "If he had power, he'd have long ago cured my legs. He's a nice old man, for all he and my daddy fussed between themselves."

"You ever tell your daddy that?"

"He won't listen. You near-about through?"

"All through, Little Anse."

It was getting on for supper time. The carpenter packed up his tools and started with Little Anse toward the house. Moving slow, the way you do with a cripple along, they hadn't gone more than a few yards when they met Mr. Absalom.

"Finished up, are you?" asked Mr. Absalom, and looked. "Well, bless us and keep us all!" he yelled.

"Don't you call that a good bridge, daddy?" Little Anse asked.

For the carpenter had driven some posts straight up in the ditch, and spiked on others like cross timbers. On those he'd laid a bridge floor from side to side. It wasn't fancy, but it looked solid to last till the Day of Judgment, mending the cutoff of the path.

"I told you I wanted—" Mr. Absalom began to say.

He stopped. For Mr. Troy Holcomb came across the bridge.

Mr. Troy's a low-built little man, with a white hangdown moustache and a face as brown as old harness leather. He came over and stopped and put out his skinny hand, and it shook like in a wind.

"Absalom," he said, choking in his throat, "you don't know how I been wanting this chance to ask your humble pardon."

Then Mr. Absalom all of a sudden reached and took that skinny hand in his big one.

"You made me so savage mad, saying I was a witchman," Mr. Troy said. "If you'd let me talk, I'd have told you the blight was in my downhill corn, too. It only just spared the uphill patches. You can come and look—"

"Troy, I don't need to look," Mr. Absalom made out to reply him. "Your word's as good to me as the yellow gold. I never rightly thought you did any witch-stuff, not even when I said it to you."

"I'm so dog-sorry I dug this ditch," Mr. Troy went on. "I hated it, right when I had the spade in my hand. Ain't my nature to be spiteful, Absalom."

"No, Troy. Ain't no drop of spite blood in you."

"But you built this bridge, Absalom, to show you never favored my cutting you off from me—"

Mr. Troy stopped talking, and wiped his brown face with the hand Mr. Absalom didn't have hold of.

"Troy," said Mr. Absalom, "I'm just as glad as you are about all this. But don't credit me with that bridge idea. This carpenter here, he thought it up."

"And now I'll be going," spoke up the carpenter in his gentle way.

They both looked on him. He'd hoisted his tool chest up on his shoulder again, and he smiled at them, and down at Little Anse. He put his hand on Little Anse's head, just half a second long.

"Fling away those crutches," he said. "You don't need them now."

All at once, Little Anse flung the crutches away, left and right. He stood up straight and strong. Fast as any boy ever ran on this earth, he ran to his daddy.

The carpenter was gone. The place he'd been at was empty.

But, looking where he'd been, they weren't frightened, the way they'd be at a haunt or devil-thing. Because they all of a sudden all three knew Who the carpenter was and how He's always with us, the way He promised in the far-back times; and how He'll do ary sort of job, if it can bring peace on earth and good will to men, among nations or just among neighbors.

It was Little Anse who remembered the whole chorus of the song—

"Shoo, John, I know that song! We sung it last night at church for Christmas Eve!"

"I know it too, John!"

"Me! Me too!"
"All right then, why don't you children join in and help me sing it?"

Go tell it on the mountain,
Tell it on the hills and everywhere,
Go tell it on the mountain
That Jesus Christ was born!

OLD DEVLINS WAS A-WAITING

All day I'd climbed through mountain country. Past Rebel Creek I'd climbed, and through Lost Cove, and up and down the slopes of Crouch and Hog Ham and Skeleton Ridge, and finally as the sun hunted the world's edge, I looked over a high saddleback and down on Flornoy College.

Flornoy's up in the hills, plain and poor, but it does good teaching. Country boys who mightn't get past common school else can come and work off the most part of their board and keep and learning. I saw a couple of brick buildings, a row of cottages, and barns for the college farm in the bottom below, with then a paved road to Hilberstown maybe eight, nine miles down valley. Climbing down was another sight farther, and longer work than you'd think, and when I got to the level it was past sundown and the night showed its stars to me.

Coming into the back of the college grounds, I saw a light somewhere this side of the buildings, and then I heard two voices quarreling at each other.

"You leave my lantern be," bade one voice, deep and hacked.

"I wasn't going to blow it out, Moon-Eye," the other voice laughed, but sharp and mean. "I just joggled up against it."

"Look out I don't joggle up against you, Rixon Pengraft."

"Maybe you're bigger than I am, but there's such a thing as the difference between a big man and a little one."

Then I was close and saw them, and they saw me. Scholars at Flornoy, I reckoned by the light of the old lantern one of them toted. He was tall, taller than I am, with broad, hunched shoulders, and in the lantern-shine his face looked good in a long, big-nosed way. The other fellow was plumpy-soft, and smoked a cigar that made an orangey coal in the night.

The cigar-smoking one turned toward where I came along with my silver-strung guitar in one hand and my possible-sack in the other.

"What you doing around here," he said to me. Didn't ask it, said it.

"I'm looking for Professor Deal," I replied him. "Any objections?"

He grinned his teeth white around the cigar. The lantern-shine flickered on them. "None I know of. Go on looking."

He turned and moved off in the night. The fellow with the lantern watched him go, then spoke to me.

"I'll take you to Professor Deal's. My name's Anderson Newlands. Folks call me Moon-Eye."

"Folks call me John," I said. "What does Moon-Eye mean?"

He smiled, tight, over the lantern glow. "It's hard for me to see in the night-time, John. I was in the Korean war, I got wounded and had a fever, and my eyes began to trouble me. They're getting better, but I need a lantern any night but when it's full moon."

We walked along. "Was that Rixon Pengraft fellow trying to give you a hard time?" I asked.

"Trying, maybe. He—well, he wants something I'm not really keeping away from him, he just thinks I am."

That's all Moon-Eye Newlands said about it, and I didn't inquire him what he meant. He went on: "I don't want any fuss with Rixon, but if he's bound to have one with me—" Again he stopped his talk. "Yonder's Professor Deal's house, the one with the porch. I'm due there some later tonight, after supper."

He headed off with his lantern, toward the brick building where the scholars slept. On the porch, Professor Deal came out and made me welcome. He's president of Flornoy, strong-built, middling tall, with white hair and a round hard chin like a water-washed rock.

"Haven't seen you since the State Fair," he boomed out, loud enough to talk to the seventy, eighty Flornoy scholars all at once. "Come in the house, John, Mrs. Deal's nearly ready with supper. I want you to meet Dr. McCoy."

I came inside and rested my guitar and possible-sack by the door. "Is he a medicine doctor or a teacher doctor?" I asked.

"She's a lady. Dr. Anda Lee McCoy. She observes how people think and how far they see."

"An eye-doctor?"

"Call her an inner-eye doctor, John. She studies what those Duke University people call ESP—extra-sensory perception."

I'd heard of that. A fellow named Rhine says folks can some way tell what other folks think to themselves. He tells it that everybody reads minds a little bit, and some folks read them a right much. Might be you've seen his cards, marked five ways— square, cross, circle, star, wavy lines. Take five of each of those cards and you've got a pack of twenty-five. Somebody shuffles them like for a game and looks at them, one after another. Then somebody else, who can't see the cards, in the next room maybe, tries to guess what's on them. Ordinary chance is for one right guess out of five. But, here and there, it gets called another sight oftener.

"Some old mountain folks would name that witch-stuff," I said to Professor Deal.

"Hypnotism was called witch-craft, until it was shown to be true science," he said back. "Or telling what dreams mean, until Dr. Freud overseas made it scientific. ESP might be a recognized science some day."

"You hold with it, do you, Professor?"

"I hold with anything that's proven," he said. "I'm not sure about ESP yet. Here's Mrs. Deal."

She's a comfortable, clever lady, as white-haired as he is. While I made my manners, Dr. Anda Lee McCoy came from the back of the house.

"Are you the ballad-singer?" she asked me.

I'd expected no doctor lady as young as Dr. Anda Lee McCoy, nor as pretty-looking. She was small and slim, but there was enough of her. She stood straight and wore good city clothes, and had lots of yellow hair and a round happy face and straight-looking blue eyes.

"Professor Deal bade me come see him," I said. "He couldn't get Mr. Bascom Lamar Lunsford to decide something or other about folk songs and tales."

"I'm glad you've come," she welcomed me.

Turned out Dr. McCoy knew Mr. Bascom Lamar Lunsford and thought well of him. Professor Deal had asked for him first, but Mr. Bascom was in Washington, making records of his songs for the Library of Congress. Some folks can't vote which they'd rather hear, Mr. Bascom's five-string banjo or my guitar; but he sure enough knows more old time songs than I do. A few more.

Mrs. Deal went to the kitchen to see was supper near about cooked. We others sat down in the front room. Dr. McCoy asked me to sing something, so I got my guitar and gave her "Shiver in the Pines."

"Pretty," she praised. "Do you know a song about killing a captain at a lonesome river ford?"

I thought. "Some of it, maybe. It's a Virginia song, I think. You relish that song, Doctor?"

"I wasn't thinking of my own taste. A student here—a man named Anderson Newlands—doesn't like it at all."

Mrs. Deal called us to supper, and while we ate, Dr. McCoy talked.

"I'll tell you why I asked for someone like you to help me, John," she began. "I've got a theory, or a hypothesis. About dreams."

"Not quite like Freud," put in Professor Deal, "though he'd be interested if he was alive and here."

"It's dreaming the future," said Dr. McCoy.

"Shoo," I said, "that's no theory, that's fact. Bible folks did it. I've done it myself. Once, during the war—"

But that was no tale to tell, what I dreamed in war time and how true it came out. So I stopped, while Dr. McCoy went on.

"There are records of prophecies coming true, even after the prophets died. And another set of records fit in, about images appearing like ghosts. Most of these are ancestors of somebody alive today. Kinship and special sympathy, you know. Sometimes these images, or ghosts, are called from the past by using diagrams and spells. You aren't laughing at me, John?"

"No, ma'am. Things like that aren't likely to be a laughing matter."

"Well, what if dreams of the future come true because somebody goes forward in time while he sleeps or drowses?" she asked us. "That ghost of Nostradamus, reported not long ago—what if Nostradamus himself was called into this present time, and then went back to his own century to set down a prophecy of what he'd seen?"

If she wanted an answer, I didn't have one for her. All I said was: "Do you want to call somebody from the past, ma'am? Or maybe go yourself into a time that's coming?"

She shook her yellow head.

"Put it one way, John, I'm not psychic. Put it another way, the scientific way, I'm not adapted. But this young man Anderson Newlands is the best adapted I've ever found."

She told how some Flornoy students scored high at guessing the cards and their markings. I was right interested to hear that Rixon Pengraft called them well, though Dr. McCoy said his mind got on other things—I reckoned his mind got on her; pretty thing as she was, she could take a man's mind. But Anderson Newlands, Moon-Eye Newlands, guessed every card right off as she held the pack, time after time, with nary miss.

"And he dreams of the future, I know," she said. "If he can see the future, he might call to the past."

"By the diagrams and the words?" I inquired her. "How about the science explanation for that?"

It so happened she had one. She told it while we ate our custard pie.

First, that idea that time's the fourth dimension. You're six feet tall, twenty inches wide, twelve inches thick and thirty-five years old; and the thirty-five years of you reach from where you were born one place, across the land and maybe over the sea where you've traveled, and finally to right where you are now, from thousands of miles ago. Then the idea that just a dot here in this second of time we're living in can be a wire back and back and forever back, or a five-inch line is a five-inch bar reaching forever back thataway, or a circle is a tube, and so on. It did make some sense to me, and I asked Dr. McCoy what it added up to.

It added up to the diagram witch-folks draw, with circles and six-pointed stars and letters from an alphabet nobody on this earth can spell out. Well, that diagram might be a cross-section, here in our three dimensions, of something reaching backward or forward, a machine to travel you through time.

"You certain sure about this?" I inquired Dr. McCoy at last. And she smiled, then she frowned, and shook her yellow head again.

"I'm only guessing," she said, "as I might guess with the ESP cards. But I'd like to find out whether the right man could call his ancestor out of the past."

"I still don't figure out about those spoken spell words the witch-folks use," I said.

"A special sound can start a machine," said Professor Deal. "I've seen such things."

"Like the words of the old magic square?" asked Dr. McCoy. "The one they use in spells to call up the dead?"

She got a pencil and scrap of paper, and wrote it out:

S	A	T	O	R
A	R	E	P	O
T	E	N	E	T
O	P	E	R	A
R	O	T	A	S

"I've been seeing that thing a many years," I said. "Witch-folks use it, and it's in witch-books like *The Long Lost Friend.*"

"You'll notice," said Dr. McCoy, "that it reads the same, whether you start at the upper left and work down word by word, or at the lower right and read the words one by one upward; or if you read it straight down or straight up."

Professor Deal looked, too. "The first two words—SATOR and AREPO—are reversals of the last two. SATOR for ROTAS, and AREPO for OPERA."

"I've heard that before," I braved up to say. "The first two words being the last two, turned around. But the third, fourth and fifth are all right—I've heard tell that TENET means *faith* and OPERA is *works,* and ROTAS something about wheels."

"But SATOR and AREPO are more than just reversed words," Professor Deal said. "I'm no profound Latinist, but I know that SATOR means a sower—a planter—or a beginner or creator."

"*Creator,*" Dr. McCoy jumped on his last word. "That would fit into this if it's a real sentence."

"A sentence, and a palindrome," nodded Professor Deal. "Know what a palindrome is, John?"

I knew that, too, from somewhere. "A sentence that reads the same back and forward," I told him. "Like Napoleon saying, *Able was I ere I saw Elba.* Or the first words Mother Eve heard in the Garden of Eden, *Madam, I'm Adam.* Those are old grandma jokes to pleasure young children."

"If these words are a sentence, they're more than a palindrome," said Dr. McCoy. "They're a double palindrome because they read the same from any place you start—backward, forward, up or down. Fourfold meaning would be fourfold power as a spell or formula."

"But what's the meaning?" I wanted to know again.

She began to write on a paper, "sator," she said out loud, *"the creator.* Whether that's the creator of some machine, or the Creator of all things . . . I suppose it's a machine-creator."

"I reckon the same," I agreed her, "because this doesn't sound to me the kind of way the Creator of all things does His works."

Mrs. Deal smiled and excused herself. We could talk and talk, she said, but she had sewing to do.

"arepo," Professor Deal kind of hummed to himself. "I wish I had a Latin dictionary, though even then I might not find it. Maybe that's a corruption of *repo* or *erepo*—to crawl or climb—a vulgar form of the word—"

I said nothing. I didn't think Professor Deal would say anything vulgar in front of a lady. But all Dr. McCoy remarked him was: "arepo—wouldn't that be a noun ablative? By means of?"

"Write it down like that," nodded Professor Deal. *"By means of creeping, climbing, by means of great effort.* And tenet is the verb *to hold. He holds, the creator holds."*

"opera is *works,* and rotas is *wheels,"* Dr. McCoy tried to finish up, but this time Professor Deal shook his head.

"rotas probably is accusative plural, in apposition." He cleared his throat, long and loud. "Maybe I never will be sure, but let's read it something like this: *The creator, by means of great effort, holds the wheels for his works."*

I'd not said a word in all this scholar-talk, till then, "tenet might still be *faith, "* I offered them. "Faith's needed to help the workings. Folks without faith might call the thing foolishness."

"That's sound psychology," said Professor Deal.

"And it fits in with the making of spells," Dr. McCoy added on.

"Double meanings, you know. Maybe there are double meanings all along, or triple or fourfold meanings, and all of them true." She read from her paper. *"The creator, by means of great effort, holds the wheels for his works."*

"It might even refer to the orbits of planets," said Professor Deal.

"Where do I come in?" I asked. "Why was I bid here?"

"You can sing something for us," Dr. McCoy replied me, "and you can have faith."

A knocking at the door, and Professor Deal went to let the visitor in. Moon-Eye Newlands walked into the house, lifted his lantern chimney and blew out his light. He looked tall, the way he'd looked when first I met him in the outside dark, and he wore a hickory shirt and blue duckins pants. He smiled, friendly, and moon-eyed or not, he looked first of all at Dr. McCoy, clear and honest and glad to see her.

"You said you wanted me to help you, Doctor," he greeted her.

"Thank you, Mr. Newlands," she said, gentler and warmer than I'd heard her so far.

"You can call me Moon-Eye, like the rest," he told her.

He was a college scholar, and she was a doctor lady, but they were near about the same age. He'd been off to the Korean War, I remembered.

"Shall we go out on the porch?" she asked us. "Professor Deal said I could draw my diagram there. Bring your guitar, John."

We went out. Moon-Eye lighted his lantern again, and Dr. McCoy knelt down to draw with a piece of chalk.

First she made the word square, in big letters:

S	A	T	O	R
A	R	E	P	O
T	E	N	E	T
O	P	E	R	A
R	O	T	A	S

Around these she made a triangle, a good four feet from base to point. And another triangle across it, pointing the other way, so that the two made what learned folks call the Star of David.

Around that, a big circle, with writing along the edge of it, and another big circle around that, to close in the writing. I put my back to a porch post. From where I sat I could read the word square all right, but of the writing around the circle I couldn't spell ary letter.

"Folks," said Moon-Eye, "I still can't say I like this."

Kneeling where she drew, Dr. McCoy looked up at him with her blue eyes. "You said you'd help if you could."

"But what if it's not right? My old folks, my grandsires—I don't know if they ought to be called up."

"Moon-Eye," said Professor Deal, "I'm just watching, observing. I haven't yet been convinced of anything due to happen here tonight. But if it should happen—I know your ancestors must have been good country people, nobody to be ashamed of, dead or alive."

"I'm not ashamed of them," Moon-Eye told us all, with a sort of sudden clip in his voice. "I just don't think they were the sort to be stirred up without a good reason."

"Moon-Eye," said Dr. McCoy, talking the way any man who's a man would want a woman to talk to him, "science is the best of reasons in itself."

He didn't speak, didn't deny her, didn't nod his head or either shake it. He just looked at her blue eyes with his dark ones. She got up from where she'd knelt.

"John," she spoke to where I was sitting, "that song we mentioned. About the lonesome river ford. It may put things in the right tune and tempo."

Moon-Eye sat on the edge of the porch, his lantern beside him. The light made our shadows big and jumpy. I began to pick the tune the best I could recollect it, and sang:

> *Old Devlins was a-waiting*
> *By the lonesome river ford,*
> *When he spied the Mackey captain*
> *With a pistol and a sword. . . .*

I stopped, for Moon-Eye had tensed himself tight. "I'm not sure of how it goes from there," I said.

"I'm sure of where it goes," said someone in the dark, and up to the porch ambled Rixon Pengraft.

He was smoking that cigar, or maybe a fresh one, grinning around it. He wore a brown corduroy shirt with officers' straps to the shoulders, and brown corduroy pants tucked into shiny half-boots worth maybe twenty-five dollars, the pair of them. His hair was brown, too, and curly, and his eyes were sneaking all over Dr. Anda Lee McCoy.

"Nobody here knows what that song means," said Moon-Eye.

Rixon Pengraft sat down beside Dr. McCoy, on the step below Moon-Eye, and the way he did it, I harked back in my mind to something Moon-Eye had said: about something Rixon Pengraft wanted, and why he hated Moon-Eye over it.

"I've wondered wasn't the song about the Confederate War," said Rixon. "Maybe *Mackey captain* means Yankee captain."

"No, it doesn't," said Moon-Eye, and his teeth sounded on each other.

"I can sing it, anyway," said Rixon, twiddling his cigar in his teeth and winking at Dr. McCoy. "Go on picking."

"Go on," Dr. McCoy repeated, and Moon-Eye said nothing. I touched the silver strings, and Rixon Pengraft sang:

> Old Devlins, Old Devlins,
> I know you mighty well,
> You're six foot three of Satan,
> Two hundred pounds of hell ...

And he stopped. "Devils—Satan," he said. "Might be it's a song about the Devil. Think we ought to go on singing about him, with no proper respect?"

He went on:

> Old Devlins was ready,
> He feared not beast or man,
> He shot the sword and pistol
> From the Mackey captain's hand. ....

Moon-Eye looked once at the diagram, chalked out on the

floor of the porch. He didn't seem to hear Rixon Pengraft's mocking voice with the next verse:

> *Old Devlins, Old Devlins,*
> *Oh, won't you spare my life?*
> *I've got three little children*
> *And a kind and loving wife.*
>
> *God bless them little children,*
> *And I'm sorry for your wife,*
> *But turn your back and close your eyes,*
> *I'm going to take your—*

"Leave off that singing!" yelled Moon-Eye Newlands, and he was on his feet in the yard so quick we hadn't seen him move. He took a long step toward where Rixon Pengraft sat beside Dr. McCoy, and Rixon got up quick, too, and dropped his cigar and moved away.

"You know the song," blared out Moon-Eye. "Maybe you know what man you're singing about!"

"Maybe I do know," said Rixon.

"You want to bring him here to look at you?"

We were all up on our feet. We watched Moon-Eye standing over Rixon, and Moon-Eye just then looked about two feet taller than he had before. Maybe even more than that, to Rixon.

"If that's how you're going to be—" began Rixon.

"That's how I'm going to be," Moon-Eye told him, his voice right quiet again. "I'm honest to tell you, that's how I'm going to be."

"Then I won't stay here," said Rixon. "I'll leave, because you're making so much noise in front of a lady. But, Moon-Eye, I'm not scared of you. Nor yet the ghost of any ancestor you ever had, Devlins or anybody else."

Rixon smiled at Dr. McCoy and walked away. We heard him start to whistle in the dark. He meant it for banter, but I couldn't help but think about the boy whistling his way through the grave-yard.

Then I happened to look back at the diagram on the porch.

And it didn't seem right for a moment, it looked like something else. The two circles, with the string of writing between them, the six-point star, and in the very middle of everything the word square:

```
S V T O Я
A Я Ǝ ꓒ O
T Ǝ N Ǝ T
O ꓒ Ǝ Я A
Я O T A S
```

"Shoo," I said. "Look, folks, that word square's turned around."

"Naturally," said Professor Deal, plain glad to talk and think about something besides how Moon-Eye and Rixon had acted. "The first two words are reversals of the—"

"I don't mean that, Professor." I pointed. "Look. I take my Bible oath that Dr. McCoy wrote it out so that it read rightly from where I am now. But it's gone upside down."

"That's the truth," Moon-Eye agreed me.

"Yes," said Dr. McCoy. "Yes. You know what that means?"

"The square's turned around?" asked Professor Deal.

"The whole thing's turned around. The whole diagram. Spun a whole hundred and eighty degrees—maybe several times—and stopped again. Why?" She put her hand on Moon-Eye's elbow, and the hand trembled. "The thing was beginning to work, to revolve, the machine was going to operate—"

"You're right." Moon-Eye put his big hand over her little one. "Just when the singing stopped."

He moved away from her and picked up his lantern. He started away.

"Come back, Moon-Eye!" she called after him. "It can't work without you!"

"I've got something to see Rixon Pengraft about," he said.

"You can't hit him, you're bigger than he is!" I thought she was going to run and catch up with him.

"Stay here," I told her. "I'll go talk to him."

I walked quick to catch up with Moon-Eye. "Big things were near about to happen just now," I said.

"I realize that, Mr. John. But it won't go on, because I won't be there to help it." He lifted his lantern and stared at me. "I said my old folks weren't the sort you ruffle up for no reason."

"Was the song about your folks?"

"Sort of."

"You mean, Old Devlins?"

"That's not just exactly his name, but he was my great-grandsire on my mother's side. Rixon Pengraft caught onto that, and after what he said—"

"You heard that doctor lady say Rixon isn't as big as you are, Moon-Eye," I argued him. "You hit him and she won't like it."

He stalked on toward the brick building where the scholars had their rooms.

Bang!

The lantern went out with a smash of glass.

The two of us stopped still in the dark and stared. Up ahead, in the brick building, a head and shoulders made itself black in a lighted window, and a cigar-coal glowed.

"I said I didn't fear you, Moon-Eye!" laughed the voice of Rixon Pengraft. "Nor I don't fear Old Devlins, whatever kin he is to you!"

A black arm waved something. It was a rifle. Moon-Eye drew himself up tall in the dark.

"Help me, John," he said. "I can't see a hand before me."

"You going to fight him, Moon-Eye? When he has that gun?"

"Help me back to Professor Deal's." He put his hand on my shoulder and gripped down hard. "Get me into the light."

"What do you aim to do?"

"Something there wasn't a reason to do, till now."

That was the last the either of us said. We walked back. Nobody was on the porch, but the door was open. We stepped across the chalk-drawn diagram and into the front room. Professor Deal and Dr. McCoy stood looking at us.

"You've come back," Dr. McCoy said to Moon-Eye, the gladdest you'd ever call for a lady to say. She made a step toward him and put out her hand.

"I heard a gun go off out there," she said.

"My lantern got shot to pieces," Moon-Eye told her. "I've

come back to do what you bid me do. John, if you don't know the song—"

"I do know it, Moon-Eye," I said. "I stopped because I thought you didn't want it."

"I want it now," he rang out his voice. "If my great-grandsire can be called here tonight, call him. Sing it, John."

I still carried my guitar. I slanted it across me and picked the strings:

> *He killed the Mackey captain,*
> *He went behind the hill,*
> *Them Mackeys never caught him,*
> *And I know they never will . . .*

"Great-grandsire!" yelled out Moon-Eye, so that the walls shook with his cry. "I've taken a right much around here, because I thought it might be best thataway. But tonight Rixon Pengraft dared you, said he didn't fear you! Come and show him what it's like to be afraid!"

"Now, now—" began Professor Deal, then stopped it.

I sang on:

> *When there's no moon in heaven*
> *And you hear the hound-dogs bark,*
> *You can guess that it's Old Devlins*
> *A-scrambling in the dark. . . .*

Far off outside, a hound-dog barked in the moonless night.

And on the door sounded a thumpety-bang knock, the way you'd think the hand that knocked had knuckles of mountain rock.

I saw Dr. McCoy weave and sway on her little feet like a bush in a wind, and her blue eyes got the biggest they'd been yet. But Moon-Eye just smiled, hard and sure, as Professor Deal walked heavy to the door and opened it.

Next moment he sort of gobbled in his throat, and tried to shove the door closed again, but he wasn't quick enough. A wide hat with a long dark beard under it showed through the door, then big, hunched shoulders like Moon-Eye's. And, spite of the Professor's shoving, the door came open all the way, and in slid the long-bearded, big-shouldered man among us.

He stood without moving inside the door. He was six feet three, all right, and I reckoned he'd weigh at two hundred pounds. He wore a frocktail coat and knee boots of cowhide. His left arm cradled a rifle-gun near about as long as he was, and its barrel was eight-squared, the way you hardly see any more. His big broad right hand came up and took off the wide hat.

Then we could see his face, such a face as I'm not likely to forget. Big nose and bright glaring eyes, and that beard I tell you about, that fell down like a curtain from the high cheekbones and just under the nose. Wild, he looked, and proud, and deadly as his weight in blasting powder with the fuse already spitting. I reckon that old Stonewall Jackson might have had something of that favor, if ever he'd turned his back on the Lord God.

"I thought I was dreaming this," he said to us, deep as somebody talking from a well-bottom, "but I begin to figure the dream's come true."

His eyes came around to me, those terrible eyes, that shone like two drawn knives.

"You called me a certain name in your song," he said. "I've been made mad by that name, on the wrong mouth."

"Devlins?" I said.

"Devil Anse," he nodded. "The McCoy crowd named me that. My right name's Captain Anderson Hatfield, and I hear that somebody around here took a shoot at my great-grandboy." He studied Moon-Eye. "That's you, ain't it, son?"

"Now wait, whoever you are—" began Professor Deal.

"I'm Captain Anderson Hatfield," he named himself again, and lowered his rifle-gun. Its butt thumped the floor like a falling tree.

"That shooting," Professor Deal made out to yammer. "I didn't hear it."

"I heard it," said Devil Anse, "and likewise I heard the slight put on me by the shooter."

"I—I don't want any trouble—" the Professor still tried to argue.

"Nor you won't have none, if you hear me," said Devil Anse. "But keep quiet. And look out yonder."

We looked out the open door. Just at the porch stood the shadows of three men, wide-hatted, tall, leaning on their guns.

"Since I was obliged to come," said Devil Anse Hatfield, and his voice was as deep now as Moon-Eye's, "I reckoned not to come alone." He spoke into the night. "Jonce?"

"Yes, pa."

"You'll be running things here. You and Vic and Cotton Top keep your eyes cut this way. Nobody's to go from this house, for the law nor for nothing else."

"Yes, pa."

Devil Anse Hatfield turned back to face us. We looked at him, and thought about who he was.

All those years back, sixty, seventy, we thought to the Big Sandy that flows between West Virginia and Kentucky. And the fighting between the Hatfields and the McCoys, over what beginning nobody can rightly say today, but fighting that brought blood and death and sorrow to all that part of the world. And the efforts to make it cease, by every kind of arguer and officer, that couldn't keep the Hatfields and the McCoys apart from each other's throats. And here he was, Devil Anse Hatfield, from that time and place, picking me out with his eyes.

"You who sung the song," he nodded me. "Come along."

I put down my guitar. "Proud to come with you, Captain," I said.

His hand on my shoulder gripped like Moon-Eye's, a bear-trap grip there. We walked out the door, and off the porch past the three waiting tall shadows, and on across the grounds in the night toward that brick sleeping building.

"You know where we're going?" I inquired him.

"Seems to me I do. This seems like the way. What's your name?"

"John, Captain."

"John, I left Moon-Eye back there because he called for me to come handle things. He felt it was my business, talking to that fellow. I can't lay tongue to his name right off."

"Rixon Pengraft?"

"Rixon Pengraft," he repeated me. "Yes, I dreamed that name. Here we are. Open that door for us."

I'd never been in that building. Nor either had Devil Anse Hatfield, except maybe in what dreams he'd had to bring him there. But, if he'd found his way from the long ago, he found the way to where he was headed. We walked along the hallway inside between doors, until he stopped me at one. "Knock," he bade me, and I put my fist to the wood.

A laugh inside, mean and shaky. "That you, Moon-Eye Newlands?" said Rixon Pengraft's voice. "You think you dare come in here? I've not locked myself in. Turn the knob, if you're man enough."

Devil Anse nudged my shoulder, and I opened the door and shoved it in, and we came across the threshold together.

Rixon sat on his bed, with a little old twenty-two rifle across his lap.

"Glad you had the nerve, Moon-Eye," he began to say, "because there's only room for one of us to sit next to Anda Lee McCoy—"

Then his mouth stayed open, with the words ceasing to come out.

"Rixon," said Devil Anse, "you know who I am?"

Rixon's eyes hung out of his head like two scuppernong grapes on a vine. They twitchy-climbed up Devil Anse, from his boots to his hat, and they got bigger and scareder all the time.

"I don't believe it," said Rixon Pengraft, almost too sick and weak for an ear to hear him.

"You'd better have the man to believe it. You sang about me. Named me Devil Anse in the song, and knew it was about me. Thought it would be right funny if I did come where you were."

At last that big hand quitted my shoulder, and moved to bring that long eight-square rifle to the ready.

"Don't!"

Rixon was on his knees, and his own little toy gun spilled on the floor between us. He was able to believe now.

"Listen," Rixon jibber-jabbered, "I didn't mean anything. It was just a joke on Moon-Eye."

"A mighty sorry joke," said Devil Anse. "I never yet laughed at a gun going off." His boot-toe shoved the twenty-two. "Not even a baby-boy gun like that."

"I—" Rixon tried to say, and he had to stop to get strength. "I'll—"

"You'll break up that there gun," Devil Anse decreed him.

"Break my gun?" Rixon was still on his knees, but his scared eyes managed to get an argue-look.

"Break it," said Devil Anse. "I'm a-waiting, Rixon. Just like that time I waited by a lonesome river ford."

And his words were as cold and slow as chunks of ice floating down a half-choked stream in winter.

Rixon put out his hand for the twenty-two. His eyes kept hold on Devil Anse. Rixon lifted one knee from the floor, and laid the twenty-two across it. He tugged at barrel and stock.

"Harder than that," said Devil Anse. "Let's see if you got any muscle to match your loud mouth."

Rixon tugged again, and then Devil Anse's rifle stirred. Rixon saw, and really made out to work at it. The little rifle broke at the balance. I heard the wood crack and splinter.

"All right now," said Devil Anse, still deep and cold and slow. "You're through with them jokes you think are so funny. Fling them chunks of gun out yonder."

He wagged his head at the open door, and Rixon flung the broken pieces into the hall.

"Stay on your knees," Devil Anse bade him. "You got praying to do. Pray the good Lord your thanks you got off so lucky. Because if there's another time you see me, I'll be the last thing you see this side of the hell I'm six foot three of."

To me he said: "Come on, John. We've done with this no-excuse for a man who's broke his own gun."

Back we went, and nary word between us. The other three Hatfields stood by Professor Deal's porch, quiet as painted shadows of three gun-carrying men. In at the door we walked, and there was Professor Deal, and over against the other side of the room stood Moon-Eye and Dr. McCoy.

"Rixon named somebody McCoy here," said Devil Anse. "Who owns up to the name?"

"I do," said she, gentle but steady.

"You hold away from her, Great-grandsire," spoke up Moon-Eye.

"Boy," said Devil Anse, "you telling me what to do and not do?"

"I'm telling you, Great-grandsire."

I looked at those two tall big-nosed men from two times in the same family's story, and, saving Devil Anse's beard, and maybe thirty-some-odd years, you couldn't have called for two folks who favored each other's looks more.

"Boy," said Devil Anse, "you trying to scare me?"

"No, Great-grandsire. I'm not trying to scare you."

Devil Anse smiled. His smile made his face look the terriblest he'd looked so far.

"Now, that's good. Because I never been scared in all my days on this earth."

"I'm just telling you, Great-grandsire," said Moon-Eye. "You hold away from her."

Dr. McCoy stood close to Moon-Eye, and all of a sudden Moon-Eye put his hickory-sleeved arm round her and drew her closer still.

Devil Anse put his eyes on them. That terrible smile crawled away out of his beard, like a deadly poison snake out of grass, and we saw it no more.

"Great-grandboy," he said, "it wasn't needful for you to get me told. I made a mistake once with a McCoy girl. Jonce—my son standing out yonder—loved and courted her. Roseanna was her name."

"Roseanna," said the voice of Jonce Hatfield outside.

"I never gave them leave to marry," said Devil Anse. "Wish I had now. It would have saved a sight of trouble and grief and killing. And nobody yet ever heared me say that."

His eyes relished Dr. McCoy, and it was amazing to see that they could be quiet eyes, kind eyes.

"Now, girl," he said, "even if you might be close kin to Old Ran McCoy—"

"I'm not sure of the relationship," she said. "If it's there, I'm not ashamed."

"Nor you needn't be." His beard went down and up as he nodded her. "I've fit the McCoy set for years, and not once found ary scared soul among them. Ain't no least drop of coward blood in their veins." He turned. "I'll be going."

"Going?" asked Professor Deal.

"Yes, sir. Goodnight to the all of you."

He went through the door, hat, beard and rifle, and closed it behind him, and off far again we could hear that hound-dog bark.

We were quiet as a dead hog there in the room. Finally:

"Well, God bless my soul!" said Professor Deal.

"It happened," I said.

"But it won't be believed, John," he went on. "No sane person will ever believe who wasn't here."

I turned to say something to Moon-Eye and Dr. McCoy. But they were looking at each other, and Moon-Eye's both arms were around that doctor lady. And if I had said whatever I had in mind to say, they'd not have been hearing me.

Mrs. Deal said something from that room where she'd gone to do her sewing, and Professor Deal walked off to join her. I felt I might be one too many, too, just then. I picked up my silver-strung guitar and went outside after Devil Anse Hatfield.

He wasn't there, nor yet those who'd come with him. But on the porch was the diagram in chalk, and I had enough light to see that the word-square read right side up again, the way it had been first set down by Dr. Anda Lee McCoy.

McCoy. Mackey. Devlins. Devil Anse. Names change in the old songs, but the power is still there. Naturally, the way my habit is, I began to pick at my silver strings, another song I'd heared from time to time as I'd wandered the hills and hollows:

> *Up on the top of the mountain,*
> *Away from the sins of this world,*
> *Anse Hatfield's son, he laid down his gun*
> *And dreamed about Ran McCoy's girl . . .*

NINE YARDS OF OTHER CLOTH

High up that almighty steep rocky slope with the sun just sunk, I turned as I knelt by my little campfire. Looking down slope and down to where the river crawled like a snake in the valley bottom, I saw her little black figure splash across the shallow place I'd found an hour back. At noontime I'd looked from the mountain yonder across the valley and I'd seen her then, too, on another height I'd left behind. And I'd thought of a song with my name in it:

> On yonder hill there stands a creature,
> Who she is I do not know . . .
> Oh no, John, no, John, no! . . .

But I knew she was Evadare. I'd fled from before her pretty face as never I'd fled from any living thing, not from evil spell-throwers nor murder-doers, nor either from my country's enemies when I'd soldiered in foreign parts and seen battle as the Bible prophet-book tells it, confused noises and garments rolled in blood. Since dawn I'd run from Evadare like a rabbit from a fox, and still she followed, climbing now along the trail I'd tried not to leave, toward the smoke of the fire I'd built before I knew she was still coming.

No getaway from her now, for night dropped on the world, and to climb higher would be to fall from some steep hidden place. I could wait where I was or I could head down and face her. Wondering which to do, I recollected how first we'd come on each other in Hosea's Hollow.

I'd not rightly known how I'd wandered there—Hosea's Hollow. I hadn't meant to, that was certain sure. No good-sensed man or woman would mean to. Folks wished Hosea's Hollow was a lost hollow, tried to stay out of it and not think about it.

Not even the old Indians relished to go there. When the white folks ran the Indians off, the Indians grinned over their shoulders as they went, calling out how Kalu would give white men the same hard times he'd given Indians.

Kalu. The Indian word means a bone. Why Kalu was named that nobody could rightly say, for nobody who saw him lived to tell what he looked to be. He came from his place when he was mad or just hungry. Who he met he snatched away, to eat or worse than eat. The folks who'd stolen the Indians' country near about loaded their wagons to go the way they'd come. Then— and this was before the time of the oldest man I'd heard tell of it—young Hosea Palmer said he'd take Kalu's curse away.

Folks hadn't wanted Hosea to try such. Hosea's father was a preacher—he begged him. So did Hosea's mother and so did a girl who'd dreamed to marry Hosea. They said if Hosea went where Kalu denned, he'd not come back, but Hosea allowed Kalu was the downright evil and couldn't prevail against a pure heart. He went in the hollow, and true he didn't come out, but no more did Kalu, from that day on. Both vanished from folks' sight and knowledge, and folks named the place Hosea's Hollow, and nary path led there.

How I myself had come to the hollow, the first soul in long years as I reckoned, it wondered me. What outside had been the broad open light of the day was cloudy gray light here among funny-growing trees. Somewhere I heard an owl hoot, not waiting for night. Likewise I half-heard music, and it came to me that was why I'd walked there without meaning to.

Later, while I watched Evadare climb up trail to me, I recollected how, in Hosea's Hollow, I'd recollected hearing the sure enough music, two days before and forty-fifty miles off.

At Haynie's Fork, hunters had shot a hog that belonged to nobody, and butchered it up while the lady-folks baked pones of corn bread and sliced up coleslaw, and from here and yonder came folks carrying jugs of beady white liquor and music instruments. I was there, too, I enjoy to aid at such doings. We ate and drank and had dancing, and the most skilled men gave us music. Obray Ramsey picked his banjo and sang *O where is pretty Polly, O yonder she stands, with rings on the fingers of her lily-white hands,* on to the last line that's near about the frighteningest last line ary song had. Then they devilled me to play my silver-strung guitar and give them *Vandy, Vandy* and *The Little Black Train*. That led to tale-tellings, and one tale was of Hosea's Hollow and fifty different notions of what might could have gone with Hosea and whatever bore the name of Kalu. Then more music, with Byard Ray fiddling his possible best, the way we never thought to hear better.

But a tall thin stranger was there, with a chin like a skinny fist and sooty-colored hair. When Byard Ray had done, the stranger took from a bag a shiny black fiddle. I offered to pick guitar to harmony with him, but he said sharp, "No, I thank you." Alone he fiddled, and, gentlemen, he purely fiddled better than Byard Ray. When he'd done, I inquired him his name.

"Shull Cobart," he replied me. "You're John, is that right? We'll meet again, it's possible, John."

His smile was no way likeable as he walked off, while folks swore no living soul could fiddle Byard Ray down without some special fiddle-secret. That had been two days before, and here I was in Hosea's Hollow, seeming to hear music that was some way like the music of Shull Cobart's black fiddle.

The gray air shimmered, but not the least hot or bright, there where owls hooted by day. I looked at a funny-growing tree, and such flowers as it had I'd not seen before. Might be they grew from the tree, might be from a vine scrabbled up. They were cup-shape, shiny black like new shoes—or like Shull Cobart's shiny-black fiddle, and I felt I could hear him still play, could see him still grin.

Was that why I half-heard the ghost of his music, why I'd come to these black-flowered trees in the shimmery gray air? Anyway, there was a trail, showing that something moved in Hosea's Hollow, between the trees so close-grown on each side you wondered could you put a knife blade among them. I headed along the trail, and the gray dancing shimmer seemed to slow me as I walked.

That tune in my head; I swung my guitar around from where it hung with my soogin sack and blanket roll, and tweaked the music from the silver strings. The shimmer dulled off, or at least

I moved faster, picking up my feet to my own playing, around a curve bunched with more black flowers. And there, under the trees to one side, was a grave.

Years old it had to be, for vines and scrub grew on it. A wooden cross showed it was sure enough a grave. The straight stick was as tall as my chin and as big around as my both hands could grab, and the crosspiece wasn't nailed or tied on, it grew on. I stopped.

You've seen branches grown to each other like that. Two sorts of wood, the straight-up piece darker than the crosspiece. But both pieces looked alive, though the ends had been cut or broken so long back the raw was gone and the splinters rubbed off. Little-bitty twigs sprouted, with broad light-green leaves on the cross-piece and narrow dark laurel-looking ones on the straight pole. Roots reached into the grave, to sprout the cross. And letters were carved on, shaky and deep-dug and different sizes:

PRAy
foR
HosEA PALMeR

So here was where Hosea Palmer had lain down the last time, and some friend had buried him with the word to pray for him. Standing alone in the unchanciness, I did what the cross bade. In my heart I prayed, *Let the good man rest as he's earned the right and when it's my time, O Lord, let me rest as I've earned the right; and bless the kind soul who made and marked a long home for Hosea Palmer, amen.*

While always my hands moved to pick that inner-heard tune, slow and quiet like a hymn. Still picking, I strolled around another curve, and there before me was a cabin.

I reckoned one main room with clay chinking, with a split-plank door on leather hinges and a window curtained inside with tanned hide. A shed-roofed leanto was tacked to the left, and it and the main cabin had shake shingles pegged on.

The door opened, and I popped behind a tree as a girl came out.

Small-made; yet you saw she was grown and you saw she was

proud, though the color was faded from her cotton dress till it was gray as a dove. Her bright, sun-colored hair was tied behind her neck with a blue ribbon. She brought a rusty old axe with her, walking proud toward a skimpy woodpile, and on her feet were flat, homemade shoes with the hair still on the cowhide. The axe was wobble-handled, but there was strength in her little round arms. She made the axe chew the wood into pieces enough for an armful, carried the wood back into the cabin, and came out again with an old hoe on her shoulder.

From the dug well she drew the bucket—it was old, too, with a couple of silver trickles leaking from it. She dipped a drink with a gourd dipper and lowered the bucket again. Then she went to the cleared patch past the cabin, and leaned on the hoe to look at the plants growing.

There was shin-high corn, and what looked like cabbages. She studied them, and her face was lovely. I saw that she yearned for her little crop to grow into food for her. She began to chop the ground up along a row, and I slid off down trail again, past the grave to where I heard water talking to itself.

I found a way through the trees to the waterside. Lay flat and took a big drink, and washed my face and hands. I dropped my gear on a flat rock, then unlaced my shoes and let the water wash my feet. Finally I cut a pole, tied on a string and hook and baited it with a scrap of smoke meat.

Fishing was good. Gentlemen, fresh fish are pretty things, they show you the reason for the names they've earned—shiner, sun-fish, rainbow trout. Not that I caught any such, but what I caught was all right. When I had six I opened my knife to clean them, and built a fire and propped a stone beside it to fry meat on and then a couple of fish for supper. They ate good, just as the sun went down across the funny trees, and I wondered about the bright-haired girl, if she had a plenty to eat.

Finally, in the last dim light, I took my handaxe and chopped as much dry wood as I could tote. I wrapped the four other fish in leaves. I slung on my guitar, for I never walk off from that. Back I went along the trail to the cabin. Firelight danced in the window as I sneaked through the door-yard, and bent to stack the wood by the threshold log and lay the fish on it.

NINE YARDS OF OTHER CLOTH   171

"What are you doing?"

She'd ripped the door open, and she had the axe in her hand. I took a long jump away before she could swing that rusty blade.

She stood with feet apart and elbows square, to fill the door as much as her small self could. Her hair was down around her shoulders, and shone like gold fire in the light from inside.

"Oh," she said, and let the axe sink. "You're not—"

"Whom am I not?" I inquired her, trying hard to sound laughy.

She leaned tired on the axe. "Not Shull Cobart," she said.

"No, ma'am," I said. "You can say for me that I'm not Shull Cobart, nor I wouldn't be. I saw him once, and I'm honest to tell you he doesn't suit me." I pointed at what I'd brought. "I'm camped by the branch yonder. Had more fish and wood than I needed, and figured you might like them." I bowed to her. "Good night."

"Wait." There was a plea in that, and I waited. "What brought you here, Mr.—"

"I'm named John. And I just roamed in here, without thought of why."

"I'm wondered, Mr.—"

"John," I named myself again.

"I'm wondered if you're the man I've heard tell of, named John, with a silver-strung guitar."

"Why," I said, "I'd not be amazed if I had the only silver-strung guitar there is. Nobody these days strings with silver but me."

"Then I've heard you called a good man." She looked down at the wood and the fish. "You've had your supper?" she asked, soft.

"Yes, ma'am, I've had my supper."

She picked up a fish. "I've not eaten. If you—maybe you'd like some coffee—"

"Coffee," I repeated her. "I'd mightily relish a cup."

She picked up the rest of the fish. "Come in, John," she bade me, and I gathered the wood in my arms and walked in after her.

"My name's Evadare," she told me.

The inside of the cabin was what I might expect from the outside. Chinked walls, a stone fire-place with wood burning in it, a table home-pegged together, two stools made of split chunks with tough branches for legs. In a corner was a pallet bed, made up on the floor with two old patch quilts. A mirror was stuck to the wall chinking—a woman purely has to have a mirror. Evadare took a fire-splinter from the hearth and lighted a candle stuck on the table in its own tallow. I saw by the glow how pinky-soft her skin was, how young and pretty; and bigger, bluer eyes than Evadare's you couldn't call for. At last she smiled, just a little hopeful smile.

I laid more wood to the fire, found a skillet and a chunk of fat meat. I rolled two fish in cornmeal and commenced frying them. She poured coffee from a tin pot into two tin cups. Watching, I had it in mind that the bottom of the pot was as sooty black as Shull Cobart's hair.

Finally I forked the fish on to an old cracked white plate for her. She ate, and I saw she was hungry. Again she smiled that little small smile, and filled my cup again.

"I'd not expected ary soul to come into Hosea's Hollow," she finally said.

"You expected Shull Cobart," I told her to recollect. "You said so."

"He'd come if anybody would, John."

"He didn't," I said. "And I did. Do you care to talk about it?"

She acted glad to talk about it, once she started.

She'd worked at weaving for Shull Cobart, with maybe nine-ten others, in a little town off in the hills. He took the cloth to places like Asheville and sold at a high mark to the touristers that came there. Once or twice he made to court Evadare, but she paid him no mind. But one day he went on a trip, and came again with the black fiddle.

"And he was different," she said. "He'd been scared and polite to folks before that. But the fiddle made him somebody else. He played at dances and folks danced their highest and fastest, but they were scared by his music, even when they flocked to it. He won prizes at fiddle-playing. He'd stand by the shop door and play to us girls, and the cloth we wove was more cloth and better cloth—but it was strange. Funny feel and funny look to it."

"Did the touristers still buy it?" I inquired her.

"Yes, and payed more for it, but they seemed scared while they were buying it. So I've heard tell from folks who saw."

"And Shull Cobart made you run off."

"It was when he said he wanted me to light his darkness."

I saw what those words meant. An evil man speaking them to a good girl, because his evil was hungry for good. "What did you reply him?"

"I said I wanted to be quiet and good, he wanted to be showy and scary. And he said that was just his reason, he wanted me for my goodness to his scariness." She shivered, the way folks shiver when ice falls outside the window. "I swore to go where he'd not follow. Then he played his fiddle, it somehow made to bind me hand and foot. I felt he'd tole me off with him then and there, but I pretended—"

She looked sad and ashamed of pretending, even in peril.

"I said I'd go with him next day. He was ready to wait. That night I ran off."

"And you came to Hosea's Hollow," I said. "How did you make yourself able?"

"I feared Kalu another sight less than I fear Shull Cobart," Evadare replied me. "And I've not seen Kalu—I've seen nothing. I heard a couple of things, though. Once something knocked at the door at night."

"What was it knocked, Evadare?"

"I wasn't so foolish for the lack of sense that I went to see." She shivered again, from her little toes up to her bright hair. "I dragged up the quilt and spoke the strongest prayer I remember, the old-timey one about God gives His angels charge over us by day and by night." Her blue eyes fluttered, remembering. "Whatever knocked gave one knock more and never again, that night or ary night since."

I was purely ready to talk of something else. "Who made this cabin for you?" I asked, looking around.

"It was here when I came—empty. But I knew good folks had made it, by the cross."

I saw where her eyes went, to the inside of the half-shut door. A cross was cut there, putting me in mind of the grave by the trail.

"It must have been Hosea Palmer's cabin. He's dead and buried now. Who buried him?"

She shook her head. "That wonders me, too. All I know is, a good friend did it years ago. Sometimes, when I reckon maybe it's a Sunday, I say a prayer by the grave and sing a hymn. It seems brighter when I sing, looking up to the sky."

"Maybe I can guess the song you sing, Evadare." And I touched the guitar again, and both of us sang it:

> Lights in the valley outshine the sun—
> Look away beyond the blue!

As we sang I kept thinking in my heart—how pretty her voice, and how sweet the words in Evadare's mouth.

She went on to tell me how she hoped to live. She'd fetched in meal and salt and not much else, and she'd stretched it by picking wild greens, and there were some nuts here and there around the old cabin, poked away in little handfuls like the work of squirrels; though neither of us had seen a squirrel in Hosea's Hollow. She had planted cabbages and seed corn, and reckoned these would be worth eating by deep summer. She was made up in her mind to stay in Hosea's Hollow till she had some notion that Shull Cobart didn't lie in wait for her coming back.

"He's waiting," she felt sure. "He laughed when I spoke of running off. Said he'd know all I meant to do, all he needed was to wonder a thing while he played his fiddle and the answer was in his mind." Her pink tongue wet her lips. "He had a song he played, said it had power—"

"Was it maybe this one?" I asked, trying to jolly her, and again I touched the strings. I sang old words to the music I heard inside:

> My pretty little pink, I once did think
> That you and I would marry,
> But now I've lost all hope of you,
> And I've no time to tarry.
>
> I'll take my sack upon my back,
> My rifle on my shoulder,
> And I'll be off to the Western States
> To view the country over . . .

"That's the tune," she said, "but not the words." Again she shivered. "They were like something in a dream, while he played and sang along, and I felt I was trapped and tangled and webbed."

"Like something in a dream," I repeated her, and made up words like another thing I'd heard once, to fit the same music:

> I dreamed last night of my true love,
> All in my arms I had her,
> And her locks of hair, all long and fair,
> Hung round me like a shadow . . .

"That's not his song, either," said Evadare.

"No, it isn't," a voice I'd heard before came to agree her.

In through that half-open door stepped Shull Cobart, with his sooty hair and his grin, and his shiny black fiddle in his hand.

"Why don't you say me a welcome?" he asked Evadare, and cut his eyes across at me. "John, I counted on you being here, too."

Quick I leaned my guitar to the wall and got up. "Then you counted on trouble with me," I said. "Lay aside that fiddle so I won't break it when I break you."

But it was to his chin, and the bow across. "Hark before we fight," he said, and gentlemen, hush! how Shull Cobart could play.

It was the same tune, fiddled beyond my tongue's power to tell how wild and lovely. And the cabin that had had red-gold light from the fire and soft-gold light from Evadare's hair, it looked that quick to glow silver-pale, in jumping, throbbing sweeps as he played. Once, a cold clear dry winter night, I saw in the sky the Northern Lights; and the air in that cabin beat and throbbed and quivered the same way, but pale silver, I say, not warm red. And it came to my mind, harking helpless, that the air turned colder all at once than that winter night when I'd watched the Northern Lights in the sky.

I couldn't come at Shull Cobart. Somehow, to move at him was like moving neck-deep against a flooding river. I couldn't wear my way a foot closer. I sat on the stool again, and he stripped his teeth at me, grinning like a dog above a trapped rabbit.

"I wish the best for you, John," he said through the music. "Look how I make you welcome and at rest here."

I knew what way he wanted me to rest, the same way Hosea Palmer rested out yonder. I knew it wouldn't help to get up again, so I took back my guitar and sat quiet. I looked him up and down. He wore a suit of dark cloth with a red stripe, a suit that looked worth money, and his shoes were as shiny as his fiddle, ready to make manners before rich city folks. His mean dark eyes, close together above that singing, spell-casting fiddle, read my thoughts inside me.

"Yes, John, it's good cloth," he said. "My own weaving."

"I know how it was woven," Evadare barely whispered, the first words she'd spoken since Shull came in.

She'd moved halfway into a corner. Scared white—but she was a prettier thing than I'd ever seen in my life.

"Like me to weave for you?" he inquired me, mocking; and then he sang a trifly few words to his tune:

> I wove this suit and I cut this suit,
> And I put this suit right on,
> And I'll weave nine yards of other cloth
> To make a suit for John . . .

"Nine yards," I repeated after him.

"Would that be enough fine cloth for your suit?" he grinned across the droning fiddle strings. "You're long and tall, a right much of a man, but—"

"Nobody needs nine yards but for one kind of suit," I kept on figuring. "And that's no suit at all."

"A shroud," said Evadare, barely making herself heard, and how Shull Cobart laughed at her wide eyes and the fright in her voice!

"You reckon there'll be a grave for him here in Kalu's own place, Evadare?" he gobbled at her. "Would Kalu leave enough of John to be worth burying? I know about old Barebones Kalu."

"He's not hereabouts," Evadare half-begged to be believed. "Never once he bothered me."

"Maybe he's just spared you, hoping for something better,"

said Shull. "But he won't be of a mind to spare all of us that came here making a fuss in his home place. That's why I toled John here."

"You toled me?" I asked, and again he nodded.

"I played a little tune so you'd come alone, John. I reckoned Kalu would relish finding you here. Being he's the sort he is, and I'm the sort I am, it's you he'd make way with instead of me. That lets me free to take Evadare away."

"I'll not go with you," Evadare said, sharper and louder than I thought possible for her.

"Won't you, though?" Shull laughed.

His fiddle-music came up, and Evadare drew herself tight and strong, as if she leaned back against ropes on her. The music took on wild-sounding notes to fit into itself. Evadare's hands made fists, her teeth bit together, her eyes shut tight. She took a step, or maybe she was dragged. Another step she took, another, toward Shull.

I tried to get up, too, but I couldn't move as she was moving. I had to sit and watch, and I had the thought of that saying about how a snake draws a bird to his coil. I'd never believed such a thing till I saw Evadare move, step by step she didn't want to take, toward Shull Cobart.

Suddenly he stopped playing, and breathed hard, like a man who's been working in the fields. Evadare stood still and rocked on her feet. I took up my muscles to make a jump, but Shull pointed his fiddle-bow at me, like a gun.

"Have sense!" he slung out. "You've both learned I can make you go or stay, whichever I want, when I fiddle as I know how. Sit down, Evadare, and I'll silence my playing for the time. But make a foolish move, John, and I might play a note that would have the bones out of your body without ary bit of help from Kalu."

Bad man as he was, he told the truth, and both of us knew it. Evadare sat on the other stool, and I put my guitar across my knees. Shull Cobart leaned against the doorjamb, his fiddle low against his chest, and looked sure of himself. At that instant I was dead sure I'd never seen a wickeder face, not among all the wicked faces of the wide world.

"Know where I got this fiddle, you two?" he asked.

"I can guess," I said, "and it spoils my notion of how good a trader a certain old somebody is. He didn't make much of a swap, that fiddle for your soul; for the soul was lost before you bargained."

"It wasn't a trade, John." He plucked a fiddle-string with his thumbnail. "Just a sort of little present between friends."

"I've heard the fiddle called the devil's instrument," said Evadare, back to her soft whisper; and once again Shull Cobart laughed at her, and then at me.

"Folks have got a sight to learn about fiddles. This fiddle will make you and me rich, Evadare. We'll go to the land's great cities, and I'll play the dollars out of folks' pockets and the hearts out of folks' bodies. They'll honor me, and they'll bow their faces in the dirt before your feet."

"I'll not go with you," she told him again.

"No? Want me to play you right into my arms this minute? The only reason I don't, Evadare—and my arms want you, and that's a fact—I'd have to put down my fiddle to hold you right."

"And I'd be on you and twist your neck around like the stem on a watch," I added onto that. "You know I can do it, and so do I. Any moment it's liable to happen."

As he'd picked his fiddle-string, I touched a silver string of my guitar, and it sang like a honey-bee.

"Don't do that any more, John," he snapped. "Your guitar and my fiddle don't tune together. I'm a lone player."

To his chin went that shiny black thing, and the music he made lay heavy on me. He sang:

> I'll weave nine yards of other cloth
> For John to have and keep,
> He'll need it where he's going to lie,
> To warm him in his sleep . . .

"What are we waiting for?" I broke in. "You might kill me somehow with your fiddling, but you won't scare me."

"Kalu will do the scaring," he said as he stopped again. "Scare you purely to death. We're just a-waiting for him to come."

"How will we know—" began Evadare.

"We'll know," said Shull, the way he'd promise a baby child something. "We'll hear him. Then I'll play John out of here to stand face to face with Kalu, if it's really a face Kalu has."

I laughed myself, and heaven pardon me the lie I put into my laugh, trying to sound as if naught pestered me. Shull frowned; he didn't like how my laugh hit his ear.

"Just for argument's sake," I said to him, "how do you explain what you say your music can do?"

"I don't do any explaining. I just do the playing."

"I've heard tell how a fiddler can be skilled to where he plays a note and breaks a glass window," I recollected. "I've heard tell he might possibly even make a house fall down."

"Dogs howl when fiddles play," said Evadare. "From pain it makes."

Shull nodded at us both. "You folks are right. There's been power-music long before this. Ever hear of a man named Orpheus?"

"He was an old-timey Greek," I said.

"He played his harp, and trees danced for him. He played his way down to the floor of hell, and back out again. Maybe I've got some of that power. A fiddle can sing extra sharp or extra sweet, and its sound's solid—like a knife or club or rope, if you can work it."

I remembered in my mind that sound goes in waves like light, and can be measured; and a wave is power, whether of sound or light. Waves can wash, like the waves of the sea that strike down tall walls and strong men. Too bad, I decided, that educated folks couldn't use that black fiddle, to make its power good and useful. In devil-taught hands, it was the devil's instrument. Not like my silver-strung guitar, the way harps, certain harps in a certain high place, are said to be strung with gold . . .

Shull listened. You could almost see his ears stick up, like the ears of an animal. "Something's out there," he said.

I heard it, too. Not a step or a scramble, but a movement.

"Kalu," said Evadare, her eyes the widest yet in the firelight.

"Yes, it's Kalu," said Shull. "John, wouldn't it be kindlier to the lady if you met him outside?"

"Much kindlier," I agreed him, and got up.

"You know this isn't personal, John," Shull said, fiddle at his chin. "But Kalu's bound to have somebody. It won't be Evadare, because some way he's let her be. And it won't be me, with you here. You've got a reputation, John, for doing things against what Kalu stands to represent. I figure he wants something good, because he's got plenty of the strong evil."

"The way you think you've got to have Evadare," I said.

"That's it. You're in the line of what he wants to devour." He began to play again. "Come on, John."

I was coming. I'd made up my mind. The weight of the music was on me, but not quite as deadening and binding as before. Shull Cobart walked out, fiddling. I just winked at Evadare, as if I figured it would be all right. Then I walked out, too.

The light was greeny-pale, though I saw no moon. Maybe the trees hid it, or the haze in the sky.

"Where will you face him?" asked Shull, almost polite above his soft playing.

"There's a grave down yonder—" I began to say.

"Yes, just the place. Come on."

I followed after him on the trail. My left hand chorded my guitar at the neck, my right-hand fingers found the strings. What was it Evadare had told me? . . . *I say a prayer by the grave and sing a hymn. It seems brighter when I sing* . . .

Then there could be two kinds of power-music.

I began to pick the tune along with Shull, softer even than Evadare's whisper. He didn't hear; and, because I followed him like a calf to the slaughter-pen, he didn't guess.

Around the bend was the grave, the green light paler around it. Shull stopped. All of a quick, I knew Kalu was in the trees over us. Somewhere up there, he made a heaviness in the branches.

"Stand where you want to, John. I vow, you've played the man so far."

I moved past him, close to the cross, though there wasn't light enough to see the name or the prayer.

"Drop that guitar!" Shull howled at me.

For I began to play loud, and I sang to his tune, changing the rhythm for my own quick-made-up words:

I came to where the pilgrim lay,
Though he was dead and gone,
And I could hear his comrade say,
He rests in peace alone—

"Hush up with that!"

Shull Cobart stopped playing and ran at me. I ducked away and around the cross, and quick I sang the second verse:

Winds may come and thunders roll
And stormy tempests rise,
But here he sleeps with a restful soul
And the tears wiped from his eyes—

"Come for him, Kalu!" Shull screamed.

Kalu drop-leaped out of the branches between us.

Gentlemen, don't ask me to say too much what Kalu was. Bones, yes—something like man-bones, but bigger and thicker, also something like bear-bones, or big ape-bones from a foreign land. And a rotten light to them, so I saw for a moment that the bones weren't empty. Inside the ribs were caged puffy things, like guts and lungs and maybe a heart that skipped and wiggled. The skull had a snout like I can't say what, and in its eye-holes burned blue-green fire. Out came the arm-bones, and the finger-bones were on Shull Cobart.

I heard Shull Cobart scream one more time, and then Kalu had him, like a bullfrog with a minnow. And Kalu was back up in the branches. Standing by the grave, still tweaking my strings, I heard the branches rustle, and no more sounds after that from Shull Cobart.

After while, I walked to where the black fiddle lay. I stomped with my foot, heard it smash, and kicked the pieces away.

Walking back to the cabin seemed to take an hour. I stopped at the door.

"No!" moaned Evadare, and then she just looked at me. "John—but—"

"That's twice you thought I was Shull Cobart," I said.

"Kalu—"

"Kalu took *him*, not me."

"But—" she stopped again.

"I figured the truth about Kalu and Hosea Palmer, walking out with Shull," I began to explain. "All at once I knew why Kalu never pestered you. You'll wonder why you didn't know it, too."

"But—" she tried once more.

"Think," I bade her. "Who buried Hosea Palmer, with a cross and a prayer? What dear friend could he have, when he came in here alone? Who was left alive here when it was Hosea Palmer's time to die?"

She just shook her head from side to side.

"It was Kalu," I said. "Remember the story, all of it. Hosea Palmer said he knew how to stop Kalu's wickedness. Folks think Hosea destroyed Kalu some way. But what he did was teach him the good part of things. They weren't enemies. They were friends."

"Oh," she said. "Then—"

"Kalu buried Hosea Palmer," I finished for her, "and cut his name and the prayer. Hosea must have taught him his letters. But how could Shull Cobart understand that? It wasn't for us to know, even, till the last minute. And Kalu took the evil man, to punish him."

I sat on the door-log, my arms around my guitar.

"You can go home now, Evadare," I said. "Shull Cobart won't vex you again, by word of mouth or by sight of his face."

She'd been sitting all drawn up, as small as she could make herself. Now she managed to stand.

"Where will you go, John?"

"There's all the world for me to go through. I'll view the country over. Think me a kind thought once in a while when we're parted."

"Parted?" she said after me, and took a step, but not as if a web of music dragged her. "John. Let me come with you."

I jumped up. "With me? You don't want to go with me, Evadare."

"Let me come." Her hand touched my arm, trembling like a bird.

"How could I do that, take you with me? I live hard."

"I've not lived soft, John." But she said it soft and lovely, and it made my heart ache with what I hadn't had time before to feel for her.

"I don't have a home," I said.

"Folks make you welcome everywhere. You're happy. You have enough of what you need. There's music wherever you go. John, I want to hear the music and help the song."

I wanted to try to laugh that thought away, but I couldn't laugh. "You don't know what you say. Listen, I'll go now. Back to my camp, and I'll be out of here before sunup. Evadare, God bless you wherever you go."

"Don't you want me to go with you, John?"

I couldn't dare reply her the truth of that. Make her a wanderer of the earth, like me? I ran off. She called my name once, but I didn't stop. At my camp again, I sat by my died-out fire, wondering, then wishing, then driving the wish from me.

In the black hour before dawn, I got my stuff together and started out of Hosea's Hollow. I came clear of it as the light rose, and mounted up a trail to a ridge above. Something made me look back.

Far down the trail I'd come, I saw her. She leaned on a stick, and she carried some kind of bundle—maybe her quilts, and what little food she had. She was following.

"That fool-headed girl," I said, all alone to myself, and I up and ran down the far side. It was hours until I crossed the bottom below and mounted another ridge beyond. On the ridge I'd left behind I saw Evadare still moving after me, her little shape barely bigger than a fly. Then I thought of that song I've told you before:

> On yonder hill there stands a creature,
> Who she is I do not know,
> I will ask her if she'll marry . . .
> Oh, no, John, no, John, no!

But she didn't stand, she came on. And I knew who she was. And if I asked her to marry she wouldn't answer no.

The rest of that day I fled from her, not stopping to eat, only to grab mouthfuls of water from streams. And in the dusky last end of the day I sat quiet and watched her still coming, leaning on her stick for weariness, and knew I must go down trail to meet her.

She was at the moment when she'd drop. She'd lost her ribbon, and the locks of her hair fell round her like a shadow. Her dress was torn, her face was white-tired, and the rocks had cut her shoes to pieces and the blood seeped out of her torn feet.

She couldn't even speak. She just sagged into my arms when I held them out to her.

I carried her to my camp. The spring trickled enough so I could wash her poor cut feet. I put down her quilt and my blanket for her to sit on, with her back to a big rock. I mixed a pone of cornmeal to bake on a flat stone, and strung a few pieces of meat on a green twig. I brought her water in my cupped hand.

"John," she managed at last to speak my name.

"Evadare," I said, and we both smiled at each other, and I sat down beside her.

"I'll cease from wandering," I vowed to her. "I'll get a piece of land and put up a cabin. I'll plant and hoe a crop for us—"

"No such thing, John! I'm tired now—so tired—but I'll get over that. Let's just—view the country over."

I pulled my guitar to me, and remembered another verse to the old song that fitted Shull Cobart's tune:

> *And don't you think she's a pretty little pink,*
> *And don't you think she's clever,*
> *And don't you think that she and I*
> *Could make a match forever?*

WONDER AS I WANDER

Some Footprints on John's Trail Through
Magic Mountains

Then I Wasn't Alone

Reckoning I had that woodsy place all to myself, I began to pick *Pretty Saro* on my guitar's silver strings for company. But then I wasn't alone; for soft fluty music began to play along with me.

Looking sharp, I saw him through the green laurels right in front. He was young. He hadn't a shirt on. Nary razor had ever touched his soft yellowy young beard. To his mouth he held a sort of hollow twig and his slim fingers danced on and off a line of holes to make notes. Playing, he smiled at me.

I smiled back, and started *The Ring That Has No End*. Right away quick he was playing that with me, too, soft and sweet and high, but not shrill.

He must want to be friends, I told myself, and got up and held out a hand to him.

He whirled around and ran. Just for a second before he was gone, I saw that he was a man only to his waist. Below that he had the legs of a horse, four of them.

You Know the Tale of Hoph

The noon sun was hot on the thickets, but in his cabin was only blue dim light. His black brows made one streak above iron-colored eyes. "Yes, ma'am?" he said.

"I'm writing a book of stories," she said, and she was rose-faced and butter-haired. "I hear you know the tale of Hoph. How sailors threw him off a ship in a terrible storm a hundred years ago, but the sea swept him ashore and then he walked and walked until he reached these mountains. How he troubled the mountain people with spells and curses and sendings of nightmares."

His long white teeth smiled in his long white face. "But you know that story already."

"No, not all of it. What was Hoph's motivation in tormenting the people?"

"His food was the blood of pretty women," was what he replied her. "Each year he made them give him a pretty woman. When she died at the year's end, with the last drop of her blood gone, he made them give him another."

"Until he died too," she tried to finish.

"He didn't die. They didn't know that he had to be shot with a silver bullet."

Up came his hands into her sight, shaggy-haired, long-clawed. She screamed once.

From the dark corner where I hid I shot Hoph with a silver bullet.

Blue Monkey

"I'll turn this potful of pebbles into gold," the fat man told us at midnight, "if you all keep from thinking about a blue monkey."

He poured in wine, olive oil, salt, and with each he said a certain word. He put the lid on and walked three times around the pot, singing a certain song. But when he turned the pot over, just the pebbles poured out.

"Which of you was thinking about a blue monkey?"

They all admitted they'd thought of nothing else. Except me—I'd striven to remember exactly what he'd said and done. Then everybody vowed the fat man's gold-making joke was the laughingest thing they'd seen in a long spell.

One midnight a year later and far away, I shovelled pebbles into another pot at another doings, and told the folks: "I'll turn them into gold if you all can keep from thinking about a red fish."

I poured in the wine, the olive oil, the salt, saying the word that went with each. I covered the pot, walked the three times, sang the song. Then I asked: "Did anybody think about a blue monkey?"

"But, John," said the prettiest lady, "you said not to think about a red fish, and that's what I couldn't put from my mind."

"I said that to keep you from thinking about a blue monkey," I said, and tried to tip the pot over.

But it had turned too heavy to move. I lifted the lid. There inside the pebbles shone yellow. The prettiest lady picked up two or three. They clinked together in her pink palm.

"Gold!" she squeaked. "Enough to make you rich, John!"

"Divide it up among yourselves," I said. "Gold's not what I want, nor yet richness."

The Stars Down There

"I mean it," she said again. "You can't go any farther, because here's where the world comes to its end."

She might could have been a few years older than I was, or a few years younger. She was thin-pretty, with all that dark hair and those wide-stretched eyes. The evening was cool around us, and the sun's last edge faded back on the way I'd come.

"The world's round as a ball," and I kicked a rock off the cliff. "It goes on forever."

And I harked for the rock to hit bottom, but it didn't.

"I'm not trying to fool you," she said. "Here's the ending place of the world. Don't step any closer."

"Just making to look down into the valley," I told her. "I see mist down there."

"It isn't mist."

And it wasn't.

For down there popped out stars in all their faithful beauty, the same way they were popping out over our heads. A skyful of stars. No man could say how far down they were.

"I ask your pardon for doubting you," I said. "It's sure enough the ending place of the world. If you jumped off here, you'd fall forever and ever."

"Forever and ever," she repeated me. "That's what I think. That's what I hope. That's why I came here this evening."

Before I could catch hold of her, she'd jumped. Stooping, I saw her falling, littler and littler against the stars down there, till at last I could see her no more.

Find the Place Yourself

It might be true that there's a curse on that house. It's up a mountain cove that not many know of, and those who do know won't talk to you about it. So if you want to go there you'll have to find the place yourself.

When you reach it, you won't think at first it's any great much. Just a little house, half logs and half whip-sawed planks, standing quiet and gray and dry, the open door daring you to come in.

But don't you go taking any such a dare. Nor don't look too long at the bush by the door-stone, the one with flowers of three different colors. Those flowers will look back at you like hard, mean faces, with eyes that hold yours.

In the trees over you will be wings fluttering, but not bird wings. Round about you will whisper voices, so soft and faint they're like voices you remember from some long-ago time, saying things you wish you could forget.

If you get past the place, look back and you'll see the path wiggle behind you like a snake after a lizard. Then's when to run like a lizard, run your fastest and hope it's fast enough.

I Can't Claim That

When I called Joss Kift's witch-talk a lie, Joss swore he'd witch-kill me in thirteen days.

Then in my path a rag doll looking like me, with a pin stuck through the heart. Then a black rooster flopping across my way with his throat cut, then a black dog hung to a tree, then other things. The thirteenth dawn, a whisper from nowhere that at midnight a stick with my soul in it would be broken thirteen times and burnt in a special kind of fire.

I lay on a pallet bed in Tram Colley's cabin, not moving, not speaking, not opening my mouth for the water Tram tried to spoon to me. Midnight. A fire blazed outside. Its smoke stunk. My friends around me heard the stick break and break and break, heard Joss laugh. Then Joss stuck his head in the window above me to snicker and say: "Ain't he natural-looking?"

I grabbed his neck with both hands. He dropped and hung

across the sill like a sock. When they touched him, his heart had stopped, scared out of beating.

I got up. "Sorry he ended thataway," I said. "I was just making out that I was under his spell, to fool him."

Tram Colley looked at me alive and Joss dead. "He'll speak no more wild words and frightful commands," he said.

"I reckon it's as I've heard you say, Grandsire," said a boy. "Witch-folks can't prevail against a pure heart."

"I can't claim that," I said.

For I can't. My heart's sinful, and each day I hope it's less sinful than yesterday.

Who Else Could I Count On

"I reckon I'm bound to believe you," I admitted to the old man at last. "You've given me too many proofs. It couldn't be any otherwise but that you've come back from the times forty years ahead of now."

"You believe because you can believe wonders, John," he said. "Not many could be made to believe anything I've said."

"This war that's going to be," I started to inquire him, "the one that nobody's going to win—"

"The war that everybody's going to lose," he broke in. "I've come back to this day and time to keep it from starting if I can. Come with me, John. We'll go to the men that rule this world. We'll make them believe, too, make them see that the war mustn't start."

"Explain me one thing first," I said.

"What's that?" he asked.

"If you were an old man forty years ahead of now, then you must have been young right in these times." I talked slowly, trying to clear the idea for both of us. "If that's so, what if you meet the young man you used to be?"

So softly he smiled: "John," he said, "why do you reckon I sought you out of all men living today?"

"Lord have mercy!" I said.

"Who else could I count on?"

"Lord have mercy!" I said again.

FARTHER DOWN THE TRAIL

JOHN'S MY NAME

Where I've been is places and what I've seen is things, and there've been times I've run off from seeing them, off to other places and things. I keep moving, me and this guitar with the silver strings to it, slung behind my shoulder. Sometimes I've got food with me and an extra shirt maybe, but most times just the guitar, and trust to God for what I need else.

I don't claim much. John's my name, and about that I'll only say I hope I've got some of the goodness of good men who've been named it. I'm no more than just a natural man; well, maybe taller than some. Sure enough, I fought in the war across the sea, but so does near about every man in war times. Now I go here and go there, and up and down, from place to place and from thing to thing, here in among the mountains.

Up these heights and down these hollows you'd best go expecting anything. Maybe everything. What's long time ago left off happening outside still goes on here, and the tales the mountain folks tell sound truer here than outside. About what I tell, if you believe it you might could get some good thing out of it. If you don't believe it, well, I don't have a gun out to you to make you stop and hark at it.

WHY THEY'RE NAMED THAT

If the gardinel's an old folks' tale, I'm honest to tell you it's a true one.

Few words about them are best, I should reckon. They look some way like a shed or cabin, snug and rightly made, except the open door might could be a mouth, the two little windows might could be eyes. Never you'll see one on main roads or near towns;

only back in the thicketty places, by high trails among tall ridges, and they show themselves there when it rains and storms and a lone farer hopes to come to a house to shelter him.

The few that's lucky enough to have gone into a gardinel and win out again, helped maybe by friends with axes and corn knives to chop in to them, tell that inside it's pinky-walled and dippy-floored, with on the floor all the skulls and bones of those who never did win out; and from the floor and the walls come spouting rivers of wet juice that stings, and as they tell this, why, all at once you know that inside a gardinel is like a stomach.

Down in the lowlands I've seen things grow they name the Venus flytrap and the pitcher plant, that can tole in bugs and flies to eat. It's just a possible chance that the gardinel is some way the same species, only it's so big it can tole in people.

Gardinel. Why they're named that I can't tell you, so don't inquire me.

NONE WISER FOR THE TRIP

Jabe Mawks howdied Sol Gentry, cutting up a fat deer in his yard. Sol sliced off enough for a supper and did it up in newspaper for Jabe to carry home, past Morg McGeehee's place that you can see from Sol's gate, and from where you can see Jabe's cabin.

Jabe never got home that day. As if the earth had opened, he was swallowed up. Only that wrapped-up meat lay on the trail in front of Morg's. The high sheriff questioned. Jabe's wife sought but did not find. Some reckoned Jabe to be killed and hid, some told he'd fled off with some woman. Twenty-eight long years died.

When one day Morg hollered from his door: "Jabe Mawks!"

"Where's the meat?" Jabe asked to know. "Where's it gone?"

He looked no older than when last he was there. He wore old wool pants, new checked shirt, broad brown hat, he'd worn that other day. "Where's the meat?" he wondered Morg.

Jabe's wife was dead and gone, and he didn't know his children, grown up with children of their own. He just knew he didn't have that deer meat he'd been fetching home for supper.

Science men allow maybe there's a nook in space and time you can stumble in and be lost beyond power to follow or seek, till by chance you stumble out again. But if that's so, Jabe is none wiser for the trip.

Last time I saw him, he talked about that deer meat Sol gave him. "It was prime," he said, "I had my mouth all set for it. Wish we had it now, John, for you and me to eat up. But if twenty-eight years sure enough passed me on my way home, why, they passed me in the blink of an eye."

NARY SPELL

Fifty of us paid a dollar to be in the Walnut Gap beef shoot, and Deputy Noble set the target, a two-inch diamond cut in white paper on a black-charred board, and a cross marked in the diamond for us to try at from sixty steps away.

All reckoned first choice of beef quarters was betwixt Niles Lashly and Eby Coffle. Niles aimed, and we knew he'd loaded a bat's heart and liver in with his bullet. Bang!

Deputy Noble went to look. "Drove the cross," he hollered us. "The up-and-down-mark, just above the sideways one."

Then Eby. He'd dug a skull from an old burying ground and poured lead through the eye-hole into his bullet mold. Bang!

Deputy Noble looked and hollered: "Drove the cross, too, just under that there line-joining."

Eby and Niles fussed over who'd won, while I took my turn, with Luns Lamar's borrowed rifle. Bang! Deputy Noble looked, and looked again.

"John's drove the cross plumb center!" he yelled. "Right where them two lines cross, betwixt the other two best shots!"

Niles and Eby bug-eyed at me. "Whatever was your spell, John?" they wondered to know.

"Nary spell," I said. "But in the army I was the foremost shot in my regiment, foremost shot in my brigade, foremost shot in my division. Preacher Ricks, won't you cut up this quarter of beef for whoever's families need it most round Walnut Gap?"

TRILL COSTER'S BURDEN

After Evadare caught up with me on that high mountain, her poor feet were worn so sore that we stayed there all next day. I snared a rabbit for dinner and dried its sinews by the fire and sewed up her torn shoes with them. Our love talk to one another would have sounded stupid to air other soul on earth. Next morning we ate our last smoked meat and corn pone, and Evadare allowed, "I can walk with a staff, John." So I bundled our two packs behind my back and slung my guitar on top. Off southwest, we reckoned, was another state line. Across that, folks could marry without a long wait or a visit to the county seat.

For hours we made it slantways down the mountain side and then across rocks in a river. We climbed a ridge beyond, midway towards evening, and saw a narrower stream below. There was a wagon track across and cabins here and yonder and, on the stream's far side, a white steepled church and folks there, little as ants.

"We'll head there," I said, and she smiled up from under the bright toss of her hair. Down we came, Evadare a-limping with her staff. At the stream I picked her up like a flower and waded over. Not one look did the folks at the church give us, so hard they harked at what a skinny little man tried to say.

"Here's sixty dollars in money bills," he hollered, "for who'll take her sins and set her soul free."

I set Evadare down. We saw a dark-painted pine coffin among those dozen ladies and men. Shadow looked to lie on and around the coffin, more shadow than it could cast by itself. The man who talked looked pitiful, and his hair was gravel-gray.

"Who'll do it?" he begged to them. "I'll pay seventy-five. No, a hundred—my last cent." He dug money from his jeans pocket. "Here's a hundred. Somebody do it for Trill and I'll pray your name in my prayers forevermore."

He looked at a squatty man in a brown umbrella hat. "Bart, if—"

"Not for a thousand dollars, Jake," said the squatty man. "Not for a million."

The man called Jake spoke to a well-grown young woman with brown hair down on her bare shoulders. "Nollie," he said, "I'd take Trill's sins on myself if I could, but I can't. I stayed by her, a-knowing what she was."

"You should ought to have thought of that when you had the chance, Jake," she said, and turned her straight back.

In the open coffin lay a woman wrapped in a quilt. Her hair was smoky-red. Her shut-eyed face had a proud beauty look, straight-nose and full-lipped. The man called Jake held out the money to us.

"A hundred dollars," he whined. "Promise to take her sins, keep her from being damned to everlasting."

I knew what it was then, I'd seen it once before. Sin-eating. Somebody dies after a bad life, and a friend or a paid person agrees the sin will be his, not the dead one's. It's still done here and there, far back off from towns and main roads.

"I'll take her sins on me, John," said Evadare to me.

Silence then, so you might could hear a leaf drop. Jake started in to cry. "Oh, ma'am," he said, "tell me your name so's I can bless it to all the angels."

Somebody laughed a short laugh, but when I turned round, nair face had nair laugh on it.

"I'm called Evadare, and this is John with me."

"Take it." Jake pushed the money at her.

"I wouldn't do such a thing for money," Evadare said. "Only to give comfort by it, if I can."

Jake blinked his wet eyes at her. The squatty man shut the coffin lid. "All right, folks," he said, and he and three others took hold and lifted. The whole bunch headed in past the church, to where I could see the stones of a burying ground. Round us the air turned dull, like as if a cloud had come up in the bright evening sky.

Jake hung back a moment. "Better you don't come in," he mumbled, and followed the others.

"I do hope I did right," said Evadare, to herself and me both.

"You always do right," I replied her.

We walked to where some trees bunched on the far side of the wagon road. I dropped our bundles under a sycamore. We could see the folks a-digging amongst the graves. I got sticks and made us a fire. Evadare sat on a root. Chill had come into the air, along with that dimness. We talked, love talk but not purely cheerful talk. The sunset looked bloody-red in the west.

The folks finished the burying and headed off this way and that. I'd hope to speak to somebody, maybe see if Evadare could stay the night in a house. But they made wide turns not to come near us. I looked in my soogin sack to see if we had aught left to eat. But nair crumb.

"There's still some coffee in my bundle," said Evadare.

"That'll taste good." I took the pot to the stream and scooped up water. Somebody made a laughing noise and I looked up.

"I didn't get your name," said the bare-shouldered woman, a-smiling her mouth at me.

"John," I said. "I heard you called Miss Nollie."

"Nollie Willoughby."

Her eyes combed me up and down in that last light of day. They were brown eyes, with hard, pale lights behind them.

"Long and tall, ain't you, John?" she said. "You nair took Trill Coster's sins—only that little snip you're with did that. If you've got the sense you look to have, you'll leave her and them both, right now."

"I've got the sense not to leave her," I said.

"Come with me," she bade me, a-smiling wider.

"No, ma'am, I thank you."

I walked off from her. As I came near the trees, I heard Evadare say something, then a man's voice. Quick I moved the coffeepot to my left hand and fisted up my right and hurried there to see what was what.

The fire burned with blue in its red. It showed me the Jake fellow, a-talking to Evadare where she sat on the root. He had a bucket of something in one hand and some tin dishes in the other.

"John," he said as I came up, "I reckoned I'd fetch youins some supper."

"We do thank you," I replied him, a-meaning it. "Coffee will be ready directly. Sit down with us and have a cup," and I set the pot on a stone amongst the fire and Evadare poured in the most part of our coffee.

Jake dropped down like somebody weary of this world. "I won't stay long," he said. "I'd only fetch more sins on you." He looked at Evadare. "On her, who's got such a sight of them to pray out the way it is."

Evadare took the bucket. It was hot squirrel stew and made two big bowls full. We were glad for it, I tell you, and for the coffee when it boiled. Jake's cup trembled in his hand. He told us about Trill Coster, the woman he still loved in her grave, and it wasn't what you'd call a nice tale to hear.

She'd been as beautiful as a she-lion, and she'd used her beauty like a she-lion, a-gobbling men. She could make men swear away their families and lives and hopes of heaven. For her they'd thieve or even kill, and go to jail for it. And not a damn she'd given for what was good. She'd dared lightning to strike her; she'd danced round the church and called down a curse on it. Finally all folks turned from her—all but Jake, who loved her though she'd treated him like a dog. And when she'd died on a night of storm, they said bats flew round her bed.

Jake had stayed true to her who was so false. And that's how come him to want to get somebody to take her sins.

"For her sins run wild round this place, like foxes round a hen roost," he said. "I can hear them."

I heard them too, not so much with my ears as with my bones.

"I promised I'd pray them away," Evadare reminded him. "You'd best go, Jake. Leave me to deal with them."

He thanked her again and left.

Full dark by then outside the ring of firelight, and we weren't alone there. I didn't see or hear plain at first, it was more like just a sense of what came. Lots of them. They felt to be a-moving close, the way wolves would shove around a campfire in the old days, to get up their nerve to rush in. A sort of low crouch of them in the dark, and here and there some sort of height half-guessed. Like as if one or other of them stood high, or possibly climbed a tree branch. I stared and tried to reckon if there were shapes there, blacker than the night, and couldn't be sure one way or the other.

"I'm not about to be afraid," said Evadare, and she knew she had to say that thing out loud for it to be true.

"Don't be," I said. "I've heard say that evil can't prevail against a pure heart. And your heart's pure. I wish mine was halfway as pure as yours."

I pulled my guitar to me and touched the silver strings, to help us both.

"They say there are seven deadly sins," said Evadare. "I've heard them named, but I can't recollect them all."

"I can," I said. "Pride. Covetousness. Lust. Envy. Greed. Anger. Gluttony. Who is there that mustn't fight to keep free from all of them?"

I began to pick and sing, words of my own making to the tune of "Nine Yards of Other Cloth":

> *And she's my love, my star above,*
> *And she's my heart's delight,*
> *And when she's here I need not fear*
> *The terror in the night.*

"Who was that laughed?" Evadare cried out.

For there'd been a laugh, that died away when she spoke. I stopped my music and harked. A different noise now. A stir, like something that tried not to make a sound but made one anyway, the ghost of a sound you had to strain to hear.

I set down my guitar and stood up. I said, loud and clear:

"Whoever or whatever's in sound of my voice, step up here close and look at the color of my eyes."

The noise had died. I looked all the way round.

Deep night now, beyond where the fire shone. But I saw a sort of foggy-muddy cloud at a slink there. I thought maybe somebody had set a smudge fire and the wind blew the smoke to us. Only there was no wind. The air was as still as a shut-up room. I looked at the sky. There were little chunks of stars and about half a moon, with a twitch of dim cloud on it. But down where I was, silence and stillness.

"Look at those sparks," said Evadare's whispery voice.

First sight of them, they sure enough might could have been sparks—greeny ones. Then you made out they were two and two in that low dark mist, two and two and two, like eyes, like the green eyes of meat-eating things on the look for food. All the way round they were caught and set by pairs in the mist that bunched and clotted everywhere, close to the ground, a-beginning to flow in, crowd in.

And it wasn't just mist. There were shapes in it. One or two stood up to maybe a man's height, others made you think of dogs, only they weren't dogs. They huddled up, they were sort of stuck together—jellied together, you might say, the way a hobby of frog's eggs lie in a sticky bunch in the water. If it had been just at one place; but it was all the way round.

I tried to think of a good charm to say, and I've known some, but right then they didn't come to mind. I grabbed up a stick from the pile for whatever good might come of it. I heard Evadare, her voice strong now:

"Thou shalt not be afraid for the terror by night."

The dark things churned, the eye-sparks blinked. I could swear that they gave back for the length of a step.

"Nor for the arrow that flieth by day," Evadare said on. "Nor for the pestilence that walketh in darkness."

They shrank back on themselves again. They surrounded us, but they were back from where they'd been.

"What did you say to them?" I inquired Evadare, still with the stick ready.

"The Ninety-first Psalm," she said back. "It was all I could think of that might could possibly help."

"It helped," I said, and thought how I'd stood like a gone gump, not able to call up one good word to save us. "If those were sins a-sneaking in," I said, "there was a sight of them, but good words made them wait."

"How long will they wait?" she wondered me, little and huddled down by the fire. She was scared, gentlemen; and, now I reckon about it, so was I.

Those many sins, a-taking shape and hungry to grab onto somebody. One might not be too bad. You'd face up to one, maybe drive it back, maybe get it down and stomp it. But all of those together all sides of you, gummed into one misty mass. Being scared didn't help. You had to think of something to do.

Think what?

No way to run off from Trill Coster's sins, bunched all round us. Maybe the firelight slowed them some, slowed the terror by night, the pestilence in darkness. Evadare had taken them on her, and here they were. She kept whispering prayers. Meanwhile, they'd pulled back some. Now their eye-sparks showed thirty or forty feet away, all directions. I put wood on the fire. The flames stood up, not so much blue in the red now.

I took up my guitar and dared sit down. Old folks allow the devil is afraid of music. I picked and I sang:

> The needle's eye that doth supply
> The thread that runs so true,
> And many a lass have I let pass
> Because I thought of you.
>
> And many a dark and stormy night
> I walked these mountains through;
> I'd stub my toe and down I'd go
> Because I thought of you.

Then again a loud, rattling laugh, and I got up. The laugh again. Into the firelight there walked that bare-shouldered woman called Nollie Willoughby, a-weaving herself while she walked, a-clapping her hands while she tossed her syrupy hair.

"I call that pretty singing, John," she laughed to me. "You aim to sleep here tonight? The ground makes a hard bed, that's a natural fact. Let me make you up a soft bed at my place."

"I mustn't go from here right now," said Evadare's soft voice. "I've got me something to do hereabouts."

Nollie quartered her eyes round to me. "Then just you come, John. I done told you it'll be a soft bed."

"I thank you most to death," I said, "but no, ma'am, I stay here with Evadare."

"You're just a damned fool," she scorned me.

"A fool, likely enough," I agreed her. "But not damned. Not yet."

She sat down at the fire without being bid to. There was enough of her to make one and a half of Evadare, and pretty too, but no way as pretty as Evadare—no way.

"All the folks act pure scared to come near youins," she told us. "I came to show there's naught to fear from Trill Coster's sins. I nair feared her nor her ways when she lived. I don't fear them now she's down under the dirt. All the men that followed her round—they'll follow me round now."

"Which is why you're glad she's dead," Evadare guessed. "You were jealous of her."

Nollie looked at her, fit to strike her dead. "Not for those sorry men," she said. "I don't touch other women's leavings." She put her eyes to me. "You don't look nor act like that sort of man, John. I'll warrant you're a right much of a man."

"I do my best most times," I said.

"I might could help you along," she smiled with her wide lips.

"Think that if it pleasures you," I said. I thought back on women I'd known. Donie Carawan, who'd sweet-talked me the night the Little Black Train came for her; Winnie, who'd blessed my name for how I'd finished the Ugly Bird; Vandy, whose song I still sang now and then; but above and past them all, little Evadare, a-sitting tired and worried there by the fire, with the crowd and cloud of another woman's sins she'd taken, all round her, a-trying to dare come get hold of her.

"If I'd listen to you," I said to Nollie. "If I heeded one mumbling word of your talk."

"Jake said you're named Evadare," said Nollie across the fire. "You came here with John and spoke up big to take Trill's sin-burden and pray it out. What if I took that burden off you and took John along with it?"

"You done already made John that offer," said Evadare, quiet and gentle, "and he told you what he thought of it."

"Sure enough," Nollie laughed her laugh, with hardness in it. "John's just a-playing hard to get."

"He's hard to get, I agree you," said Evadare, "but he's not a-playing."

"Getting right cloudy round here," Nollie said, a-looking over that smooth bare shoulder of hers.

She spoke truth. The clumpy mist with its eye-greens was on the move again, like before. It hung close to the ground. I saw tree branches above it. The shapes in it were half-shapes. I saw one like what children make out of snow for a man, but this was dark, not snowy. It had head, shoulders, two shiny green eyes. Webbed next to it, a bunch of the things that minded you of dogs without being dogs. Green eyes too, and white flashes that looked like teeth.

Those dog things had tongues too, out at us, like as if to lap at us. Evadare was a-praying under her breath, and Nollie laughed again.

"If you fear sin," she mocked us, "you go afraid air minute of your life."

That was the truth too, as I reckoned, so I said nothing. I looked on the half-made hike of the man shape. It molded itself while I looked. Up came two steamy rags like arms. I wondered myself if it had hands, if it could take hold; if it could grab Evadare, grab me.

One arm-rag curled up high and whipped itself at us. It threw something—a whole mess of something. A little rain of twinkles round the root where Evadare had sat since first we built the fire.

"Oh," she whispered, not loud enough for a cry.

I ran to her, to see if she'd been hit and hurt. She looked down at the scatter of bright things round her. I knelt to snatch one up.

By the firelight, I saw that it was a jewel. Red as blood, bright as fire. I'm no jeweler, but I've seen rubies in my time. This was a big one.

Evadare bent with both hands out, to pick the things up. From the mist stole out soft noises, noises like laughter—not as loud as Nollie could laugh, but meaner, uglier.

"Don't take those things," I said to Evadare. "Not from what wants to give them to you." I sent myself to throw that big ruby.

"No," said Evadare, and got up, too. "I must do it. I'm the one who took the sins. I'm the one to say no to them."

She made a flinging motion with her arm, underhand, the way girls are apt to throw. I saw those jewels wink in the firelight as they sailed through the air. Red for rubies, white for diamonds, other colors for other ones. They struck in among the misty shapes. I swear they plopped, like stones flung in greasy water.

"Give me," she said, and took the big ruby from me. She flung it after the others. It made a singy sound in the air. Back from the cloudy mass beat a tired, hunting breath, like somebody pained and sorrowed.

"All right," said Evadare, the strongest she'd spoken since first we'd made out camp. "I've given them back their pay, refused all of it."

"Did you?" Nollie sort of whinnied.

"You saw me give them back," Evadare said. "All of them."

"No, not all of them, look at this."

Nollie held out her open palm. There lay a ruby, big as a walnut, twice the size of the one I'd taken up.

"How many thousands do you reckon that's worth?" Nollie jabbered at us, her teeth shining. "I got it when it fell, and I'm a-going to keep it."

"Miss Nollie," I said, "you should ought to have seen enough here tonight to know you can't keep air such a thing."

"Can't I?" she jeered me. "Just watch me, John. I'll take it to a big town and sell it. I'll be the richest somebody in all these parts."

"Better give it to Evadare to throw back," I said.

"Give it to little half-portion, milky-face Evadare? Not me."

She poked the ruby down the front of her dress, deep down there.

"It'll be safe where it's at," she snickered at us. "Unless you want to reach a hand down yonder for it, John."

"Not me," I said. "I want no part of it, nor yet of where you put it."

"John," said Evadare, "look at how the cloud bunches away."

I looked; it drew back with all its shapes, like the ebb tide on the shore of the sea.

"Sure enough," I said. "It's a-leaving out of here."

"And so am I," spoke up Nollie. "I came here to talk sense to you, John. You ain't got the gift to know sense where you hear it. Come visit me when I get my money and put up my big house here."

She swung, she switched away, a-moving three directions at once, the way some women think they look pretty when they do it. She laughed at us once, over her shoulder so bare. Evadare made a move, like as if to try to fetch her back, but I put my hand on Evadare's arm.

"You've done more than your duty tonight," I said. "Let her go."

So Evadare stood beside me while Nollie switch-tailed off amongst the trees. I reckoned the misty shapes thickened up at Nollie, but I couldn't be dead sure. What I did make out was, they didn't fence us in now. I saw clearness all the way round. The moon washed the earth with its light.

Evadare sat down on the root again, dead tired. I built up the fire to comfort us. I struck a chord on the guitar to sing to her, I don't recollect what. It might could as well have been a lullaby. She sank down asleep as I sang. I put my soogin sack under her head for a pillow and spread a blanket on her.

But I didn't sleep. I sat there, awaiting for whatever possibly happened, and nothing happened. Nothing at all, all night. The dawn grayed the sky and far off away I heard a rooster crow. I put the last of our coffee in the pot to brew for us, all we could count on for breakfast. While I watched by the fire, three men came toward us. Evadare rose up and yawned.

"John," said Jake in his timid voice, "I bless the high heavens to see you and your lady all safe here. This here is Preacher Frank Ricks, and here's Squire Hamp Dolby, come along with me to make your acquaintance."

Preacher Ricks I'd met before. We shook hands together. He was thin and old, but still a-riding here and there to do what good was in his power. Squire Dolby was a chunk of a man with white hair and black brows. "Proud to know you, John," he said to me.

"I hurried in here just at sunrise," said Preacher Ricks. "I'd heard tell of poor Trill Coster's death, and I find she's already buried. And I heard tell, too, of the brave, kind thing your lady agreed to do to rest her soul."

"I hoped it would be merciful," said Evadare.

"How true you speak, ma'am," said Squire Dolby. "But the sins you said you'd take, they never came to you. They fastened somewhere else. Nollie Willoughby's gone out of her mind. Round her house it's all dark-shadowy, and she's in there, she laughs and cries at one and the same time. She hangs onto a little flint rock and says it's a ruby, richer than all dreams on this earth."

"Isn't it a ruby?" I inquired him.

"Why," he said, "the gravelly path to my house is strewed with rocks like that, fit for naught but just to be trod on."

"I fetched these folks here on your account, John," said Jake. "You done told me you and Evadare hoped to be married."

"And we can do that for you," allowed Preacher Ricks, with a smile to his old face. "Squire Dolby here has the legal authority to give you a license here and now."

"It's sure enough my pleasure," said Squire Dolby.

He had a pad of printed blanks. He put down Evadare's name and mine, and he and Jake signed for the witnesses.

"Why not right now, under these trees and this sky?" said Preacher Ricks, and opened his book. "Stand together here, you two. John, take Evadare's right hand in your right hand. Say these words after me when I tell you."

THE SPRING

Time had passed, two years of it, when I got back to those mountains again and took a notion to visit the spring.

When I was first there, there'd been just a muddy, weedy hole amongst rocks. A young fellow named Zeb Gossett lay there, a-burning with fever, a-trying-to drink at it. I pulled him onto some ferns and put my blanket over him. Then I knelt down and dragged out the mud with my hands, picked weeds away and bailed with a canteen cup. Third time I emptied the hole to the bottom, water came clear and sweet. I let Zeb Gossett have some, and then I built us a fire and stirred up a hoecake. By the time it was brown on both sides, he was able to sit up and eat half of it.

Again and again that night, I fetched him water, and it did him good. When I picked my silver-strung guitar, he even joined in to sing. Next day he allowed he was well, and said he'd stay right where such a good thing happened to him. I went on, for I had something else to do. But I left Zeb a little sack of meal and a chunk of bacon and some salt in a tin can. Now, returned amongst mountains named Hark and Wolter and Dogged, not far from Yandro, I went up the trail I recollected to see how the spring came on.

The high slope caved in there, to make a hollow grown with walnut and pine and hickory, and the spring showed four feet across, with stones set in all the way round. Beside the shining water hung a gourd ladle. Across the trail was a cabin, and from the cabin door came Zeb Gossett. "John," he called my name, "how you come on?"

We shook hands. He was fine-looking, young, about as tall as I am. His face was tanned and he'd grown a short brown beard. He wore jeans and a home-sewn blue shirt. "Who'd expect I'd find Zeb Gossett here?" I said.

"I live here, John. Built that cabin myself, and I've got title to two acres of land. A corn patch, potatoes and cabbages and beans and tomatoes. It's home. When you knelt down to make that spring give the water that healed me, I knew this was where I'd live. But come on in. I see you still tote that guitar."

His cabin was small but rightly made, of straight poles with neat-notched corner joints, whitewash on the clay chinking. There was glass in the windows to each side of the split-slab door. He led me into a square room with a stone fireplace and two chairs and a table. Three-four books on a shelf. The bed had a blazing-star quilt. Over the fire bubbled an iron pot with what smelled like stewing deer meat.

"Yes, I live here, and the neighborhood folks make me welcome," he said when we sat down. "I knew that spring had holy power. I watch over it and let others heal their ills with it."

"It was just a place I scooped out," I reminded him. "We had to have water for you, so I did it."

"It's cured hundreds of sick folks," he said. "I carried some to the Fleming family when they had flu, then others heard tell of it and came here. They come all the time. I don't take pay. I tell them, 'Kneel down before you drink, the way John did while he was a-digging. And pray before you drink, and give thanks afterwards.'"

"You shouldn't ought to give me such credit, Zeb."

"John," he said, "that's healing water. It washes away air bad thing whatsoever. It helps mend up broken bones even. Why, I've known folks drink it and settle family quarrels and lawsuits. It's a miracle, and you did it."

I wouldn't have that. I said, "Likely the power was in the water before you and I came here. I just cleaned the mud out."

"I know better, and so do you," Zeb grinned at me.

Outside, a sweet voice: "Hello, the house," it spoke. "Hello, Zeb, might could I take some water?"

He jumped up and went out like as if he expected to see angels. I followed him out, and I reckon it was an angel he figured he saw.

She was a slim girl, but not right small. In her straight blue dress and canvas shoes, with her yellow curls waterfalled down her back, she was pretty to see. In one hand she toted a two-gallon bucket. She smiled, and that smile made Zeb's knees buck.

"Tilda"—he said her name like a song—"you don't have to ask for water, just dip it. Somebody in your family ailing?"

"No, not exactly." Then her blue eyes saw me and she waited.

"This is my friend John, Tilda," said Zeb. "He dug the spring. John, this is Tilda Fleming. Her folks neighbor with me just round the trail bend."

"Proud to be known to you, ma'am," I made my manners, but she was a-looking at Zeb, half nervous, half happy.

"Who's the water for, then?" he inquired her.

"Why," she said, shy with every word, "that's why I wondered if you'd let me have it. You see, our chickens—" and she stopped again, like as if she felt shamed to tell it.

"Ailing chickens should ought to have whatever will help them, Zeb." I put in a word.

"That's a fact," said Zeb, "and a many a fresh egg your folks have given me, Tilda. So take water for them, please."

She dropped down on her knees and bowed her head above the spring. She was a pretty sight, a-doing that. I could tell that Zeb thought so.

But somebody else watched. I saw a stir beyond some laurel, and looked hard thataway.

It was another girl, older than Tilda, taller. Her hair was blacker than storm, and her pointy-chinned, pale face was lovely. She looked at Tilda a-kneeling by the spring and she sneered, and it showed her teeth as bright as glass beads.

Zeb didn't see her. He bent over Tilda where she knelt, was near about ready to kneel with her. I walked through the yard toward the laurel. That tall, black-haired girl moved into the open and waited for me.

She wore a long dress of tawny, silky stuff, hardly what you'd look for in the mountains. It hung down to her feet, but it held to her figure, and the figure was fine. She looked at me, impudent-faced. "I declare," she said in a sugary-deep voice, "this is the John we hear so much about. A fine-looking man, no doubt in the world about that. But that's a common name."

"I always reckoned it's been borne by a many a good man," I said. "How come you to know me?"

"I heard you and Zeb Gossett a-talking. I can hear at a considerable distance." Her wide, dark eyes crawled over me like spiders. "My name's Craye Sawtelle, John. You and I might could be profitable acquaintances to each other."

"I'm proud to be on good terms with most folks," I said. "You come to visit with Zeb, yonder?"

"Maybe, when that little snip trots her water bucket home." Craye Sawtelle looked at Tilda a-filling the pail, and for a second those bright teeth showed. "I have business to talk with Zeb. Maybe he'll find the wit to hark to it."

Zeb walked Tilda to the trail. Craye Sawtelle had come into the yard with me, and when Tilda walked on and Zeb turned back, Craye said, "Good day to you, Zeb Gossett," and he jumped like as if he'd been stuck with a pin.

"What can I do for you, Miss Craye?" he said.

She ran her eyes over him, too. "You know the answer to that. I'll make you a good offer for this house and this spring."

He shook his head till his young beard flicked in the air. "You know the place isn't for sale, and the spring water's free to all."

"Only if they kneel and pray by it." She smiled a chilly smile. "I'm not a praying sort, Zeb."

"Nobody's heart to kneel before God," said Zeb.

"I don't kneel to your God," she said.

"What god do you kneel to?" I inquired her, and her black eyes blazed round to me.

"You make what educated folks call an educated guess," she said to me. "If you know so much, why should I answer you?"

She turned back to Zeb. "What if I told you there's a question about your title here, that I could gain possession?"

"I'd say, let's go to the court house and find out."

"You're impossible," she shrilled at him. "But I'm reasonable. I'll give you time to think it over. Like sundown tomorrow."

Then she went off away, the other direction from Tilda. In that tawny dress, air line of her swayed.

Just then, the sun looked murkier over us. Here and there amongst the trees, the leaves showed their pale undersides, like before a storm comes.

"Let's go in and have something to eat," Zeb said to me.

It was a good deer-meat stew, with cornmeal dumplings. I had two helps. Zeb said he'd put in onions and garlic and thyme and bay leaf, with a dollop of wine from a bottle he kept for that. We finished up and drank black coffee. While we sipped, a sort of lonesome whinnying sound rose outside.

"That's an owl," said Zeb. "Bad luck this time of day."

"I figured this was the sort of place where owls hoot in the daytime and they have possums for yard dogs." I tried to crack the old joke, but Zeb didn't laugh.

"Let me say what's been here," he said. "The trouble's with that witch-girl, Craye Sawtelle. She makes profit by this and that—says strings of words supposed to make your crops grow, allows she can turn your cows or pigs sick unless you pay her. What she wants is this spring, this holy spring. Naturally, she figures it would make her rich."

"And you won't give it over."

"It's not mine to give, John. I reckon it saved my life—I'd have died without you knelt to scoop it clear for me. So I owe it to folks to let them cure themselves with it. Oh, Craye's tried everything. You've seen what sort she is. First off, she wanted us to be partners—in the spring and other things. That didn't work with me, and she got ugly. I'll banter you she's done things to the Flemings, like those sick chickens you heard tell of from Tilda. And she told me she'd put a curse on my corn patch. Things don't go right well there just now."

I picked my guitar. "Hark at this," I said:

> Three holy kings, four holy saints,
> At heaven's high gate that stand,
> Speak out to bid all evil wait
> And stir no foot or hand . . .

"Where'd you catch that song, John?"

"Long ago, from old Uncle T. P. Hinnard. He allowed it was a good song against bad stuff."

Zeb crinkled his eyes. "Like enough it is, but it sort of chills the blood. You know one of a different kind?"

The owl quivered its voice outside as I touched the strings again.

> *Her hair is of a brightsome color*
> *And her cheeks are rosy red,*
> *On her breast are two white lilies*
> *Where you long to lay your head.*

"Tilda," said Zeb, a-brightening up. "You made that song about Tilda."

"It's older than Tilda's great-grandsire," I told him, "but it'll do for her. I saw how she and you lean to one another."

"If it wasn't for Craye Sawtelle—" And he stopped.

"Tell me about her," I bade him, and he did.

She'd lived thereabouts before Zeb built his cabin. She followed witchcraft and didn't care a shuck who knew it. Some folks went to her for charms and helps, others were scared to say her name out loud. When Zeb began a-letting sick folks drink from the spring, she tried air way she knew to cut herself in. She'd tried to sweet-talk Zeb, even tried to move into his cabin with him. But by then he'd met Tilda Fleming and couldn't think of air girl but her.

"When she saw I wouldn't love her, she started in to make me fear her," he said. "She's done that thing, pretty much. You wonder yourself why I don't speak up to Tilda. I've got it in mind that if I did, Craye would do something awful to her. I don't know what it would be, likely I don't want to know."

I made the guitar string whisper to drown out the owl's voice. "What would she do with the spring if she had it?"

"Make folks pay for its water, I told you. Maybe turn its power round to do bad instead of good. I can't rightly say."

I leaned my guitar on the wall. "Maybe I'll just go out and walk round your place before the sun goes down."

"Be careful, John."

"Shoo," I said, "I'll do that. I may not be the smartest man in these mountains, but I'm sure enough the carefullest."

I went out at the door. The sun had dropped to a fold of the mountains. I walked back and looked at Zeb's rows of corn, his bean patch with pods a-coming on, the other beds of vegetables. Past his garden grew up trees, tall and close together, with shadowy dark amongst them.

"We meet again, John," said a voice I'd come to know.

"I reckoned we might, Miss Craye," I said, and out she came from betwixt two pines. She carried a stick of fresh wood, its bark peeled off.

"If I pointed this wand at you and said a spell," she said, "what would happen?"

"We'll never know without you try it."

She tossed her hair, black as a yard up a chimney on a dark night. Her teeth showed, bright and sharp. "That means you figure you've got help against spells," she said. "I'm not without help myself. I don't go air place without help."

"Then you must be hard pushed when it's not nigh."

I felt the presence of what she talked about. Back in the thicket, I knew, were gathered things. I couldn't see them, just felt them. A stir and a sigh back yonder.

"John," she said, "you could go farther and fare worse than by making a friend of me. You understand things these country hodges nair dreamt of. You've been up and down the world and grabbed onto truths here and there."

"I've done that thing," I agreed her, "and the poet wasn't right all the time when he said beauty was truth and truth was beauty. Truth can be right ugly now and then."

"Suppose Zeb Gossett was shown a quick way out of here," she said. "Suppose you and I got to be partners in the spring and other matters."

"What kind of partners?"

She winnowed close then. I made out she didn't have on air stitch under her silky dress. She was proudly made, and well she knew it. She stood so close she near about touched me.

"What kind of partners would you like us to be?" she whispered.

"Miss Craye," said I, "no, thank you. No partnerships in the spring or in you, either one."

If she'd had the power to kill me with a look, I'd have died then and there. For hell's worst fury is a woman scorned, says another poet.

"I don't know why I don't raise my voice and set my pack on you," she breathed out in my face, and drew off a step.

"Maybe I can make one of those educated guesses," I said. "Your pack might not be friendly to you, not when you've just failed at something."

"You're the failure!" she squeaked like a bat.

"A failure for you, like Zeb Gossett. Isn't the third time the charm? If it doesn't work the third time, where will the charm put you?"

"I gave you and Zeb Gossett till sundown tomorrow," she gritted out with her pointy teeth. "Just about twenty-four hours."

"We'll be here," I said.

She backed off amongst the trees. They tossed their branches, like as if in a high wind. I turned and went back to the cabin. As I helped Zeb do the dishes, I related him what had passed.

"You bluffed her out of something she might try on you," said Zeb.

"I wasn't a-bluffing. If she's got the power of evil, I've been up against that in my time, and folks will say evil nair truly won over me. I hope some power of good is in me."

"Sure it is," he said. "Look out yonder at that healing spring. But she says bad will fall on us by sundown tomorrow. How can we go all right against that?"

"I don't rightly know how to answer that," I made confession. "We'll play it by ear, same as I play this guitar." And I picked it up to change the subject.

Out yonder was a sound, like a whisper, but too soft and sneaky to be a real voice. And a shadow passed outside a window.

I stopped my picking. Zeb had taken a dark-covered book from the shelf and was opening it. "What's that?" I asked.

"The Bible." He flung the covers wide and stabbed down his finger. "I'm a-going to cast a sign for us."

I knew about that, open the Bible anywhere and put your finger on a text and look for guidance in it.

"Here, the last verse in thirteenth Mark." Zeb read it out: " 'And what I say unto you I say unto all, Watch.' "

"Watch," I repeated. "That's what we'll do tonight."

Shadows at the window again. Zeb looked in the Bible, but didn't read from it anymore. I picked my guitar, the tune of "Never Trust a Stranger." Outside rose a rush of wind, and when

I looked out it was darkened. Night, and, from what I could judge, no moon. The owl hooted. On the hearth, the fire burnt blue. Zeb got up and lit a candle. Its flame fluttered like a yellow leaf.

Then a scratchy peck at the door. Zeb looked at me, his eyes as wide as sunflowers. I put down the guitar and went to the door.

It opened by hiking the latch on a string. I cracked it inward a tad and looked at what was out there. A dog? It was as big as a big one, black and bristly-haired. Its eyes shone, likewise its teeth. It looked to be a-getting up on its hind legs, and for a second I thought its front paws were hairy hands.

"Thanks," I said to it, "whatever you got to sell, we don't want any."

I closed the door and the latch fell into place. I heard that big body a-pressing against the wood. A whiney little sound, then the wind again. Zeb put more wood on the fire, though it wasn't cold. "What must we do?" he asked.

"Watch, the way the Bible told us," I replied him.

Things moved heavily all round the cabin. A scratch at a window-pane. Feet tippy-toed on the roof.

"I reckon it's up to you, John," said Zeb, his Bible back in his hand. "Up to you to see us through this night. You've got good in you to stand off the bad."

I thought of saying that Craye had given us to sundown the next day, which should ought to mean we'd last till then. As to the good in me, I hoped it was there. But it's not a right thing to claim aught for yourself, just be thankful if it helps.

Zeb gave us both a whet out of a jug of good blockade, and again I picked guitar. He joined in with me to sing "Lonesome River Shore" and "Call Me from the Valley," and wanted me to do the one that had minded him of Tilda. Things quietened outside while we sang. The devil's afraid of music. I'd heard tell from a preacher in a church house one time.

But when I put the guitar by, I heard another kind of singing. It was outside, it was a moanish tune and a woman's voice a-doing it. I tried to make out the words:

> *Cummer, go ye before, cummer, go ye,*
> *Gif ye not go before, cummer, let me . . .*

And I'd heard that same song before. It was sung, folks said, near about four hundred years back, at North Berwick, in Scotland, to witch a king on his throne and the princess he wanted to marry. I didn't reckon I'd tell Zeb that.

"Sounds like Craye Sawtelle's voice," he said as he listened. "What does cummer mean, John?"

"I think that's an old-timey word for a chum, a friend," I replied him.

"Then what cummers are out there with Craye?" His face was white—so white I never mentioned the dog-thing that had come to the door.

"She'd better not fetch her cummers in here," I said to hearten him. "They might could hear what wouldn't please them."

"Hear what?"

I had to tell him something, so I took the guitar and sang:

> *Lights in the valley outshine the sun,*
> *Look away beyond the blue . . .*

He looked to feel better. Outside, the other singing died out.

"Would it help if we had crosses at the windows?" he asked, and I nodded him it wouldn't hurt. He tied splinters of firewood crosswise with twine string and put two at the windows and hung another to the latch of the door. Out yonder, somebody moaned like as if the somebody had felt a pain somewhere. Zeb actually grinned at that.

Time dragged by, and the wind sighed round the cabin, or anyway something with a voice like wind. I yawned and stretched, and told him I felt like sleep.

"Take the bed yonder," Zeb bade me. "I'll sit up. I won't be able to sleep."

"That's what you think," I said. "Get into your bed. I'll put down this blanket I fetched with me, just inside the door."

And I did, and wropped up in it. I didn't stay awake long, though once it sounded like as if something sniffed at where the door came down to the bottom. Shoo, gentlemen, you can sleep if you're tired enough.

What woke me up was the far-off crow of a rooster. I was glad to hear that, because a rooster's crow makes bad spirits leave. I rolled over and got up. Zeb was at the fireplace, with an iron fork to toast pieces of bread. A saucepan was a-boiling eggs.

"We're still here," he said. "It wonders me what Craye Sawtelle was up to last night."

"Just a try at scaring us," I said. "She gave us till sundown tonight, you recollect."

Somehow, that pestered him. He didn't talk much while we ate. I said I'd fetch a pail of water, and out I went with it to the spring. There, at the spring but not right close up beside it, stood Craye Sawtelle. This time she wore a long black dress, with black sandals on her bare feet, and her hair was tied up with a string of red beads.

"Good day, ma'am," I said. "How did you fare last night?"

"I was a trifle busy," she answered. "A-getting ready for sundown."

I dipped my bucket in the spring. The water looked sweet.

"I note by your tracks that you've been round and round here," I said, "but you nair once got close enough to dip in the spring."

"That will come," she promised me. "It will come when the spring's mine, when there's no bar against me. How does that sound to you, John?"

"Why, since you ask, it sounds like the same old song by the same old mockingbird. Like a try at scaring us out. Miss Craye, I've been a-figuring on you since we met up yesterday, and I'll give you my straight-out notion. There's nothing you can do to me or Zeb Gossett, no matter how you try."

"You'll be sorry you said that."

"I'm already sorry," I said. "I hate to talk thisaway to lady-folks, but some things purely have to be said."

"And yonder comes Zeb Gossett," she said, pointing. "He'll do like you, try to talk himself out of being afraid."

Zeb came along to where I stood with the bucket in my hand. He looked tight-mouthed and pale under his brown beard.

"Have you come to talk business?" Craye inquired him, and showed him her pointy teeth.

"I talk no business with you," he said.

"Wait until the sun slides down behind the mountain," she mocked at him. "Wait until dark. See what I make happen then."

"I don't have to wait," he said. "I've made my mind up."

"Then why should I wait, either?" she snarled out. "Why not do the thing now?"

She lifted up her hands, crooked like claws. She began to say a string of wild words, in whatever language I don't know. Zeb gave back from her.

"I hate things like this, folks," I said, and I upped with the bucket and flung that water from the spring all over her.

She screamed like an animal caught in a trap. I saw yellow foam come a-slathering out of her mouth. She whirled round and whirled round again and slammed down, and by then you couldn't see her on account of the thick dark steam that rose.

Zeb ran back off a dozen steps, but I stood there to watch, the empty bucket in my hand.

The steam thinned, but you couldn't see Craye Sawtelle. She was gone.

Only that black dress, twisted and empty, and only those two black sandals on the soaked ground, with no feet in them. Naught else. Not a sigh of Craye Sawtelle. The last of the steam drifted off, and Zeb and I stared at each other.

"She's gone," Zeb gobbled in his throat. "Gone. How did you—"

"Well"—I steadied my voice—"yesterday you said it washed away air bad thing whatever. So I thought I'd see if it would do that. No doubt about it, Craye Sawtelle was badness through and through."

He looked down at the empty dress and empty sandals.

"Blessed water," he said. "Holy water. You made it so."

"I can't claim that, Zeb. More likely it was your doing, when you started in to use it for help to sick and troubled folks."

"But you knew that if you threw it on her—"

"No." I shook my head. "I just only hoped it would work, and it did. Wherever Craye Sawtelle's been washed to, I don't reckon she'll be back from there."

He looked up along the trail. Yonder came Tilda Fleming.

"Tilda," he said her name. "What shall I tell Tilda?"

"Why not tell her what's in your heart for her?" I asked. "I reckon she's plumb ready to hark at you."

He started to walk toward her and I headed back to the cabin.

OWLS HOOT IN THE DAYTIME

That time back yonder, I found the place myself, the way folks in those mountains allowed I had to.

I was rough hours on the way, high up and then down, over ridges and across bottoms, where once there'd been a road. I found a bridge across a creek, but it was busted down in the middle, like a warning not to use it. I splashed across there. It got late when I reached a cove pushed in amongst close-grown trees on a climbing slope.

An owl hooted toward where the sun sank, so maybe I was on the right track, a path faint through the woods. I found where a gate had been, a rotted post with rusty hinges on it. The trees beyond looked dark as the way to hell, but I headed along that snaky-winding path till I saw the housefront. The owl hooted again, off where the gloom grayed off for the last of daylight.

That house was half logs, half ancient whipsawed planks, weathered to dust color. Trees crowded the sides, branches crossed above the shake roof. The frontsill timber squatted on pale rocks. The door had come down off its old leather hinges. Darkness inside. Two windows stared, with flowered bushes beneath them. The grassy yard space wasn't a great much bigger than a parlor floor.

"What ye wish, young sir?" a scrapy voice inquired me, and I saw somebody a-sitting on a slaty rock at the house's left corner.

"I didn't know anybody was here," I said, and looked at him and he looked at me.

I saw a gnarly old man, his ruined face half-hid in a blizzardy white beard, his body wrapped in a brown robe. Beside him hunkered down what looked like a dark-haired dog. Both of them looked with bright, squinty eyes, a-making me recollect that my shirt was rumpled, that I sweated under my pack straps, that I had mud on my boots and my dungaree pant cuffs.

"If ye nair knowed nobody was here, why'd ye come?" scraped his voice.

"It might could be hard to explain."

"I got a lavish of time to hark at yore explanation."

I grinned at him. "I go up and down, a-viewing the country over. I've heard time and again about a place so far off of the beaten way that owls hoot in the daytime and they have possums for yard dogs."

An owl hooted somewhere.

"That's a saying amongst folks here and yonder," said the old man, his broad brown hand a-stroking his beard.

"Yes, sir," I agreed him, "but I heard tell it was in this part of the country, so I thought I'd find out."

The beard stirred as he clamped his mouth. "Is that all ye got to do with yore young life?"

"Mostly so," I told him the truth. "I find out things."

The animal alongside him hiked up its long snout.

It was the almightiest big possum I'd ever seen, big as a middling-sized dog. Likely it weighed more than fifty pounds. Its eyes dug at me.

"Folks at the county seat just gave me general directions," I went on. "I found an old road in the woods. Then I heard the owl hoot and it was still daytime, so I followed the sound here."

I felt funny, a-standing with my pack straps galled into me, to say all that.

"I've heard tell an owl hoot by daytime is bad luck," scraped the voice in the beard. "Heap of that a-going, if it's so."

"Over in Wales, they say an owl hooting means that a girl's a-losing her virginity," I tried to make a joke.

"Hum." Not exactly a laugh. "Owls must be kept busy a-hooting for that, too." He and the possum looked me up and down. "Well, since ye come from so far off, why don't me bid ye set and rest?"

"Thank you, sir." I unslung my pack and put it down and laid my guitar on it. Then I stepped toward the dark door hole.

"Stay out of yonder," came quick warning words. "What's inside is one reason why nobody comes here but me. Set down on that stump acrost from me. What might I call ye?"

I dropped down on the stump. "My name's John. And I wish you'd tell me more about how is it folks don't come here."

"I'm Maltby Sanger, and this here good friend I got with me is named Ung. The rest of the saying's fact, too. I keep him for a yard dog."

Ung kept his black eyes on me. His coarse fur was grizzled gray. His forepaws clasped like hands under his shallow chin.

"Maybe I'd ought to fix us some supper while we talk," said Maltby Sanger.

"Don't bother," I said. "I'll be a-heading back directly."

"Hark at me," he said, scrapier than ever. "There ain't no luck a-walking these here woods by night."

"There'll be a good moon."

"That there's the worst part. The moon shows ye to what's afoot in the woods. Eat here tonight and then sleep here."

"Well, all right." I leaned down and unbuckled my pack. "But let me fix the supper, since I came without bidding." I fetched out a little poke of meal, a big old can of sardines in tomatoes. "If I could have some water, Mr. Sanger."

"'Round here, there's water where I stay at."

He got off his rock, and I saw that he was dwarfed. His legs under that robe couldn't be much more than knees and feet. He wouldn't stand higher than my elbow.

"Come on, John," he said, and I picked up a tin pan and followed him round the house corner.

Betwixt two trees was built a little shackly hut, poles up and down and clay-daubed for walls, other poles laid up top and covered with twigs and grass for a roof. In front of it, in what light was left, flowed a spring. I filled my pan and started back.

"Is that all the water ye want?" he asked after me.

"Just to make us some pone. I've got two bottles of beer to drink."

"Beer," he said, like as if he loved the word.

He waddled back, a-picking up wood as he came. We piled twigs for me to light with a match, then put bigger pieces on top. I poured meal into the water in the pan and worked up a batter. Then I found a flat rock and rubbed it with ham rind and propped it close to the fire to pour the batter on. Afterward I opened the

sardines and got my fork for Maltby Sanger and took my spoon
for myself. When the top of the pone looked brown enough, I
turned it over with my spoon and knife, and I dug out those bottles of beer and twisted off the caps.

We ate, squatted on two sides of the fire. Maltby Sanger
appeared to enjoy the sardines and pone, and he gave some to
Ung, who held chunks in his paws to eat. When we'd done, not a
crumb was left. "I relished that," allowed Maltby Sanger.

It had turned full dark, and I was glad for the fire.

"Ye pick that guitar, John?" he inquired. "Why not pick it some
right now?"

I tuned my silver strings and struck chords for an old song I
recollected. One verse went like this:

> We sang good songs that came out new,
> But now they're old amongst the young,
> And when we're gone, it's just a few
> Will know the songs that we have sung.

"I God and that's a true word," said Maltby Sanger when I finished. "Them old songs is a-dying like flies."

I hushed the silver strings with my palm. "I don't hear that owl
hoot," I said.

"It ain't daytime no more," said Maltby Sanger.

"Hark at me, sir," I spoke up. "Why don't you tell me just
what's a-happening here, or anyway a-trying to happen?"

He gave me one of his beady looks and sighed a tired-out sigh.
"How'll I start in to tell ye?"

"Start in at the beginning."

"Ain't no beginning I know of. The business is as old as this
here mountain itself."

"Then it's right old, Mr. Sanger," I said. "I've heard say these
are the oldest mountains on all this earth. They go back before
Adam and Eve, before the first of living things. But here we've
got a house, made with hands." I looked at the logs, the planks.
"Some man's hands."

"John," he said, "that there's just a housefront, built up against
the rock, and maybe not by no man's hands, no such thing. I

reckon it was put there to tole folks in. But I been here all these years to warn folks off, the way I tried to warn ye." He looked at me, and so did Ung, next to him. "Till I seen ye was set in yore mind to stay, so I let ye."

I studied the open door hole, so dark inside. "Why should folks be toled in, Mr. Sanger?"

"I've thought on that, and come to reckon the mountain wants folks right into its heart or its belly." He sort of stared his words into me. "Science allows this here whole earth started out just a ball of fire. The outside cooled down. Water come in for the sea, and trees and living things got born onto the land. But they say the fire's still inside. And fire's got to have something to feed on."

I looked at our own fire. It was burning small and hot, but if it got loose it could eat up that whole woods. "You remind me of old history things," I said, "when gods had furnaces inside them and sacrifices were flung into them."

"Right, John," he nodded me. "Moloch's the name in the Bible, fifth chapter of Amos, and I likewise think somewheres in Acts."

"The name's Molech another place," I said. "Second Kings; Preacher Ricks had it for a text one time. How King Joash ruled that no man would make his son or daughter pass through the fire to Molech. You reckon this place is some way like that?"

"Might could be this here place, and places like it in other lands, gave men the idee of fiery gods to burn up their children."

I hugged my guitar to me, for what comfort it could give. "You wouldn't tell me all this," I said, "if you wanted to fool me into the belly of the mountain."

"I don't worship no such," he snapped. "I told ye, I'm here to keep folks from a-meddling into there and not come out no more. It was long years back when I come here to get away from outside things. I wasn't much good at a man's work, and folks laughed at how dwarfished-down I was."

"I don't laugh," I said.

"No, I see ye don't. But don't either pity me. I wouldn't like that no more than I'd like laughter."

"I don't either pity you, Mr. Sanger. I judge you play the man, the best you can, and nobody can do more than that."

He patted Ung's grizzled back. "I come here," he said again, "and I heard tell about this place from the old man who was here then. I allowed I'd take over from him if he wanted to leave, so he left. It wonders me if this sounds like a made-up tale to ye."

"No, sir, I hark at air word you speak."

"If ye reckon this here is just some common spot, look on them flowers at the window by ye."

It was a shaggy bush in the firelight. There were blue flowers. But likewise pinky ones, the color of blood-drawn meat. And dead white ones, with dark spots in them, like eyes.

"Three different flowers on one bush," he said. "I don't reckon there's the like of that, nowheres else on this earth."

"Sassafras has three different leaves on one branch," I said. "There'll be a mitten leaf, and a toad-foot leaf next to it, and then just a plain smooth-edged leaf." I studied the bush. "But those flowers would be special, even if there was just one of a kind on a twig."

"Ye done harked at what I told, John," said Maltby Sanger, and put his bottle up to his beard to drink the last drop. "Suit yoreself if it makes sense."

"Sense is what it makes," I said. "All right, you've been here for years. I reckon you live in that little cabin 'round the corner. Does that suit you?"

"It's got to suit somebody. Somebody's needed. To guard folks off from a-going in yonder and then not come out."

I strummed my guitar, tried to think of what to sing. Finally:

> Yonder comes the Devil
> From hell's last bottom floor,
> A-shouting and a-singing,
> There's room for many a more.

"I enjoy to hear ye make music, John," said Maltby Sanger. "It was all right for ye to come here tonight. No foolishness. I won't say no danger, but ye'll escape danger, I reckon."

I looked toward the open door. It was all black inside—no, not all black. I saw a couple of red points in there. I told myself they were reflected from our fire.

"I've been a-putting my mind on what's likely to be down

yonder," I said. "Recollected all I was told when I was little, about how hell was an everlasting fire down under our feet, like the way heaven was up in the sky over us."

"Have ye thought lately, the sky ain't truly up over us no more?" he inquired me. "It's more like off from us now, since men have gone a-flying off to the moon and are a-fixing to fly farther than that, to the stars. Stars is what's in the sky, and heaven's got to be somewheres else. But I ain't made up my mind on hell, not yet. Maybe it's truly a-burning away, down below our feet, right this minute."

"Or either, the fire down in there is what made folks decide what hell was."

"Maybe that," he halfway agreed me. "John, it's nigh onto when I go to sleep. I wish there was two beds in my cabin, but—"

"Just let me sleep out here and keep our fire a-going," I said. "Keep it a-going and not let it get away and seek what it might devour."

"Sure thing, if ye want to." He got up on his stumpy legs and dragged something out from under that robe he wore. "Ye might could like to have this with ye."

I took it. It was a great big Bible, so old its leather covers were worn and scrapped near about away.

"I thank you, sir," I said. "I'll lay a little lightwood on the fire and read in this."

"Then I'll see ye when the sun comes up."

He shuffled off to his shack. Ung stayed there and looked at me. I didn't mind that, I was a-getting used to him.

Well, gentlemen, I stirred up the fire and put on some chunks of pine so it would burn up strong and bright. I opened the Bible and looked through to the Book of Isaiah, thirty-fourth chapter. I found what I'd recollected to be there:

It shall not be quenched night nor day: the smoke thereof shall go up for ever; from generation to generation it shall lie waste . . .

On past that verse, there's talk about dragons and satyrs and such like things they don't want you to believe in these days. In the midst of my reading, I heard something from that open door, a long, grumbling sigh of sound, and I looked over to see what.

The two red lights moved closer together, and this time they seemed to be set in a lump of something, like eyes in a head.

I got up quick, the Bible in my hand. Those eyes looked out at me, and the red of them burned up bright, then went dim, then bright again. Ung, at my foot, made a burbling noise, like as if it pestered him.

I put down the Bible and picked up a burning chunk from the fire. I made myself walk to the door. My chunk gave me some light to see inside. Sure enough it was a cave in there; what looked like a house outside was just a front, built on by whatever had built it for whatever reason. The cave was hollowed back into the mountain and it had a smooth-looking floor, almost polished, of black rock. Inside, the space slanted inward both ways, to narrowness farther in. It was more like a throat than anything I could say for it. A great big throat, big enough to swallow a man, or more than one man.

Far back hung whatever it was had those eyes. I saw the eyes shine, not just from my flashlight. They had light of their own.

"All right," I said out loud to the eyes. "Here I am. I look for the truth. What's the truth about you?"

No answer but a grumble. The thing moved, deep in there. I saw it had, not just that black head with red eyes, it had shoulders and things like arms. It didn't come close, but it didn't pull back. It waited for me.

"What's the truth about you?" I inquired it again. "Might could your name be Molech?"

It made nair sound, but it lifted those long arms. I saw hands like pitchforks. It was bigger than I was, maybe half again bigger. Was it stronger?

A man's got to be a man sometime, I told myself inside me. I'd come there to find out what was what. There was some strange old truth in there, not a pretty truth maybe, but I'd come to see what it was.

I walked to where the door was fallen off the leather hinges. The red eyes came up bright and died down dull and watched me a-coming. They waited for me, they hoped I'd get close.

I put my foot on where the door-log had been once. It was long ago rotted to punk, it crumbled under my boot. I took hold of the jamb and leaned in.

"You been having a time for yourself?" I asked the eyes.

There was light from the chunk I carried, but other light, a ghost of a show of it, was inside. It came from on back in there. It was a kind of smoky reddish light, I thought, you might have called it rosy. It made a glitter on something two-three steps inside.

I spared a look down there to the floor. Gentlemen, it was a jewel, a bunch of jewels, a-shining white and red and green. And big. They were like a bunch of glass bottles for size. Only they weren't bottles. They shone too bright, too clear, strewed out there by my foot.

There for the picking up—but if I bent over, there was that one with the red eyes and the black shape, and he could pick me up.

"No," I said to him, "you don't get hold of me thattaway," and I whirled my chunk of fire, to get more light.

There he was, dark and a-standing two-legged like a man, but he was taller than I was, by the height of that round head with the red eyes. And no hair to his black hide, it was as slick as a snake. Long arms and pitchfork hands sort of pawed out toward me, the way a praying mantis does. The head cocked itself. I saw it had something in it besides eyes, it had a mouth, open and as wide as a gravy boat, wet and black, like a mess of hot tar.

"You must have tricked a many a man in here with those jewels," I said.

He heard me, he knew what I said, knew that I wouldn't stoop down. He moved in on me.

Those legs straddled. Their knees bent backward, like a frog's, the feet slapped flat and wide on the floor of the cave, amongst more jewels everywhere. Enough in there to pay a country's national debt. He reached for me again. His fingers were lumpy-jointed and they had sharp claws, like on the feet of a great big hawk. I moved backward, I reckoned I'd better. And he followed right along. He wanted to get those claws into me.

I backed to the old door-log and near about tripped on it. I dropped the burning chunk and grabbed hold of the fallen-down door with both hands, to stay on my feet. I got hold of its two edges and hiked it between me and that snake-skinned thing that lived inside. I looked past one edge of the door, and all of a sudden I saw him stop.

There was the rosy light in yonder, and outside my chunk blazed where it had fallen. I could see that door rightly for the first time.

It was one of those you used to see in lots of places, made with a thick center piece running from top to bottom betwixt the panels, and two more thick pieces set midpoint of the long one to go right and left to make a cross. In amongst these were set the four old, half-rotted panels. But the cross stood there. And often, I'd heard tell, such doors were made thattaway to keep evil from a-coming through.

So, in the second I did my figuring, I saw why the front had been built on the cave, why that door had been hung there. It was to hold in whatever was inside. And it had worked right well till the door dropped down.

It was a heavy old door, but I muscled it up. I shoved on back into the cave, with the door in front of me like a shield.

Nothing shoved back. I took one step after another amongst those shining jewels, careful to keep from a-tripping on them. I cocked my head leftways to look past the door. That big black somebody moved away from me. I saw the flicker of the rose light from where it came into the cave.

The cross, was it a help? I'd been told that there were crosses long before the one on Calvary, made for power's sake in old, old lands beyond the sea. Yes, and in this land too, by Indian tribes one place and another. My foot near about skidded on a rolling jewel, but I stayed up.

"In this sign we conquer," I said, after some king in the olden days, and I believed it. And I went on forward with the door for my sign.

For as long as a breath I shoved up against him. I felt him lean against the other side, like high wind a-blowing. I fought to keep the door on him to push him back, and took a long step and dug in with my foot.

And almighty near fell down a hole all full of the rosy light.

He'd tricked me there where his light came up from. I hung

on its edge, a-looking down a hole three-four feet across, deeper than I could ask myself to judge, and away down there was fire, a-dancing and a-streaming—a world, it looked to me, of fire.

On the other side of the door he made a noise. It was a whiny buzz, what you'd expect from a bee as big as a dog. His long old arm snaked round the edge of the door, a-raking with its claws. They snagged into my shirt—I heard it rip. I managed to sidestep clear of that hole, and he buzzed and came again. I shoved hard with the door, put all I could put into it. Heat come in all round me, it was like when you sit in a close room with a hot stove. I smelt something worse than a skunk.

The pressure was there, and then the pressure was all of a sudden gone. I went down, the door in front of me, to slam on the floor with a rattly bang.

I got up quick, without the door. I wondered how to face him. But he wasn't there. Nowhere.

I stood and trembled and gulped for air. Sweat streamed all over me. I looked up, all 'round me. Sure enough, he was gone. I was all alone in that dark cave, me and the door. And the rosy light was gone.

For the door had fallen whack down on top of it.

I put a knee down on the panel. I could feel a tremble and stir underneath.

"By God Almighty, I've got you penned in!" I yelled down to what made the stir in that fiery hole.

It was a-humping to me there. I reached out and grabbed a shiny green jewel. It must have weighed eight pounds or so. I put it on a plank of the cross. I got up on my feet, found more jewels. I laid them on, one next to another, along both arms, to make the cross twice as strong.

"You're shut up in there now," I said down to the hole it covered.

The door lay still and solid. No more hum below.

I headed out toward the gleam of the cooking fire. My feet felt weak under me. Ung sat out there and looked at me. I wondered if I should ought to get a blanket. Then I didn't bother. I must have slept.

It was morning's first gray again, with the stars a-paling out of the sky, when I sat up awake. Maltby Sanger was there, a-building up the fire. "Ye look to have had ye a quiet night," he said.

"Me?" I said, and he laughed. Next to the fire he set a saucepan with eggs in it.

"Duck eggs," he told me. "Ung found them for our breakfast. And I got parched corn, and tomatoes from my garden."

"And I've got a few pinches of coffee, we can boil it in my canteen cup," I said. "Looky over yonder at the cave."

He looked. He pulled his whiskers. "Bless my soul," he said, "the door's plumb gone off it."

"The door's inside, to bottle up what was the trouble in there," I said.

While he was a-cooking, I told him what I'd met in the cave. He got up with a can of hot coffee in his hand and stumped inside. Out again, he filled one of his old buckets with dirt and stones and fetched it into the cave. Then back for another bucketful of the same stuff, and then another. Finally he came out and washed his hands and served up the eggs. We ate them before the either of us said a word.

"Moloch," Maltby Sanger said then. "Ye reckon that's who he is?"

"He didn't speak his name," I replied him. "All I guess is, he'll likely stay under that door with the cross and the weight on it, so long as it's left to pen him in."

"So long as it's left," he agreed me. "Only ye used them jewels for weight. If somebody comes a-using 'round here and sees them, he might could wag them off. So I put a heap of dirt over them to hide them best I could. Nobody's a-going to scrabble there so long's I'm here to keep them from it."

He stroked his beard and grinned his teeth at me.

"My time's been long hereabouts, and it'll be longer. Only after I'm gone can somebody stir him up in yonder. Then the world can suit itself about what to do about him."

He squinted his eyes to study me. "Now," he said, "ye'll likely be a-going yore way."

"Yes, sir, and I'm honest to thank you for a-letting me found out what I wanted to know."

I stowed my pack and strapped on the blanket roll.

"Last night," he said from across the fire, "I'd meant to ask ye to stay on watch here and let me go."

"Ask me to stay?"

"That's what. And ye'd have stayed, John, if I'd asked ye the right way. Stayed and kept the watch here."

I couldn't tell myself for certain if that was so.

"I aimed for to ask ye," he said again, "but if I was to go, where'd I go? Hellfire, John, I been here so long it's home."

Ung twinkled an eye, like as if he heard and understood.

"I'll just stay a-setting here and warn other folks off from a-messing round where that door is," said Maltby Sanger.

I slung my pack on my shoulders and picked up my guitar. "Sunrise now," I said.

"Sure enough, sunrise. Good-bye, John. I was proud to have ye here overnight."

We shook hands. He didn't seem so dwarfish right then. I found the path I'd come in by, that would take me back to people.

The sun was up. Daytime was come. Back on the way I went, I heard the long, soft hoot of an owl.

CAN THESE BONES LIVE?

I'd dropped my blanket roll and soogin sack and guitar and sat quiet on the granite lump as those eight men in rough country clothes fetched their burden along. It was a big chest of new-sawed planks, pale in the autumn afternoon, four men on each side.

As they tramped, they watched me. I got to my feet. I reckoned I was taller than any of them, probably wider through the shoulders. I wore old pants and boots and rumply hat, but I'd shaved that morning and hoped I looked respectable.

They came close to me amongst those tree-strung heights, and set the chest down with a bump. I figured it to be nine feet long and three feet wide and another three high. Rope loops were spiked to the sides for handles. The lid was fastened with a hook and staple, like what you use on a shed door. One of the eight stared me up and down. He was a chunky, grizzled man in a wide black hat, bib overalls and a denim jacket.

"Hidy," he drawled, and spit on the ground. "What you up to here?"

"I was headed for a place called Chaw Hollow," I replied him.

They all stared. "How you name yourself?" asked the one who had spoken.

"Just call me John."

"What do you follow, John?" asked another man.

I smiled my friendliest. "Well, mostly I study things. This morning, back yonder at that settlement, I heard tell about a big skeleton that had been turned up on a Chaw Hollow farm."

"You a government man?" the grizzled one inquired me.

"You mean, look for blockade stills?" I shook my head. "Not me. Call me a truth seeker, somebody who wonders himself about riddles in this life."

"A conjure man?" put in another of the bunch.

"Not me," I said again. "I've met up with that sort in my time, helped put two-three of them out of mischief. Call that part of what I follow."

"My name's Embro Hallcott," said the grizzled one. "If you came to poke round them bones, you're too late."

I waited for him to go on, and he went on:

"I dug them bones up on my place, a-scooping out for a fish pond. Some of us reckoned that, whoair he was, he should ought to be buried in holy ground, yonder at Stumber Creek church house. So we made him a box, and that's where we're a-going with him now."

"Let me give you a hand," I said, and slung my guitar and other things to my shoulders.

"He's a stranger man, Mr. Embro," said the scrawny man.

"Sure, but he looks powerful for strength." Hallcott raked me with his eye. "And you feel puny today, Oat. All right, John, grab a hold there where Oat's been a-heaving on this here thing."

I shoved my hand through the loop and we hoisted the coffin. It was right heavy, at that. I heard the others grunt as we took the trail through the ravine. On the trees, autumn leaves showed yellow, different reds and so on, like flowers. Half a mile, maybe, we bore our load along.

"Yonder we are, boys," said Hallcott.

We came out into a hollow amongst shaggy heights that showed rocky knobs. One, I thought, looked like a head and shoulders. Another jabbed up like a finger, another curved like a hawk bill. The lower ground into which we tramped was tufted with trees, with a trickle of water through it. Beside this stood a grubby white house with a steeple. Stumber Creek Church, I figured it to be.

Hallcott, at a front loop, steered us into a weedy tract with gravestones here and yonder. "Set her down," he wheezed, and we did so. "Yonder comes Preacher Travis Melick. I done sent him the word to meet up with us here."

From the church house ambled a gaunt man in a jimswinger coat, a-carrying a book covered with black leather. Hallcott walked toward him. "Evening, Preacher," he said. "Proud to have you here."

"The grave's been made ready," said the other in a deep-down voice, and nodded to where a long, dark hole gaped amongst the weeds. Then he faced me. "Don't believe I know this gentleman."

"Allows he's named John," grated the scrawny one called Oat.

"I've heard of John," said Preacher Melick, and held out his skinny hand. "Heard of good things you've done, sir. Welcome amongst us."

Hallcott's crinkly face got easy. "If you say he's all right, Preacher, that makes him all right," he said. "I'll tell you true, he made better than a good hand, a-wagging this coffin the last part of the way."

We hiked the coffin to the side of the grave. On the bank of fresh dirt lay three shovels. Oat touched the hook on the lid.

"Ain't we supposed to view the body?" he wondered us. "Ain't that the true old way?"

"I've done seen the thing," snapped out Hallcott.

"Open it for a moment if you feel that's proper," said the preacher man.

Oat worked the hook out of the staple and hoisted the lid. The hinges creaked. "Wonder who he was," he said.

The bones inside were loose from one another and half-wrapped in a Turkey Track quilt, but I saw they were laid out in order. They were big, the way Hallcott had said, big enough for an almighty big bear. I had a notion that the arms were right long; maybe all the bones were long. Thick, too. The skull at the head of the coffin was like a big gourd, with caves of eyeholes and two rows of big, lean teeth. Hallcott banged the lid shut and hooked it again.

"That there's enough of a look to last youins all day and all night," he growled round at the others.

"Brothers," said Preacher Melick, a-opening his book, "we're here to bury the remains of a poor lost creature. We don't even know his name. Yet I've searched out what I hope is the right text for this burying."

He put his knobby finger to the page. "Book of Ezekiel," he said. "Thirty-seventh chapter, third verse. 'And he said unto me, Son of man, can these bones live? And I answered, O Lord God, thou knowest.'"

He closed his book. "The Lord God knoweth all things. We're

taught that after death will come the life we deserve. Let us pray."

We bowed our heads down. Preacher Melick said, "In the midst of life we are in death," and so on. When he finished, I said, "Amen," and so did Hallcott and two-three others.

"Now lower the coffin," said Preacher Melick.

We took hold and set it in the grave. It fitted right snug, its lid was just inches below surface. Preacher Melick sprinkled a handful of dirt. "Ashes to ashes, dust to dust," he repeated, and then we all said the Lord's Prayer together. Finally the preacher man smiled round at us. The service was over.

Three men shoveled in the earth. It took just minutes to fill the grave up.

Hallcott offered some crumpled money bills to Preacher Melick, who waved them away.

"You took it on yourselves to make the stranger a coffin and bring him here to rest," he said. "The least duty I can do is speak comfortable words without expectation of pay. John, to judge from the gear you brought, you're a-looking for lodging for the night. Will you be my guest?"

"Thanks, maybe later," I said. "I reckon I'll wait here a spell."

"If you come later on, it's half a mile up the trail the far side of the church."

He walked away with his book. The coffin-makers headed the other direction. The sun was a-dropping red to the edge of the western heights.

One of the shovels had been fetched to lean under a fair-sized walnut tree. I put down my stuff next to the roots and sat with my back against the trunk. On the silver strings of my guitar I made a few chords to whisper. The air got gloomy.

"It's kindly creepy a night," said a voice at my elbow.

That quick I was up on my feet. Embro Hallcott stood there, his crinkly face a-smiling.

"For a man your height, you move quick as a cat, John," he said. "I done heard you tell Preacher Melick you'd stay round, so I decided myself to stay too, for whatever's up."

"What do you reckon's up?" I inquired him.

"If you don't know how to answer that, neither do I."

I sat down under the tree again, and Hallcott hunkered down

beside me. He dragged out a twist of home-cured tobacco and bit off a chunk the size of half a dollar.

"I was right interested by Preacher Melick's text from Ezekiel," I said. "All that about could these bones live."

"Ezekiel," Hallcott repeated me, a-folding his ridgy hands on the knees of his overalls. "I done read in that, some time back. Strange doings in Ezekiel—the wheels in the wheels. Some folks reckon that means what they call UFOs."

"They were unknown and they flew, so they were UFOs all right," I nodded him. "And all those prophecies about nation after nation, and the brass man a-walking round to measure Jerusalem. And I've heard it explained that the four faces of the living creatures meant the Four Gospels. But the strangest of all the thing is the Valley of Dry Bones, where the bones join together and come to life."

A moon rose up and shone down on the burial ground. Hallcott moved to pull together some pieces of wood and light them with a match. I went to the stream and dipped water in my canteen cup and set it on a rock where it could heat. "I don't reckon you brought aught for supper," I said.

"I've done without no supper before this."

"I've got something left from my noon lunch." I pawed through my soogin and came up with two sandwiches wrapped in foil. "Home-cured ham on white bread."

Hallcott took one and thanked me kindly. As the water grew hot, I trickled in instant coffee and stirred it with a twig. We ate and passed the cup back and forth.

"I appreciate this, John," said Hallcott as he swallowed down his last bite. "How long you aim to stop here?"

"That depends."

"I reckon you'll agree with me, them bones we buried were right curious. Great big ones, and long arms, like on an ape."

"Or maybe on Sasquatch," I said. "Or Bigfoot."

"You believe in them tales."

"I always wonder myself if there's not truth in air tale. And as for bones—I recollect something the Indians called Kalu, off in a place named Hosea's Hollow. Bones a-rattling round, and sure death to a natural man."

"You believe that, too?"

"Believe it? I saw it happen one time. Only Kalu got somebody else, not me."

"Can these bones live?" Hallcott repeated the text. "Ain't there an old song about that, the bones a-coming together alive?"

"I've sung it in my time," I said, and picked up my guitar and struck out the tune. "It goes like this:

> *Connect these bones, dry bones, dry bones,*
> *Connect these bones, dry bones, dry bones,*
> *Connect these bones, dry bones, dry bones,*
> *Hear the word of the Lord."*

Hallcott sang the verse with me, his voice rough and husky:

> *The toe bone's connected to the foot bone,*
> *The foot bone's connected to the heel bone,*
> *The heel bone's connected to the ankle bone,*
> *Hear the word of the Lord.*

And we sang the rest of it together, up to the end:

> *The shoulder bone's connected to the neck bone,*
> *The neck bone's connected to the jaw bone,*
> *The jaw bone's connected to the head bone,*
> *Hear the word of the Lord.*

> *Connect these bones, dry bones, dry bones,*
> *Connect these—*

Hallcott broke off then, and so did I. "John," he said, "looky yonder where we buried him. What's that there white stuff?"

I saw it, too. In the shine of the moon above the grave stirred a pale something or other.

It made just a sneaky blur, taller than a tall man. It came toward us with a ripple in it.

"Mist," Hallcott stuttered. "Comes from that there fresh-dug-up dirt—"

"No," I said, "that's no mist."

I leant my guitar to the walnut tree and got up on my feet as whatever it was came nearer, started to make itself into a shape.

I heard Hallcott say a quick cuss word, and then there was a scrambly noise, like as if he was a-trying to make his way off from there on hands and knees. I faced toward whatair the shape was, because I reckoned I had to.

As it came slowly along, the moonlight hit it fair. It looked scaffolded some way. That was because it was just bones. I could see a sort of baskety bunch of ribs, and big, stout arm bones with almighty huge hands a-hanging down below crooked knees. The shallowy skull had deep, dark eyeholes. The long-toothed jaws sank itself down and then snapped shut again. The skull turned on its neck bone and gave me a long, long look.

Then it reached out its right hand with fingerbones the size of table knives, and laid hold on a young tree and yanked it out by the roots, without air much a-trying. It stood and tore off branches, easy as you'd peel the shucks from an ear of corn. It made itself a club thattaway, and hiked it over the low skull and moved to close in on me again.

No point in it for me to try to run away from such a thing, and well I knew it. Turn and run from a hant or a devil, it runs after you. If it catches you, then what? I quick grabbed up the shovel where it leant on the walnut trunk. Compared to that club the bony thing had, it was like a ball bat against a wagon tongue.

"What you want of me?" I said, but I felt I didn't have to be told that.

Bones like those, long worn bare and scattered apart and now joined and made to live by words of power, they'd wake up hungry. They'd be starved for food. If they got food, maybe they'd put flesh back on themselves, be themselves as they'd been once before. What food was closer to hand than I was?

Man-eaters—such things were told of by old Indians, wise men who'd sworn to them. The wendigo, up in Northern parts. The anisgina, recollected in Cherokee tales to make you shiver. Supposed to be all died out and gone these days, but when bones rise up . . .

The bones came a-slaunching close. I heard them click.

I hiked up the shovel with both my hands, and held the blade edge forward like an axe. I'd chop with that. The bones stood a second, the whole skeleton of them, tall over me. In the glow of the moon those bones looked like frosty silver. My head wouldn't have come put to those big cliffs of shoulders. The jaws opened and shut. They made a snapping sound.

Because they wanted to bite a chunk out of me. Those teeth in the jaws, they were as long and sharp as knives. They could break a man's arm off if they jammed into it.

But I didn't run. To run nair had helped me much in such a case. I'd stand my ground, fight. If I lost the fight, maybe Hallcott could get away and tell the tale. I bent my knees and made my legs springy. I hoped I could move faster and surer than those big, lumbering bones.

Preacher Melick had said the Bible words to make them live, had said them without a-thinking. And that song, I'd have been better off if I'd nair sung it. I watched the thick, bony arms rise up and fetch the club down to bust my head.

That quick, I sidestepped and danced clear, and down came the big hunk of tree, so hard on the ground it boomed there like a slamming door. I made a swing with my own shovel, but the club was up again and in the way. My blade bounced off. Again the club hiked up over me, it made a dark blotch against the moon. I set myself to dodge again.

Then it was that Embro Hallcott, come back up just behind me, started in to sing in his husky voice:

> *The toe bone's connected from the foot bone,*
> *The foot bone's connected from the heel bone . . .*

And quick on from there, about the shin and thigh and hip bones, about the back bone and the shoulder bone. I stood with my shovel held up in both hands, and watched the thing come apart before my eyes.

It had dropped that club that would have driven me into the ground like a nail. It swayed in broken-up moonlight that shone through tree branches. It fell to pieces while I watched.

I looked at the bones, down and scattered out now. The skull stared up at me, and one more time it gave a hungry snap of those jaws. I heard:

> *The neck bone's connected from the jaw bone,*
> *The jaw bone's connected from the head bone,*
> *Hear the word of the Lord.*

The jaw bone snapped no more. It rolled free from the skull. Hallcott was up beside me. I could feel him shake all over.

"It worked," he said, in the tiredest voice you could call for.

"That song built him up," I said back. "And that song, sung different, took him back down again. Though it appears to me the word should be 'disconnected'."

"Sure enough?" he wondered me. "I don't know that word, that disconnected. But I thought on an old tale, how a man read in a magic book and devilish things came all round him, so he read the book backward and made them go away." His eyes bugged as he looked at a big thigh bone, dropped clear of its kneecap and shin. "What if it hadn't worked, John?"

"Point is, it did work and thank the good Lord for that," I told him. "Now, how you say for us to put him back in his coffin again, and not sing air note to him this time?"

Hallcott didn't relish to touch the bones, and, gentlemen, neither did I. I scooped them in the shovel, all the way along to where the grave was open and the coffin lid flung back. In I shoved them, one by one, in a heap on top of the Turkey Track quilt. I sought out air single bone, even the little separate toe bones that come in the song, a-picking them up with the shovel blade. Somewhere I've heard tell there are two hundred and eight bones in a skeleton. Finally I got all of them. I swung the lid down, and Hallcott fastened the hook into the staple. Then we stood and harked. There was just a breath of sweet, cool breeze in some bushes. Nair other sound that we made out.

Hallcott picked up another of the shovels, and quick we filled that grave in again. We patted it down smooth on top. Again we harked. Nair sound from where we'd buried the bones a second time.

"I reckon he's at rest now," I felt like a-saying. "Leastways, all disconnected again thattaway, he can't get up unless some other gone gump comes here and sings that song to him again."

"For hell's sake, whatever was he?" Hallcott asked, of the whole starry night sky.

"Maybe not even science folks could answer that," I said. "I'd reckon he was of a devil-people long gone from this country—a people that wasn't man nor either beast; a kind of people that pure down had to go, but gets recollected in ugly old tales of man-eating things. That's all I can think to say to it."

I flung down the shovel and went back to where my stuff lay against the walnut tree. I slung my blanket roll and soogin on my back, and took my guitar up under my arm. Right that moment, I sure enough didn't have a wish to play it.

"John," said Hallcott. "Where you reckon to head now?"

"Preacher Melick kindly invited me to his house. I have it in mind to go there."

"Me, too, if he's got room for me," said Hallcott. "Money wouldn't buy me to go nowheres alone in this night. No sir, nor for many a night to come."

NOBODY EVER GOES THERE

That was what Mark Banion's grandparents told him when he was a five-year-old with tousled black hair, looking from the porch and out across Catch River to a big dark building and some small dark ones clumped against the soaring face of Music Mountain, rank with its gloomy huddles of trees.

His grandparents towered high to tell him, the way grownups do when you're little, and they said, "Nobody ever goes there," without explaining, the way grownups do when you're little. Mark was a good, obedient boy. He didn't press the matter. And he sure enough didn't go over.

The town had been named Trimble for somebody who, a hundred and forty-odd years ago, had a stock stand there, entertainment for man and beast. In those old days, stagecoaches and trading wagons rolled along the road chopped through the mountains, and sometimes came great herds of cattle and horses and hogs. Later there had been the railroad that carried hardly anything anymore. Trucks rumbled along Main Street and on, northwest to Tennessee or southeast to Asheville. Trimble was no great size for a town. Maybe that was why it stayed interesting to look at. It had stores on Main Street, and Mark's grandfather's chair factory, the town hall and the *Weekly Record*. On side streets stood the bank, the high school where students came by bus from all corners of the rocky county, and three churches. All those things were on this side of Catch River.

But over yonder where nobody went, loomed the empty-windowed old textile mill, like the picture of a mined castle in an outlawed romantic novel. Once it had spun its acres of cloth. People working there had lived in the little houses you could barely see from this side. Those houses had a dusky, secret look, bunched against Music Mountain. When Mark asked why it was called Music Mountain, his grandparents said, "We never heard tell why." So once, in his bed at night, Mark thought he heard soft music from across Catch River to his window. When he mentioned that next day, they laughed and said he was making it up.

He stopped talking about that other side of the river, but he kept his curiosity as he grew older. He found out a few things from listening to talk when he played in town. He found out that a police car did cruise over there two or three times a week on the rattly old bridge that nobody else used, and that the cruise was made only by daylight. When he was in high school, tall and tanned and a hot-rock tight end on the football team, he and two classmates started to amble across one Saturday. They were nearly halfway to the other side when a policeman came puffing after them and scolded them back. That night, Mark's grandparents told him never to let them hear of doing such a fool thing again. He asked why it was foolish, and his grandmother said, "Nobody ever goes there. Ever." And shut up her mouth with a snap.

One who did tell Mark something about it was Mr. Glover Shelton, the oldest man in Trimble, who whittled birds and bear cubs and rabbits in his little shop behind the Worley Cafe. Once a month he sold a crate of such whittlings to a man who carried them to a tourist bazaar off in another county. Mr. Glover was lamed so that he had an elbow in one knee, like a cricket. He wore checked shirts and bib overalls and a pointed beard as white as dandelion fluff. And he had memories.

"Something other happened there round about seventy-five years back," he said. "I was another sight younger than you then. There was the textile mill, and thirty-forty folks a-living in them company houses and a-working two shifts. Then one day, they was all of a sudden all gone."

"Gone where?" Mark asked him.

"Don't rightly know how to answer that. Just gone. Derwood Neidger the manager, and Sam Brood the foreman, and the whole crew on shift—gone." Mr. Glover whittled at the bluejay he was making. "One night just round sundown, the whistle it blowed and blowed, and folks over here got curiosed up and next day some of 'em headed over across the bridge. And nair soul at the mill, nor neither yet in the houses. The wives and children done gone, too. Everybody."

"Are you putting me on, Mr. Glover?"

"You done asked me, boy, and I done told you the thing I recollect about it."

"They just packed up and left?"

"They left, but they sure God nair packed up. The looms was still a-running. Derwood Neidger's fifty-dollar hat was on the hook, his cigar burnt out in a tray on his desk. Even supper a-standing on the stoves, two-three places. But nair a soul to be seen anywheres."

Mark looked to see if a grin was caught in the white beard, but Mr. Glover was as solemn as a preacher. "Where did they go?" Mark asked.

"I just wish you'd tell me. There was a search made, inquiries here and yonder, but none of them folks air showed theirself again."

"And now," said Mark, "nobody ever goes there."

"Well now, a couple-three has gone, one time another . . . from here, and a hunter or so a-cooning over Music Mountain from the far side. But none air come back no more. Only them policemen that drives over quick and comes back quick—always by daylight, always three in the car, with pistols and sawed-off shotguns. Boy," said Mr. Glover, "folks just stays off from that there place, like a-staying off from a rocky patch full of snakes, a wet bottom full of chills and fever."

"And now it's a habit," said Mark. "Staying out."

"Likewise a habit not to go a-talking about it none. Don't you go a-naming it to nobody I told you this much."

Mark played good enough football to get a grant in aid at a lowland college, about enough help to make the difference between going and not going. Summers, he mostly worked hard to keep in condition, in construction and at road mending. By the time he graduated, his grandparents had sold the chair factory and had retired to Florida. Mark came back to Trimble, where they hired him to coach football and baseball and teach physical education at his old high school.

And still nobody ever went across Catch River. He felt the old interest, but he quickly became more interested in Ruth Covell, the history teacher.

She was small and slim, and her hair was blonde with a spice of red to it. She wore it more or less the length Mark wore his own black mane. She came up to about his coat lapel. Her face was round and sweet. She gave him a date, but wanted to sit and talk on the porch of the teacherage instead of driving to an outdoor movie. It was a balmy October night. She fetched them out two glasses of iced tea, flavored with lemon juice and ginger. They sat on bark-bottomed chairs, and Ruth said it was good to be in Trimble.

"I've liked it here from the first," she said, "I've thought I might write a history of this town."

"A history of Trimble?" Mark repeated, smiling. "Who'd read that?"

"You might, when I finish it. This place has stories worth putting on record. I've been to the town hall and the churches. I've found out lots of interesting things, but one thing avoids me."

"What's that, Ruth?" Mark asked, sipping.

"Why nobody ever goes across the river, and why everybody changes the subject when I bring it up."

From where they sat they could see a spattery shimmer of moonlight on the water, but Music Mountain beyond was as black as soot.

"Ruth," Mark said, "you're up against a story that just never is told in Trimble."

"But why not?" Her face hung silvery in the moonglow.

"I don't know. I never found out, and I was born here. Old Mr. Glover Shelton told me a few things, but he's dead now." He related the old man's story. "I'm unable to tell you why things are that way about the business," he wound up. "It's just not discussed, sort of the way sex didn't used to be discussed in polite society. I suspect that most people have more or less forgotten about it, pushed it to the back of their minds."

"But the police go over," she reminded him. "The chief said it was just a routine check, a tour in a deserted area. Then he changed the subject, too."

"If I were you, I'd not push anyone too hard about all this," said Mark. "It's a sort of rule of life here, staying on this side of the river. As an athletic coach, I abide by rules."

"As a historian, I look for the truth," she said back, "and I don't like to have the truth denied me."

He changed the subject. They talked cheerfully of other things. When he left that night, she let him kiss her and said he could come back and see her again.

Next Saturday evening, Ruth finished grading a sheaf of papers and just before sundown she walked out in the town with Mark. She wore snug jeans and a short, dark jacket. They had a soda at Doc Roberts's drug store and strolled on along Main Street. Mark told her about his boyhood in Trimble, pointed out the massive old town hall (twice burned down, once by accident, and rebuilt both times inside its solid brick walls), and led her behind Worley's Cafe to show her where Glover Shelton once had worked. The door of the little old shop was open. A light gleamed through it, and a voice from inside said, "Hidy."

A man sat at the ancient work bench, dressed in a blue hickory shirt and khaki pants and plow shoes, carefully shaping a slip of wood with a bright, sharp knife. He was lean, and as tall as Mark, say six feet. His long, thoughtful face was neither young nor old. In his dark hair showed silver dabs at the temples and in a brushed-back lock on top.

"Glover Shelton and I were choice friends, years back," he said. "I knew the special kinds of wood he hunted out and used here, and his nephew loaned me a key so I could come work me out a new bridge for my old guitar."

It was an old guitar indeed, seasoned as dark brown as a nut. The man set the new bridge in place, with a dab of some adhesive compound. "That'll dry right while we're a-studying it," he said. Then he laid the strings across, threaded them through the pegs, and tightened them with judicious fingers. He struck a chord, adjusted the pegs, struck and struck again. "Sounds passable," he decided.

"Those strings shine like silver," offered Ruth.

"It just so happens that silver's what they are," was the reply, with a quiet smile. "Silver's what the oldest old-timers used. Might could be I'm the last that uses it."

He achieved a chord to suit him. Tunefully, richly, he sang:

She came down the stair,
Combing back her yellow hair,
And her cheek was as red as the rose . . .

Mark had made up his mind to something.

"Sir," he said, "I knew Mr. Glover Shelton when I was a boy. This young lady wishes he had lived for her to talk to. Because he was the only man I ever heard speak of the far side of Catch River yonder, the Music Mountain side."

"I know a tad of something about that," said the guitar-picker, while the strings whispered under his long, skilled fingers. "An old Indian medicine man, name of Reuben Manco—he mentioned about it to me one time."

"Nobody here in Trimble talks about it," said Mark. "They just stay away from over there. Nobody ever goes there."

"I reckon not, son. The way Reuben Manco had it, the old Indians more or less left the place alone, too. What was there didn't relish to be pestered."

"Some other kind of men than Indians?" suggested Ruth.

"Better just only call them things. The way the old story comes down, they didn't truly look like aught a man could tell of at first. And they more or less learnt from a-studying men—Indians— how to get a little bitty bit like men, too."

"They sound weird," said Mark, interested.

"I reckon that's a good word for them. The Indians were scared of how they made themselves to look. So sometimes the Indians got up on the top of the mountain yonder and sang to the things, to make sure they wouldn't try to come out and make trouble." The long, thoughtful face brooded above the guitar's soft melody. "I reckon that's how it come to be named Music Mountain. The Indians would sing those things back off and into their place, time after time. I reckon all the way up to when the white men came in."

"Came in and took the Indians' land," said Mark. "That happened here."

"Shoo, it happened all over America—the taking of the land. All right, I've given you what Reuben Manco gave me. Music Mountain for the music the Indians used against those things."

"Why won't anybody in town tell about this?" Ruth asked.

"I don't reckon folks in town much heard of it. Especially when they might not want to hear tell of it."

"I'm glad to hear it," declared Ruth. "I'm someone who wants to know things."

"There's always a right much to get to know, ma'am," was the polite rejoinder.

Mark sat down on the work bench. "Music," he repeated. "Could the Indians control something like that—something frightening, you said—with music?"

"Well, son, with Indians the right song can make the rain to fall. An Indian hunter sings to bring him luck before he goes after game. Medicine men sing to cure a sick man or a hurt man. One time another, music's been known to do the like of such things."

Mark asked for the story of the mill that had been built under Music Mountain. It seemed that Derwood Neidger had interested some Northern financiers and had built his mill, with Trimble's townspeople shaking their heads about it. But there was good pay, and families came from other places to live in the houses built for them and to spin the cloth. Until the night they all vanished.

"What if there had been music at the mill?" Mark wondered. "In the houses?"

"Doesn't seem like as if there was much of that, so we can't rightly tell. And it's too late to figure on it now."

The sun sank over the western mountains. Dusk slid swiftly down into the town. Mark listened as his companion struck the silver strings and sang again:

> *She came down the stair,*
> *Combing back her yellow hair . . .*

He muted the melody with his palm. "Sounds like that beauty-looking young girl that came here with you. Where's she gone off to?"

Mark jumped up from where he sat. Ruth was nowhere in sight. He hurried out of the shop, around the cafe and out into the street.

"Ruth, wait—"

Far along the sidewalk, in the light of a shop window, he saw her as she turned off and out of view, where the old alley led to where the bridge was.

"Wait!" he yelled after her, and started to run.

It was a long sprint to the alley. One or two loungers gazed at Mark as he raced past. He found the alley, headed into it, stumbled in its darkness and went to one knee. He felt his trousers rip where they struck the jagged old cobbles. Up again, he hurried to the bridge.

It was already too dim to see clearly, but Ruth must be there. She must be moving along, almost as fast as he. "You damned fool," he wheezed into the darkening air as he ran. "You damned little fool, why did you do this?" And in his heart her voice seemed to answer him, *I'm someone who wants to know things.*

The old, old boards of the bridge rattled under his feet. He heard the soft, purling rush of Catch River. There she was now, at the far end, a darker point in the night that came down on them. "Ruth," he tried to call her once more, but his breath wasn't enough to carry it. He ran on after her.

Now he had come out on the other bank, where nobody ever went. He turned to his left. A road of sorts had been there once, it seemed. Its blotchy stones were rank between with grass. His shoe skidded on what must have been slippery moss and he nearly went down again. To his right climbed the steep face of Music Mountain, huddled with watching trees as black as ink. On ahead of him, small, dark houses clung together at the roadside. Farther beyond them rose the sooty pile of the old mill. He stood for a moment and wheezed to get his breath. Something came toward him. He quivered as he faced it.

"I knew you'd come too, Mark," said Ruth's merry voice.

At that moment, the moon had scrambled clear of the mountain and flung pale light around them. He saw that Ruth smiled.

"Why ever did you—" he began to say.

"I told you, Mark, I want to find things out. Nobody else here wants to. Dares to."

"You come right back to town with me," he commanded.

She laughed musically.

On into the sky swam the round, pallid moon, among a bright sprinkling of stars. Its light picked out the mill more clearly. It struck a twinkle from the glass of a window; or could there be a stealthy light inside? Ruth laughed again.

"But you came across, at least," she said, as though happy about it.

The glow of the moon beat upon her, making her hair pale. And something else moved on the road to the mill.

He hurried toward Ruth as the something drifted from between those dubious houses, a murky series of puffs, like foul smoke. He thought, for a moment hoped, that it might be fog; but it gathered into shapes as it emerged, shadowy, knobby shapes. Headlike lumps seemed to rise, narrow at the top, with, Mark thought, great loose mouths. Wisps stirred like groping arms.

"Let's get out of here," he said to Ruth, and tried to catch her by the hand.

But then she, too, saw those half-shaped things that now stole into groups and advanced. She screamed once, like an animal caught in a trap, and she lost her head and ran from them. She ran toward the mill in the moonlight that flooded the old paving stones.

Mark rushed after her because he must, because she had to be caught and hustled back toward the bridge. As the two of them fled, the creatures from among the houses slunk, stole after them, made a line across the road, cut off escape in that direction.

Ruth ran fast in her unreasoning terror, toward where a great squat doorway gaped in the old mill. But then she stopped, so suddenly that Mark nearly blundered against her as he hurried from behind.

"More—" she wimpered. "More of them—"

And more of them crept out through that door. Many more of them, crowding together into a grotesque phalanx.

Ruth pressed close against Mark. She trembled, sagged, her pert daring was gone from her. He gathered his football muscles for a fight, whatever fight he could put up. They came closing in around him and Ruth, those shapes that were only half-shapes. They churned wispily as they formed themselves into a ring.

He made out squat bodies, knobs of craniums, the green gleam of eyes, not all of the eyes set two and two. The Indians, those old Indians, had been right to fear presences like these. Everything drew near. Above the encircling, approaching horde, Mark saw things that fluttered in the air. Bats? But bats are never that big. He heard a soft mutter of sound, as of panting breath.

Even if Ruth hadn't been there to hold on her feet, Mark could never have run now. The way was cut off. It would have to be a battle. What kind of battle?

Just then, abrupt music rang out in the shining night.

And that was a brave music, a flooding burst of melody, like harps in the hands of minstrels. A powerful, tuneful voice sang words to it:

> *The cross in my right hand,*
> *That I may travel open land,*
> *That I may be charmed and blessed,*
> *And safe from any man or beast . . .*

The pressing throng ceased to press around Mark and Ruth. It ebbed away, like dark water flowing back from an island.

The song changed, the guitar and the voice changed:

> *Lights in the valley outshine the sun,*
> *Lights in the valley outshine the sun,*
> *Lights in the valley outshine the sun—*
> *Look away beyond the blue.*

Those creatures, if they could be called creatures, fell back. They fell back, as though blown by the wind. The singing voice put in words of its own, put in a message, a guidance:

> *Head for the bridge and I'll follow you,*
> *Head for the bridge and I'll follow you,*
> *Head for the bridge and I'll follow you—*
> *Look away beyond the blue.*

Ruth would have run again. Mark held her tightly by the arm, kept her to a walk. Running just now might start something else running. They stumbled back along the rough stones with the grass between the edges. The moonlight blazed upon them. Behind them, like a prayer, another verse of the song:

> Do, Lord, oh do, Lord, oh do remember me,
> Do, Lord, oh do, Lord, oh do remember me,
> Do, Lord, oh do, Lord, oh do remember me—
> Look away beyond the blue.

But this time, a confident happiness in that appeal. Mark felt like joining in and singing the song himself, but he kept silent and urged Ruth along by her arm. He thought, though he could not be sure, that soft radiances blinked on and off in the shantylike old houses strung along the road. He did not stop to look more closely. He peered ahead for the bridge, and then the bridge was there and thankfully they were upon it, their feet drumming the planks.

Still he panted for breath, as they reached the other side. He held Ruth to him, glad that he could hold her, glad for her that he was there to hold her. He looked across. There on the bridge came something dark. It was the guitar-picker, moving at a slower pace than Mark and Ruth had moved. He sang, softly now, softly. Mark could not make out the song. He came and joined them at last. He stood tall and lean with his hair rumpled, holding his guitar across himself like a rifle at the port.

"You all can be easy now," he said gently. "Looky yonder, they can't come over this far."

Over there, all the way over there at the far bridge head, a dark cluster of forms showed under the moon, standing close together and not coming.

"The fact about it is," said the guitar-picker, "they don't seem to be up to making their way across a run of water."

Mark was able to speak. "Like *Dracula*," he said numbly. "Like the witches in *Tam O'Shanter*."

"Sure enough, like them. Now, folks," and the voice was gentler than ever, "you all see they'd best be left alone on their side yonder, the way folks have mostly left them alone, all the way back to when the whole crew of the mill went off to nowhere. Old ways can be best."

"Mark, I was such a fool," Ruth mumbled against Mark's shirt.

"I told you that, dear," he said to her.

"Did you call me dear?"

"Yes."

"It makes me feel right good to hear talk like that with nice young folks like you two," said the guitar-picker.

Mark looked up above Ruth's trembling golden head. "You were able to defeat them," he said. "You knew music would hold them back."

"No, I nair rightly knew that." The big hand swept a melody from the silver string. "I hoped it, was all, and the hope wasn't vain."

Mark held out a shaking hand. "We'll never be able to thank you, Mr.—I don't even know your name."

"My name's John."

"John what?" Mark asked.

"Just call me John."

WHERE DID SHE WANDER?

That gravelly old road ran betwixt high rocks and twiny-branched trees. I tramped with my pack and silver-strung guitar past a big old dornick rock, wide as a bureau, with words chopped in with a chisel:

THIS GRAVE DUG FOR
BECKY TIL HOPPARD
HUNG BY THE TRUDO FOLKS
AUG THE 12 18 & 49
WE WILL REMEMBER YOU

And flowers piled round. Blue chicory and mountain mint and turtlehead, fresh as that morning. I wondered about them and walked on, three-four miles to the old county seat named Trudo, where I'd be picking and singing at their festival that night.

The town square had three-four stores and some cabin-built houses, a six-room auto court, a jail and courthouse and all like that. At the auto court stood Luns Lamar, the banjo man who was running the festival, in white shirt and string tie. His bristly hair was still soot-black, and he wore no glasses. Didn't need them, for all his long years.

"I knew you far down the street, John," he hailed me. "Long, tall, with the wide hat and jeans and your guitar. All that come tonight will have heard tell of you. And they'll want you to sing songs they recollect—'Vandy, Vandy,' 'Dream True,' those ones."

"Sure enough, Mr. Luns," I said. "Look, what do you know about Becky Til Hoppard's grave back yonder?"

He squinted, slanty-eyed. "Come into this room I took for us, and I'll tell you what I know of the tale."

Inside, he fetched out a fruit jar of blockade whiskey and we each of us had a whet. "Surprised you don't know about her," said Mr. Luns. "She was the second woman to get hung in this state, and it wasn't the true law did it. It was folks thought life in prison wasn't the right call on her. They strung her up in the square yonder, where we'll sing tonight."

We sipped and he talked. Becky Til Hoppard was a beauty of a girl with strange, dark ways. Junius Worral went up to her cabin to court her and didn't come back, and the law found his teeth and belt buckle in her fireplace ashes; and when the judge said just prison for life, a bunch of the folks busted into the jail and took her out and strung her to a white oak tree. When she started to say something, her daddy was there and he hollered. 'Die with your secret, Becky!' and she hushed and died with it, whatever it was."

"How came her to be buried right yonder?" I asked him.

"That Hoppard set was strange-wayed," said Mr. Luns. "Her father and mother and brothers put her there. They had dug the hole during the trial and set up the rock and cut the words into it, then set out for other places. Isaiah Hoppard, the father, died when he was cutting a tree and it fell onto him. The mother was bit by a mountain rattler and died screaming. Her brother, Harrison, went to Kentucky and got killed stealing hogs. Otway, the youngest brother, fell at Chancellorsville in the Civil War."

"Then the family was wiped out."

"No," and he shook his head again. "Otway had married and had children, who grew up and had children, too. I reckon Hoppards live hereabouts in this day and time. Have you heard the Becky Til Hoppard song?"

"No, but I'd sure enough like to."

He sang some verses, and I picked along on my silver strings and sang along with him. It was a lonesome tune, sounded like old-country bagpipes.

"I doubt if many folks know that song today," he said at last. "It's reckoned to be unlucky. Let's go eat some supper and then start the show."

They'd set up bleachers in the courthouse square for maybe a couple thousand. Mr. Luns announced act after act. Obray Ramsey was there with near about the best banjo-picking in the

known world, and Tom Hunter with near about the best country fiddling. The audience clapped after the different numbers,
especially for a dance team that seemed to have wings on their
shoes. Likewise for a gold-haired girl named Rilla something,
who picked pretty on a zither, something you don't often hear in
these mountains.

When it came my turn, I did the songs Mr. Luns had named,
and the people clapped so loud for more that I decided to try the
Becky Til Hoppard song. So I struck a chord and began:

> *Becky Til Hoppard, as sweet as a dove,*
> *Where did she wander, and who did she love?*

Right off, the crowd went still as death. I sang:

> *Becky Til Hoppard, and where can she be?*
> *Rope round her neck, swung up high on the tree.*

And that deathly silence continued as I did the rest of it:

> *On Monday she was charged, on Tuesday she was tried,*
> *By the laws of her country she had to abide.*
> *If I knew where she lay, to her side I would go,*
> *Round sweet Becky's grave pretty flowers I would strow. . . .*

When I was done, not a clap, not a voice. I went off the little
stage, wondering to myself about it. After the show, Rilla, the
zither girl, came to my room to talk.

"Folks here think it's unlucky to sing that Becky Hoppard
song, John," she said. "Even to hark at it."

"I seem to have done wrong," I said. "I didn't know."

"Well, those Hoppards are a right odd lot. Barely come into
town except to buy supplies. And they take pay for curing sick-
ness and making spells to win court cases. They're strong on that
kind of thing."

"Who made the song?" I asked.

"They say it was sung back yonder by some man who was
crazy for Becky Til Hoppard, and she never even looked his way.

None of the Hoppard blood likes it, nor either the Worral blood. I know, because I'm Worral blood myself."

"Can you tell me the tale?" I inquired. "Have some of this blockade. Mr. Luns left it in here, and it's good."

"I do thank you." She took a ladylike sip. "All I know is what my oldest folks told me. Becky Hoppard was a witch-girl, the pure quill of the article. Did all sorts of spells. Junius Worral reckoned to win her with a love charm."

"What love charm?" I asked, because such things interest me.

"I've heard tell she let him have her handkerchief, and he did something with it. Went to the Hoppard cabin, and that's the last was seen of him alive. Or dead, either—he was all burnt up except his buckle and teeth."

"The song's about flowers at her grave," I said. "I saw some there."

"Folks do that, to turn bad luck away."

I tweaked my silver guitar strings. "Where's the Hoppard place?"

"Up hill, right near the grave. A broken-off locust tree there points to the path. I hope I've told you things that'll keep you from going there."

"You've told me things that make me to want to go."

"Don't, John," she begged to me. "Recollect what happened to Junius Worral."

"I'll recollect," I said, "but I'll go." And we said goodnight.

I woke right soon in the morning and went to the dining room to eat me a good breakfast with Mr. Luns. Then I bade him good day and set out of Trudo the same way I'd come in, on the gravelly road.

Rilla had said danger was at the Hoppard place, but my guitar's silver strings had been a help against evil time and time again. Likewise in my pocket was a buckeye, given me one time by an Ozark fellow, and that's supposed to guard you, too—not just against rheumatics but all kinds of dangers. No man's ever found dead with a buckeye in his pocket, folks allow. So I was glad I had it as I tramped along with my pack and my guitar.

As I got near to the grave rock, I picked me some mountain

laurel flowers. As I put those round the stone, I noticed more flowers there, besides the ones I'd seen the day before. Beyond was the broken-off locust, and a way uphill above it.

That path went through brush, so steep I had to lean forward to climb it. Trees crowded close at the sides. They near about leaned on me, and their leaves bunched into unchancey green faces. I heard a rain crow make its rattly call, and I spied out its white vest and blotchy tail. It was supposed to warn of a storm, but the patch of sky above was clear; maybe the rain crow warned of something else than rain. I kept on, climbed a good quarter mile to where there was a cabin amongst hemlocks.

That cabin was of old, old logs chinked with clay. It must have been built before the last four wars. The roof's split shakes were cracked and curly. A lean-to was tacked on at the left. There were two smudgy windows and a cleated plank door, and on the door-log sat a man, watching me as I climbed into his sight.

He was dressed sharp, better than me in my jeans and old hat. Good-fitting pants as brown as coffee and a bright-flowered shirt. He was soft-pudgy, and I'd reckon more or less fifty years old. His cheeks bunched out. His bald brow was low and narrow. He had a shallow chin and green eyes like grape pulps. His face had the look of a mean snake.

"We been a-waiting for you," he said when I got there.

"How come you to know I'd come, Mr. Hoppard?" I asked him.

He did a creaky laugh. "You know my name, and I don't know yours yet," he said, "but we been a-waiting on you. We know when they come." He grinned, with mossy-green teeth. "What name might I call you?"

"John."

We were being watched. Two heads at one of the windows. A toss-haired woman, a skinny man. When I looked at them they drifted back, then drifted up again.

"You'll be the John we hear tell about," said Hoppard. "A-sticking your nose in here to find out a tale."

"The tale of Becky Til Hoppard," I agreed.

"Poor Becky. They hung her up and cut her down."

"And buried her below here," I added on.

"No, not exactly," he said. "That stone down yonder just satisfies folks away from the truth. They don't ask questions. But you do—ask questions about my great-great aunt Becky." He turned his ugly head to the house. "All right, youins," he bawled, "come out there and meet John."

Those two came. The young man was tall, near about my height, but so ganted he looked ready to bust in two. He wore good pants and shirt, but rumpled and grubby. His eyes were green, too. The girl's frock looked to be made of flowered curtain cloth, and it was down off one rounded bare shoulder. Her tousled hair was as red as if it had been dipped in a mountain sunset. And she looked on me with shiny green eyes, like Hoppard's, like the young man's.

"These is my son and daughter," said Hoppard, a-smirking. "I fetched them up after my fashion, taught them what counts and how to tell it from what doesn't count. She's Tullai. I call the boy Herod."

"Hidy," I told the two of them.

Hoppard got up from the door-log, on crooked legs like a toad's. "Come on in the house," he said, and we went in, all four.

The front room was big, with a puncheon floor worn down with God alone knows how many years, and hooked rag rugs on it. The furniture was home-made. I saw a long sofa woven of juniper branches at back and seat, and two stools and an arm chair made of tree chunks, and a table of old planks and trestles. At the back, a sort of statue stood on a little home-made stand. It looked to be chipped from dark rock, maybe three feet high, and it had a grinning head with horns on it. Its eyes were shiny green stones, a kind I didn't know, but the color of Hoppard's eyes.

"Is that a god?" I inquired of Hoppard.

"Yes, and it's been worshipped here for I can't tell how many generations," he said. "Walk all round the room and them eyes keep a-looking on you. Try it."

I tried it. Sure enough, the eyes followed me into every corner. But I'd seen the same thing to happen with a picture of George Washington in a museum, and a photograph of a woman called Mona Lisa. "You all pray to that idol?" I asked.

"We do, and he answers our prayers," said the girl Tullai, soft-voiced. "He sent you to us."

258   JOHN THE BALLADEER

"Pa," said the boy Herod, "you should ought to tell John about us."

"Sit down," said Hoppard, and we sat here and there while he told the tale. Tullai sat next to me.

Hoppard allowed that his folks had always been conjure folks. Way back yonder, Becky Til Hoppard had been foremost at it. Some things she'd done was good—cures for sick folks, spells to make rain fall, all like that. But about Junius Worral, he said, what I'd heard wasn't rightly so.

"They told you he'd had a charm to win Becky?" said Hoppard. "It was more the other way round. She charmed him to fetch him here."

"What for?" I asked.

"He was needed here," said Hoppard; and Tullai repeated, "Needed here," and her green eyes looked at me sidelong, the way a kitten looks at a bowl of milk.

"To help Becky to a long life," Hoppard went on. "The hanging nair truly killed her, so her folks just set her head back on its neckbone and fetched her home." He nodded to a door that led to the lean-to shed. "She's in yonder now."

"You a-telling me she's alive?" I asked him.

"Her folks did things that fetched her back. In yonder she waits, for you to talk to her."

"John's got him a guitar," spoke up Tullai all of a sudden, her green eyes still cut at me. "Can't we maybe hear him pick it?"

"Sure enough, if you all want to hark at me," I said.

I did some tuning, then I sang something I'd been thinking up:

> Long is the road on which I fare,
> Over the world afar,
> The mountains here and the valleys there,
> Me and this old guitar.
>
> The places I've been were places, yes,
> The things that I've seen were things,
> With this old guitar my soul to bless
> By the sound of its silver strings.

"Hey, you're good!" squeaked out Tullai, and clapped her hands. "Go on, sing the rest."

"That's all the song so far," I said. "Maybe more later."

"But meanwhile," said Hoppard, "Becky's a-waiting on you in yonder." He looked me up and down. "Unless you're scared to go see."

"I got over being scared some while back," I said, and hoped that was more or less a fact. "I came here to find out about her."

Herod stomped over to the inside door and opened it, and I picked up my pack and guitar and went over and into the lean-to room. The door shut behind me. I heard a click, and knew I was locked in.

The room was a big one. It was walled, front and sides, with up-and-down split slabs, with bark and knots, and as old as the day Hell was laid out. The rear wall was a rock face, gray and smooth, with a fireplace cut in it and a blaze on the hearth, with wood stacked to the side. Next to the hearth, a dark-aged wooden armchair, with above it the biggest pair of deer horns I'd ever seen, and in the chair somebody watching me.

A woman, I saw right off, tucked from chin to toes in a robe as red as blood, and round her neck a blue scarf, tight as a bandage. Her face was soft-pale, her slanty Hoppard green eyes under brows as thin as pencil marks. Her lips were redder than her red robe. They smiled, with white teeth.

"So you're John," and her voice was like flowing water. "Come round where I can look on you."

"How do you know my name?"

"Say a little bird told me," she mocked me with her smile. "A bird with teeth in its beak and poison in its claws, that tells me what I need to know. We waited for you here, John."

"You know my name, and I know yours, Miss Becky Til Hoppard. Why aren't you in your grave down by the road, Miss Becky?"

"They told you. I nair went in it. I was toted off here and my folks said some words and burnt some plants, and here I am. They left that grave for a blind. My old folks and my brothers died in right odd ways, but I do fine with these new kinfolks."

Blood-red lipped, she smiled.

"What next?" I inquired.

"You," and she kept her smile. "You're next, John. Every few years I find somebody like you, somebody with strong life in him, to keep my life going. This won't be like poor Junius Worral, my first helper—he was traced here. Nobody knows you came. But why don't you play on your pretty guitar?"

I swept my hands on the silver strings. I sang:

> Becky Til Hoppard, as sweet as a dove,
> Where did she wander, and who did she love? . . .

All the way through, and she smiled and harked at me. "You sang that in town last night. I could hear you. I'm able to hear and see things."

"You've got you a set of talents."

"So have you. When you sang that song, I did spells to fetch you here."

"I don't aim to stay," I said.

"You'll stay," she allowed, "and give me life."

I grinned down at her, with my guitar across me. "I see," I nodded to her. "You took Junius Worral's life into you to keep you young. And others . . ."

"Several," she said. "I made them glad to give me their years."

"Glad?" I repeated, my hand on the silver strings.

"Because they loved me. You'll love me, John."

"Not me, I'm sorry. I love another."

"Another what?" She laughed at her own joke. "John, you'll burn up for love of me. Look."

The fire blazed up. I saw a chunk of wood drop in on the blaze.

She quartered me with her gleamy green eyes. "I could call out just one word, and there's two Hoppard men out yonder would come in here and bust your guitar for you."

"I've seen those two men," I said, "and neither of them looks hard for me to handle."

"There'd be two of them . . ."

"I'd hit them two hard licks," I said. "Nobody puts a hand on my guitar but just me myself."

"Then take it with you, yonder to the fire. Go to the fire, John."

One hand pointed a finger at me, the other pointed to the fire. It blazed high up the chimney. Wood had come into it, without a hand to move it there. It shot up long, fierce, bright tongues of flame. The floor of Hell was what it looked like.

"Look on it," Becky Til Hoppard bade me again. "I can send you into it. I made my wish before," and her voice half-sang. "I make it now. I nair saw the day that the wish I made was not true."

That was a kind of spell. I had a sense that hands pushed me. I couldn't see them, but I could feel them. I made another step into the hot, hot air of the hearth. I was come right next to her, with her bright green eyes watching me.

"Yes," she sang. "Yes, yes."

"Yes," I said after her, and pushed the silver strings of my guitar at her face.

She screamed once, shrill and sharp as a bat, and her head fell over to the side, all the way over and hung there, and she went slack where she sat.

For I'd guessed right about her. Her neck was broken; her head wasn't fast there, it just balanced there. And she sank lower, and the flames of the fire came pouring out at us like red-hot water. I fairly scuttled away toward the door, the locked door, and the door sprang itself open.

I was caught behind the door as Hoppard and his son Herod came a-shammocking in, and after them his daughter Tullai. As they came, that fire jumped right out of its hearth into the room, onto the floor, all round where Becky Til Hoppard sunk in her chair.

"Becky!" one of them yelled, or all of them. And by then I was through the door. I grabbed up my pack as I headed out into the open. Behind me, something sounded like a blast of powder. I reached the head of the trail going down, and gave a lookback, and the cabin was spitting smoke from the door and the windows.

That was it. Becky Til Hoppard ruled the fire. When her rule came to an end, the fire ran wild. I scrambled down, down from that height.

I wondered if they all burnt up in that fire. I nair went back to see. And I don't hear that anybody by the Hoppard name has been seen or heard tell of thereabouts.

Made in the USA
Middletown, DE
01 September 2024

60147184R00156